THE
LAST
WIZARDS'
BALL

ALSO BY CHARLAINE HARRIS

Gunnie Rose series

An Easy Death
A Longer Fall
The Russian Cage
The Serpent in Heaven
All the Dead Shall Weep

A Novel of Midnight, Texas series

Midnight Crossroad
Day Shift
Night Shift

A Sookie Stackhouse Novel series

Dead until Dark
Living Dead in Dallas
Club Dead
Dead to the World
Dead as a Doornail
Definitely Dead
All Together Dead
From Dead to Worse

Dead and Gone
Dead in the Family
Dead Reckoning
Deadlocked
Dead Ever After
The Complete Sookie Stackhouse Stories
The Sookie Stackhouse Companion

An Aurora Teagarden Mystery series

Real Murders
A Bone to Pick
Three Bedrooms, One Corpse
The Julius House
Dead over Heels
A Fool and His Honey
Last Scene Alive
Poppy Done to Death
All the Little Liars
Sleep Like a Baby

Gunnie Rose:
BOOK 6

THE LAST WIZARDS' BALL

CHARLAINE HARRIS

SAGA  PRESS

LONDON   **NEW YORK**   TORONTO
AMSTERDAM/ANTWERP   NEW DELHI   SYDNEY/MELBOURNE

SAGA PRESS

AN IMPRINT OF SIMON & SCHUSTER, LLC

1230 AVENUE OF THE AMERICAS, NEW YORK, NEW YORK 10020

For more than 100 years, Simon & Schuster has championed authors and the stories they create. By respecting the copyright of an author's intellectual property, you enable Simon & Schuster and the author to continue publishing exceptional books for years to come. We thank you for supporting the author's copyright by purchasing an authorized edition of this book.

This book is a work of fiction. Any references to historical events, real people, or real places are used fictitiously. Other names, characters, places, and events are products of the author's imagination, and any resemblance to actual events or places or persons, living or dead, is entirely coincidental.

First Saga Press hardcover edition July 2025

SAGA PRESS and colophon are trademarks of Simon & Schuster, LLC

Simon & Schuster strongly believes in freedom of expression and stands against censorship in all its forms. For more information, visit BooksBelong.com.

For information about special discounts for bulk purchases, please contact Simon & Schuster Special Sales at 1-866-506-1949 or business@simonandschuster.com.

The Simon & Schuster Speakers Bureau can bring authors to your live event. For more information or to book an event, contact the Simon & Schuster Speakers Bureau at 1-866-248-3049 or visit our website at www.simonspeakers.com.

Interior design by Yvonne Taylor

Manufactured in the United States of America

1   3   5   7   9   10   8   6   4   2

Library of Congress Control Number: 2025935944

ISBN 978-1-6680-3812-3
ISBN 978-1-6680-3814-7 (ebook)

Thanks, first of all, to my readers who have followed me through the years and the stories. And lots of love to my staunch friends, who have done likewise: Dana, Toni, Treva, and Paula, who know where all the bodies are buried. My family (husband, children, grandchildren) has given me the love and strength to carry on, and so has my church. Last but not least, thanks to my wonderful agent, Joshua Bilmes, and my editor, Joe Monti, who have shepherded me through the publishing world and allowed me to arrive safe on the other side.

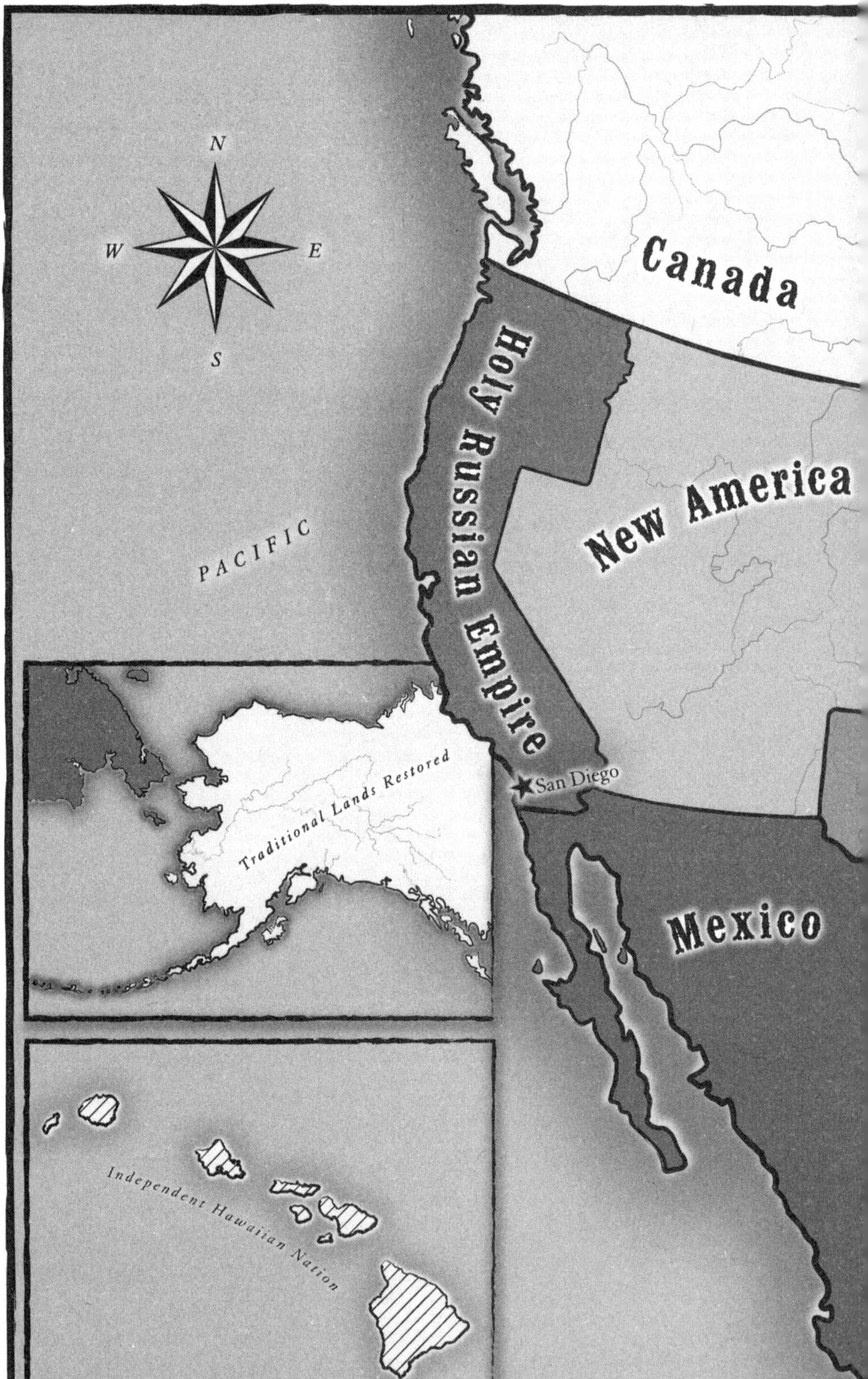
N
W
E
S
PACIFIC
Canada
Holy Russian Empire
New America
San Diego
Mexico
Traditional Lands Restored
Independent Hawaiian Nation

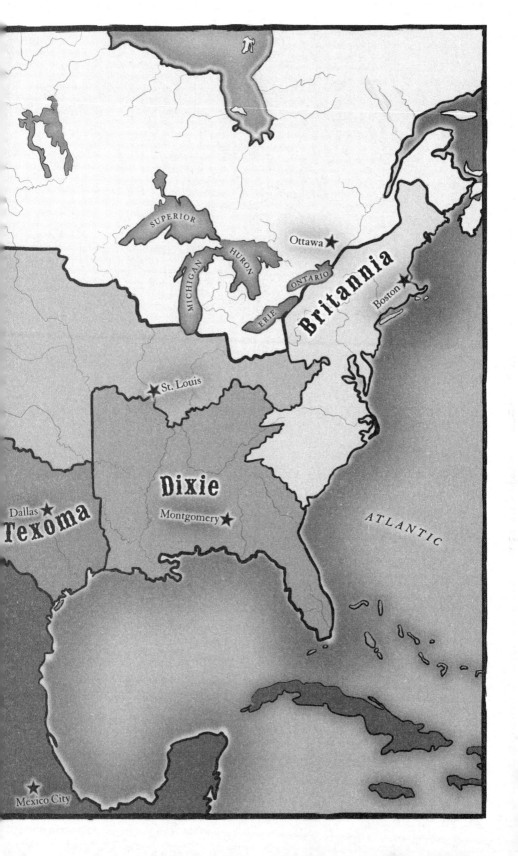

CHAPTER ONE

The first event of the triennial Wizards' Ball was being held in San Diego's Balboa Park, in the Japanese Friendship Garden. You can do that in January in San Diego. The late morning sky was clear and blue, the garden was beautiful—especially to someone who'd grown up in Texoma, which never had enough water.

This event was what my husband, Eli, called a "look and walk."

Though I was very anxious, I reminded myself that I was in a beautiful place with Eli and my sister, Felicia, both people I loved. My low heels didn't hurt much, and the outfit my mother-in-law had loaned me fit okay.

Those were the good things about today.

Everything else made me scowl. I didn't know this until my husband looked back at me and gave me a huge bright smile, a hint that I did not look pleasant. I made my lips turn up. I felt so strange and wrong: so far from home, in clothes so different from my usual jeans and shirt, my Colt .45 stuffed away in my borrowed handbag. *One* gun. Backed up by a knife hidden in the inner pocket of my coat and one strapped to my thigh. That one chafed under the dress.

Since I was wearing a light red coat and a plaid dress, I'd also had to pull on stockings, garters to hold them up, a bra, a stupid hat, and the heels. And the handbag to have a means to bring one of my guns, illegal in San Diego.

I'd rather be fined for carrying an illegal gun than see my sister killed before my eyes.

I'd looped the black leather straps of the handbag over my elbow to leave my hands free. The bag banged against my side, weighted with the fully loaded Colt. If you need to draw a gun, time is really important. I'd worked on the bag's clasp to loosen it.

Felicia turned to smile at me. It became easier to smile back. Felicia and I had different mothers, but we'd dropped the "half" some months ago. We were sisters.

Felicia looked lovely in the dark green version of my outfit. Unlike me, Felicia was absolutely at ease in her finery, though she'd grown up even poorer than I had. I'd been raised in a small town in Texoma, the poorest of the countries that had formed when the old United States broke apart. It was a plain place, as the name gave away. Texas plus Oklahoma.

Felicia had—well, she'd never been "raised," exactly. She'd lived in the poorest part of Ciudad Juárez, in Mexico, with her father and uncle. Then Eli and I had found her. Now Felicia attended the San Diego school founded in Rasputin's name. She was the school's star pupil.

The people we were here to be seen by? They were all practitioners of some kind of magic. Today's outing was the preliminary warm-up to the week of the Wizards' Ball. Every three years this was held in a different city around the world. People of all magical persuasions were able to party, make deals, swap spells, and contract engagements and marriages. On one of my trips as a gunnie, I'd found a book by Georgette Heyer at a secondhand store, so I'd learned about the London Season. The Wizards' Ball Week was the supernatural equivalent; it was the marriage market for the magically gifted. Weeks before, all those wanting to be considered for marriage were required to submit their biographies and photographs, which were required to place candidates on the List. Our Listed candidate was Felicia Karkarova Dominguez. Eli and I were there to protect her—to make sure everyone knew she had people.

Eli, wearing his brown dress slacks and jacket (under that was his grigori vest, which no Russian practitioner would be without), looked calm and at ease. He'd been born an aristocrat, though his birth had been on the long-traveling flotilla of boats carrying Russian aristocracy and their servants in their years-old quest to find a new home.

Some days I found it hard to believe he'd married me. He looked like he was the king of the world. His long, light hair was blowing in the gentle breeze.

My own black hair was covered with gook that kept it in rigid waves.

Eli gave me the overdone smile again, so I tried once more to look agreeable. Just when I'd made my lips turn up (again), I spotted Felix standing on the path ahead of us. He was talking to a man and woman, both in their midtwenties.

Felix Drozhdov was small and dark-headed. "Hello, my student!" Felix called to Felicia, who grinned when she saw him.

Felix, who was grumpy by nature, was pretending as hard as I was. He only bothered because it was for Felicia.

My sister picked up the gentle pace we'd been maintaining. She hugged Felix. The death grigori endured it.

"I can't believe you're here!" Felicia told Felix. "Where's Lucy?"

Lucy, Eli's sister, was Felix's wife.

"She had things to do at home," Felix said. "I had things to do here." She had her work, he had his.

Eli made a little hand gesture at Felix to remind him to perform introductions.

"I believe you have met Clayton Dashwood, Felicia?" Felix said. "And this is his twin sister, Camilla."

"Of course I remember Clayton. It's nice to meet you, Camilla. How are things in Virginia?"

"Still cold," the young woman said. "Give us a couple of months, though, and the farm will be beautiful." Twins didn't always look alike, but Camilla and her brother both had the same brown eyes, narrow noses, and broad faces. Even I could tell that they were dressed with expensive good taste.

"We're glad to meet up with you. I thought I'd have to track you two down," Clayton said, including me in his smile. "How is the weather in Texoma, Lizbeth?"

I was a little surprised that he remembered me. "Dry and warm. In two months, it'll be dry and hot." I shrugged. Not that much variation in my part of Texoma.

Eli looked from Clayton to me, obviously waiting for me to tell him how I knew Clayton Dashwood. "Clayton was one of the early suitors last summer," I reminded him. "Clayton and Camilla, this is my husband, Prince Eli Savarov."

Camilla looked impressed. Eli didn't use his title in Texoma, thank God, because I couldn't have borne the teasing. But here I was Princess Savarova. Which was stupid, but sometimes useful.

"Do you have your schedule lined up for the week?" Camilla asked Felicia.

"More or less. This is my first time. I understand invitations will come in as soon as everyone is in town, which should be tomorrow."

"I don't know about you, but it felt really odd to send out that much information about me and my brother," Camilla said.

Felicia's face lit up. "Is this your first Ball Week, too?"

Camilla nodded. "The family says Clayton and I need to get out of Britannia to find ourselves sweethearts. You know how families are."

We did, but maybe not in the same way as the Dashwood twins.

"We've been in Virginia for a hundred and fifty years, I guess," Camilla continued. "Our folks want some zip added to the family tree. San Diego is as close to us as the ball is ever likely to be, while we're eligible."

Eli had told me cities across the world wanted to host the Wizards' Ball. It had been quite a coup for San Diego to get the bid three years ago. Felicia was already in San Diego, and so was Eli's family, so we'd grabbed the opportunity, though Felicia was only sixteen (maybe). The youngest you could be Listed was fourteen, and that was for a contracted engagement. No actual marriage until you were at least seventeen. And after you were thirty-two, you couldn't be Listed.

"The last one was in Paris, right?" I said. "You all didn't want to go to that one?"

Felix scowled at me. He was always doing that, so I ignored him. What was rude about asking?

"We didn't," Clayton said. "My mother has a prejudice against the French. Don't ask! It's a long story."

"Your dress is real pretty, Camilla," Felicia said. It was navy with little white symbols, so with her coloring it looked cute.

"Let me return the compliment," Clayton said. "You ladies look lovely."

I had to smile. "The contrast must be what struck you."

When he'd appeared in Texoma, popping out of nowhere, we'd been wearing everyday clothes . . . at least for me. We'd worn jeans and shirts, and we'd been grubby from a day outside.

"Have a wonderful time this week," Eli said. He was trying to ease us away so we could continue our stroll and be seen by as many people as possible.

"I heard what a great grigori you are," Camilla told Felicia. "Someone's just going to snap you right up!"

"Not necessarily," Felicia said. She was well aware that she had a "danger" sign attached to her back.

"Golly, gal, you're pretty, you got a great bloodline, and you're a known whiz at magic! That's why Clayton visited you early."

"That's the way I feel," I said, hoping to cut this conversation off before it got really awkward. "We were so pleased to meet Clayton when he came to Texoma. I'm afraid we must get going now, but I'm glad we got to chat. We'll be seeing you, for sure."

The Dashwood twins said their goodbyes, and off we went in a different direction.

Eli dropped back to talk for a second.

"Everything Camilla said is true. Felicia is all the things she said." I was grousing. I knew how intimidating my sister could be.

He put his arm around my shoulders. "Lizbeth, my very dear wife, you also have an interesting bloodline: half grigori, half a lovely woman schoolteacher, and you're a famous shooter. But not everyone would think that would add to their family pool. I was not everyone, and I saw the advantage of marrying you immediately."

Just when I felt like socking Eli, he'd say something like that. He hadn't called me his dear wife in a couple of months. Or longer.

"Well, Oleg was my father in the smallest sense of the word," I said dryly. He'd put my mother under a magic spell and raped her. Then he'd left town with his little magic show, and he hadn't come back. Six years later, Oleg had eloped with Felicia's mother, who was not anything like my mom. Valentina Dominguez was the oldest daughter in a very powerful family of witches in Ciudad Juárez.

That kind of heritage and reputation were sure to attract a lot of attention. My sister already had a scary reputation. Felicia was fresh, pretty, smart, and lethal.

Last year Felicia had killed all the Dominguezes (including her grandfather, Francisco) with one exception: Isabella, the aunt who'd actually helped Felicia when she was living in Ciudad Juárez. (In Felicia's defense, her family had tried to abduct her and give her as a bride to the scion of the Ruiz clan, also based in Mexico.) My sister was a death grigori. She could kill, and she could restore life . . . sometimes. Mastery over death could give you mastery over life, under some circumstances. Felicia's power was strong and rare.

To my mind, anyone considering marrying Felicia was a moth to her flame. But the attraction of her huge magical talent outweighed her lethal reputation . . . in some circles.

As early as months before, while Felicia had been staying with me in my cabin in Texoma, interested suitors had begun to drop in—sometimes literally. They took advantage of their window of opportunity. Once my sister returned to the Rasputin School, such attempts were out of the question. A drop-in visitor at the Rasputin School, run by the magically gifted and for the magically gifted, would be dead on arrival.

Felicia had been both delighted and angry at the various attempts to get her attention, one of which had consisted of abduction. Others had been pleasant and flattering. She'd been talking about that the day before, at our planning session. She'd sounded (I had to admit) full of herself.

Felix had snapped, "My girl, you are a powerhouse. But don't let it go to your head! Nothing's more off-putting than conceit."

He should know.

Felix had continued, "There are girls as powerful as you, girls as pretty, girls with money, girls with long and honorable pedigrees. What you have is people who are interested in your power, but afraid of it, too. People who are afraid will back off at the merest sign of trouble."

Felicia had looked flattened after this truth-telling. That was better than letting it all go to her head.

Her deflation hadn't lasted long enough.

When Eli and I had come down for breakfast this morning, Felicia had been all lit up like a candle. She'd been chattering at Veronika, Eli's mother, nonstop. Veronika's new husband, Captain Ford McMurtry, had been hiding behind his newspaper. I'd only been able to see his reddish hair.

The headlines had all been about the unrest in Europe.

I spared a moment to wonder if the foofaraw this Hitler was causing might keep some of the European magicians from getting to San Diego. That was my whole scope this week.

Not that I wanted Felicia to marry someone from Spain or Switzerland and move to Europe. Any of the five countries from the divided United States would be fine: Britannia, Dixie, New America, the Holy Russian Empire, Texoma. (It would be hard to swallow Dixie, because I'd had such a bad time there, but I would.) Even Canada, which had encroached on the northern part of the United States when the collapse had come. Even Mexico, which had taken a big bite out of the southwestern United States. Anywhere a train ran.

I wanted Felicia to have all the choices she could. I was fixed on my sister's future. She would graduate from the Rasputin School in little more than a year. That was, if she didn't get to skip some classes she had already surpassed. Then it would be time for her to pick a profession or a path.

When we'd been alone in our bedroom after two hours of planning, Eli had said, "I'm surprised you are so determined that Felicia should do this. I believed you would hate the whole idea."

I heaved a sigh. "At first I did. But then I figured . . . I never had many choices." I pulled off my boots. "When I left school, I had to find a way to support myself. I wasn't about to get married that young, not after what happened to my mother. I didn't want any of

the jobs open around town, like helping at the feed and seed store."
That had sounded like slow death. "But by then I'd learned to shoot,
thanks to Jackson." Jackson Skidder was my stepfather. He was the
only father I'd ever known. "And I liked the work, the travel, being
alert, having purpose." Being a gunnie, guarding people or goods
in transit, was a good job for me. I was suited to it. Though I had a
shorter life expectancy than someone who clerked in a store, I had a
broader horizon than a clerk.

Felicia, who'd been trapped into looking ten years old by her
father's spell, had proved to be much more than a grubby little girl
with Rasputin's blood in her veins. After we'd rescued her from Ciudad Juárez and put her in the Rasputin School in San Diego, Felicia
had gone from looking like a child to looking her real age (which we
figured was fifteen or sixteen) in a matter of months.

It had been a shocking growth spurt, and it had been hard for
her emotions to catch up with her body.

Though she'd never said it out loud, Felicia had been *angry*.

Our father and his brother (Oleg and Sergei Karkarov) had
taught her to steal to support them and kept her small to avoid the
consequences. They'd left her in indifferent care for weeks at a time,
while they traveled around doing easy magic tricks and making
money from the uneducated.

And taking what they wanted from girls, like my mother. Oleg
had left something he didn't want with my mother. Me.

CHAPTER TWO

*H*ere and now, I told myself. Worry over Felicia and her future had made me think too much about my past. I am not one for looking back, as a rule.

As we walked, I took in the Japanese Friendship Garden. It was very beautiful: trees and plants I didn't know, streams with rocks arranged in patterns, graceful bridges. It had been constructed to conform to the existing landscape, and included sudden steep hillsides, narrow spaces, and open areas.

Good ambush territory.

This was why Felix, the least sociable of men, was stalking up the path ahead of Felicia. This was why Eli and I, who should have been home working in Segundo Mexia, were instead staying at his mother's home in San Diego this week.

Since I'd been half expecting her to turn up, when I saw a woman waiting on the path ahead of us, I knew instantly who it was.

"Aunt Isabella!" Felicia called, opening her arms. Isabella flowed into them like water into a ditch.

I knew a prearranged meeting when I saw one. Felicia had been holding back.

Isabella, in her early thirties, was still very attractive. When she embraced Felicia, the family likeness was undeniable.

"See and be seen," Eli muttered.

"What is she proving?" I said.

"She's proving that her remaining family stands by her."

"What's that worth?"

"A lot to Felicia, apparently."

While Isabella and Felicia unclenched to begin an apparently happy conversation, and Felix scowled at them both, Isabella glanced past Felix to Eli and me, and her face showed a . . . I didn't know what to call it. An awareness. I felt a prickle. I looked up at my husband with a sudden suspicion.

"Eli, didn't you say once that you went to the last ball, in Paris? Why didn't you pick one of the girls you met?"

"I did go to one Wizards' Ball," my husband said, but not as if he was happy to recall the time. "Not to Paris, though. My father sent me to Denmark, two balls ago. Six years."

"Tell me what happened."

He didn't meet my eyes. "I met a witch from Mexico. I liked her quite a bit, but her father thought I wasn't good enough. And she thought I was too young."

"You mean . . . you mean Isabella."

Eli gave a short nod.

"And she turned you down."

"Her father did not approve. He thought the age difference was too much. And he knew I would not live in Mexico, since I was preparing to be in service to the tsar."

There wasn't any reason Eli should have told me all this before we married, since it had come to nothing, and neither he nor Isabella had given me any sign they were in any way involved until today. I was sure the look Isabella had thrown his way was calculated. "So you and Isabella have not been in contact since then?"

"We have not. I had no idea Felicia had been talking to her aunt after my brother died, and you almost did, in Texoma. I had no idea they'd arranged this. Which, clearly, they did."

"How . . . how did you feel, then? In Denmark? When Francisco nixed the engagement?"

"I was cast down, at the time. I was very young." Then Eli smiled down at me. "But it all worked out for the best. Instead, I met a woman with guns and nerves of steel, and she did not care how much money I had or didn't have, or that my father was a traitor."

"I didn't care then, and I don't care now."

"Well, Lizbeth turned down someone, too," Felix said. He had dropped back to stand by us while the very public aunt-and-niece reunion continued. The Happy Dominguezes, all two of them.

"Felix," I said, making sure my voice was quiet and even.

"Really? Who was it?" Eli was smiling broadly.

I changed my mind. Felix could tell him, and even embroider on it.

"The baker's son," Felix said. "The handsome one. The one who came to see Lizbeth the day of his wedding, hoping that she would throw you over and take him instead."

Eli wheeled to look at me, his eyebrows all hiked up. I shrugged. It was true. I'd never felt the need to tell Eli about Dan Brick's visit. Just now, I felt fine about that decision. Especially since I knew about his thing for Isabella Dominguez.

We exchanged very level looks.

"We all need to keep walking," Felix said, bored with the drama. He set off, saying something pointed to Isabella and Felicia as he passed them. We all trailed behind him.

"Isabella would have eaten you alive," I muttered.

"Dan Brick would have bored you to tears," he replied.

The garden was even more crowded now. Many of the magically talented people seemed to know one another. I heard lots of different languages. This was not for me. This whole charade of parading around, arranging meetings for picnics and teas and dances, looking at each other, seemed just as odd and stupid to me as it had when Eli and Felix had explained it. I'd accepted their surety that this was my sister's best chance to meet the wizard of her dreams, to gain safety, security, and a future family.

Now my doubts had swum to the surface, and this was only the opening event.

I felt my handbag bang into my side again. How had I been suckered into doing this city job? But I wanted Felicia to succeed, however she felt that might be done.

I pressed my lips together and stared at every boy who came near as if I suspected he would try to kill my sister rather than woo her.

I might be right.

CHAPTER THREE

Felicia bobbed her head to a brown-haired girl with a thin face, who was surrounded by male relatives. Maybe a fellow pupil from the school? The girl bobbed back. One of the girl's escorts gave Felicia a long, long look.

She was worth it.

Felicia's hair was black like mine. Where I was fair complexioned, her skin was a creamy tan. Her eyes were deep and brown (like her mother's, I supposed), while mine were blue like our father's. Though Felicia now looked her age, middle teens, she'd always been an adult in a real sense because she'd been brought up to fend for herself.

When Eli and I had found Felicia, we'd had no idea she wasn't exactly the child she appeared to be. Eli had taken her to San Diego to the school. She'd been a charity urchin, valuable only because her blood (since she was Rasputin's illegitimate granddaughter, as I was, courtesy of our father) would keep the tsar alive. He had the bleeding disease, for which there was no cure.

Felicia seldom needed to donate to the tsar these days. Another bastard grandchild, Ruslan, was the usual donor.

My sister was not only a strong grigori, she was also a pretty good cook and a fair shot and a medium-skilled knife thrower. (Some lessons just don't take.) She could kill and butcher a chicken or a deer quite handily now, after I'd given her lessons. She could make a bomb and throw it accurately, which she really enjoyed and had taught herself. In fact, Felicia could blast people into walls with her magic.

A blond woman in her midtwenties strolled up to us, her entourage—two tough-looking men I identified as professional guards—hanging back. She was slim and hard, dressed to kill. She spoke directly to my sister. "Fraulein," she said. "If I may talk to you?"

Felicia nodded, wary and doubtful.

"I'm Hilde Bergen, from Berlin, Germany. I want to make your acquaintance."

"Felicia Karkarova Dominguez," my sister said, not extending her hand. People with magic do not shake. Another bit of etiquette I'd learned.

"I've heard great things about you. I hope we find time to talk this week." Bergen smiled, displaying a lot of white teeth.

Felicia had obviously never heard of Hilde Bergen, and just as obviously didn't feel the urge to make a date to talk. "We'll both be busy this week," Felicia said with a small smile. "But I'm sure we'll see each other at some party or another."

"I'll make sure that happens," Hilde said.

That sounded kind of threatening. Felicia's polite smile vanished. After an awkward pause, both parties started walking again.

That had been more than a little odd.

Felicia dropped back to walk beside me. I thought she'd say something about Hilde Bergen. Instead, she said, "I miss Peter, today especially." Eli's younger brother, Peter, had adored Felicia, and she had been fond of him—just not as much as he'd wanted. His death had knocked her for a loop—all of us, really. After she'd gotten the news, Veronika had not written to us for two months. I didn't know if she'd blamed us (because Peter had died in Segundo

Mexia), or if she just hadn't had the heart to talk to her other son. I still didn't know.

"We all miss Peter," I said.

Eli's brother had been very likable, especially after he'd out-grown some of his impulsiveness. He hadn't been a great grigori, but he had been a very nice guy.

"I've heard some things about the German wizards," Felicia said, still in that low voice. "I don't think I—"

But we were interrupted.

"Felicia!" The girl who had spoken was very pretty, dressed to catch the eye in a bright outfit, and properly chaperoned by a man and woman who could only be her parents.

Felicia assumed a bright smile. "Anna!" she said. "How are you?"

The two girls hugged each other, with as little body contact as you could have while you hugged.

"They make a pretty picture together," Eli murmured.

"They know that," I said.

"Anna Feodorovna is stupid," Felix said, and he didn't bother to lower his voice. Anna heard. I could tell by the way her lips pressed together before they sprang back into a broad, happy smile.

Anna's parents were standing a little aside. For the first time I noticed Anna's brother was with them. He was as handsome as Anna was lovely, but his expression wasn't animated. He was smil-ing, too, but it was vague and wondering. He reached out to pat Felicia's hair. "Hello, Felicia," he said.

"Nikolai, how are you?" Felicia said politely. Her hands twitched, and I knew she was wondering if he'd disarranged her hair. She had a Ginger Rogers grown-out bob look, with the bottom all fluffed up.

"He'd better leave her hair alone," Eli muttered. He had two sisters and me, so he knew how women feel about their hairstyles.

"He doesn't know any better."

"Lucky Nikolai's good-looking. Maybe some older woman will want him around for sex," Felix said.

He kept his voice low this time. He didn't mind insulting able people, but he did not show scorn to the feeble. That was something I could say in Felix's favor. I added it to the short list.

I spied a woman Felicia needed to pay her respects to. I stepped forward. "Excuse me, Anna, Nikolai, Mr. and Mrs. Feodorov. Felicia's being summoned."

Felicia followed my gesture. Tom O'Day, who had long been the lobby watchdog at the Rasputin School, was setting up a lawn chair for Madame Semyonova, the ancient headmistress. Hovering next to her was a red-haired young woman.

"Tom, Callista!" Felicia called, smiling. The redhead waved back, and she seemed just as happy to see Felicia as Felicia was to see her. My sister strode across the grass to the shady spot where Madame was being situated.

Settled into her folding chair, Madame beckoned to Felicia with a hand like a claw. Madame Semyonova might be failing, but she remained the head of the school and was given great respect.

I glanced back at the Feodorovs. They were watching my sister, and they were not happy with the attention she'd been given. Anna had gotten none. But I had to dismiss them so I could listen to Felicia's conversation with Madame.

"Child, where have you been?" the old woman asked. Her voice was feeble. Madame looked like a skinny bundle of brittle sticks. I hoped she would last through the end of the next school year to see Felicia graduate.

"Good afternoon, Madame," Felicia said, dipping her head. "Like everyone else my age, I am taking two weeks off for the ball. We are staying with Eli's mother and her new husband."

Madame nodded and said, "Have a good time and meet good people."

That was a neat way to put it.

Madame spied Felicia's male companions. "Eli and Felix! Are you escorting our star student?"

"Yes, Madame. It's so good to see you."

"Why are you two squiring Felicia around the grounds?"

There was a moment of confused silence.

Eli said, "As you may remember, Felix is Felicia's mentor, and I am her brother-in-law."

Madame looked doubtful.

"I am married to Felicia's sister, Lizbeth," Eli explained. He stepped to one side so Madame could see me.

"It's good to see you again, Madame," I said, kind of bobbing my head as my sister had done.

Madame looked at me, her face still clouded. Then she said, "Of course. The gunslinger."

"Yes, ma'am."

"What have you been doing today, Felicia?" Madame said.

"I spent all morning getting ready to walk around here, to give anyone interested a good look at me." My sister did not mince words.

Madame cackled, and Callista laughed out loud. Tom O'Day almost smiled. That was a stretch for him.

While we three stood by, Felicia had a chat about the school with Madame, Tom, and Callista.

Just when we were about to say our farewells, Madame looked past Felicia directly at me and said, "Remember Klementina?"

I froze. After a little pause to switch my brain to a new track, I said, "Yes, ma'am. I remember Klementina very well. We fought together, and she saved my life."

I remembered too well.

In my dreams, I was standing on the train platform in Ciudad Juárez in the bright sun, sweating and afraid, knowing I was about to die. My sister had to get out of the city, had to find safety in San Diego, and Eli had to take her. The rogue grigoris who wanted to kill every descendant of Rasputin (so the tsar would die from lack of healing blood) were running toward the train station. There were many of them. The ancient grigori Klementina made the stand with me. There were only two of us.

I saw plenty of blood that day.

I could not remember how many people Klementina and I killed, her with her spells and me with my guns, but I could see them, over and over, falling onto the stones of the plaza around the station, their blood flowing.

In the end, Klementina had been struck with a spell. I'd shot the grigori who'd thrown it at her. Our last enemy was dead, but so was my only ally. I was alone with many dead people. The train had left while the battle raged on. The police must be on their way.

It would have been better to die on the spot than to stay in a Mexican jail.

Klementina had lived long enough to make me invisible so I could escape.

I came back to the here and now with a shocking suddenness. The memory had never been so real before, the grigoris falling to their deaths had never been so clear. I realized Madame had made me have that memory so she could share it.

"So that was how Klementina died," the old woman said. "Brave to the end."

"Yes, ma'am, she was a lion," I said, not managing to get my voice louder than a whisper. But the old woman heard me, and she nodded, and let me go. Felicia, Eli, and Felix bade her farewell. I said nothing. I could hardly wait to get away from her. Madame Semyonova scared the tar out of me.

"Want to tell me?" Eli murmured as we strolled away.

"Not even a little bit," I said. Old people deserved respect. Old and demented grigoris deserved fear. No wonder Madame had been such a successful headmistress, if she could read students' thoughts.

It took me a good five minutes to calm down.

I had had other terrible times—the day everyone in my gun crew had been killed but me, the day the train I was on had been derailed and attacked—but I hadn't realized that day in Mexico had been the worst.

I knew it now.

As my breathing evened out, my head came back completely to this day, this garden. Soon after that, I was able to smile, or at least look pleasant. I think.

We resumed our stroll so more of Felicia's prospective suitors could take a good look. And there were a few she wanted to have a gander at herself. She'd pored over the pictures and biographies, like any girl would. Both the photographs and the life stories were probably over-flattering.

A dark-haired young man was bold enough to approach us directly. "Do I have the honor of addressing Senorita Dominguez?" He bowed gracefully. He wasn't tall, he wasn't broad, but he was young and easy on the eyes. From his accent and clothes, he was from somewhere in Latin America.

Felicia had definitely noticed the easy-on-the-eyes part. "You do," she said. I gave her marks for sounding calm.

"I am your *very* distant kinsman, Mateo Medina Dominguez."

Felicia's smile vanished as quick as a wink, and her hands flew up.

I'd already unlatched my handbag. My hand had plunged in to grip my Colt. Eli and Felix were at the ready, too.

"I beg your pardon. I do not know what I have said that was offensive." Mateo, who appeared to be no fool, stood absolutely still.

"I didn't know I had more family," Felicia said. I was proud of how matter-of-fact she seemed. "What is our connection?"

"My great-grandmother was half sister to your great-grandfather. They shared a father but had different mothers."

So this Mateo was only a second cousin, right? I'd never had to keep track of extended family connections. My own family was so small.

"Why the long name?" Felix muttered in my ear.

"Mexican last names start with the father's, then add the mother's," I whispered back. "In Mexico, my sister's Felicia Karkarova Dominguez. Mateo's dad is a Medina."

"Where does your family live?" Felicia sounded relaxed, which I thought was premature.

"We moved north in the last thirty years. The Medinas are now centered in Baja Mexico."

"I've heard it's very beautiful," Felicia said.

Mateo beamed. His body lost its tension. "We think so. We live on the beach. We have a row of houses all belonging to family or family connections. Quite safe."

"You live with your parents?"

"That's our custom until we marry." And his smile this time was brilliant.

Felicia decided Mateo was at least satisfactory. "Mateo, this is my brother-in-law, Prince Savarov." She indicated my husband. "And my sister, his wife, Lizbeth Savarova. This is my tutor, Felix Drozhdov."

Mateo bowed to each of us in turn. "May I walk with you?" he asked Felicia. "I would not want to hold you from your exercise."

"Of course," Felicia said. She took a little step forward. So we all did. It was like a little train. Eli was our cattle guard. Felicia was our engine. Right now, Felix and I were the caboose.

Felicia and Mateo resorted to Spanish before too long. I was able to follow their conversation, more or less. I kept my ears open so I'd know if their back-and-forth hit on some unsuitable topic. Felix, who spoke English and Russian, glanced at me uneasily from time to time. I nodded, to tell him all was well.

The kids' exchange was light as air and almost as empty: the weather, the upcoming social events of the week, Mateo's journey to San Diego with his uncle. "I am eighteen," Mateo said.

"I believe I am sixteen now." Felicia did not explain. Mateo's only response was a widening of the eyes.

After a moment, Mateo said, "I can tell my mother's name is . . . distressing to you. It's true you have severed connections with your mother's family?"

Felicia laughed. I smothered a smile.

Mateo was very interested in this reaction.

"I severed them permanently," Felicia said. "Aunt Isabella is the only one left, because she helped me when I needed it, as much as she could. The others did not. I don't like it when people try to kidnap me and force me into a marriage."

"Understandable," Mateo said. "Especially to the Ruiz heir."

I gave him credit for that, too.

Glancing from side to side, I observed other young men drawing near, after seeing Mateo received in a friendly way.

They began to walk parallel to us at a polite distance, waiting for their turn to charm Felicia. Mateo was aware, of course. Though the young man smiled in an impish way, he had the courtesy to excuse himself with the flowery wish that we would be able to meet him and his uncle during this week for lunch, perhaps?

Felicia glanced at me with a question on her face.

"If you will tell me his name and your hotel, I will send a note to let you know if we can accept," I told him.

Mateo passed me a card with the information already on it, while he told with his eyes that I was lovely, though perhaps not quite as lovely as my sister (quite true).

Mateo was the first rock in an avalanche of suitors.

Felicia met a young man from Panama, two cousins from Hungary who were in their twenties, a boy her own age from Kiev, an older suitor from Spain who had to be at least thirty, and a very strange man from Romania who made my skin crawl (Felicia's too, I could tell).

Throughout all this socializing and vigilance, we had the chance to look at many beautiful scenes in the garden. The streams, in particular, were very restful. I come from a place of little water, and the water we have isn't pretty. The different colors and shapes of the trees, the careful arrangement of the rocks and plants . . . I could have looked forever. I promised myself I'd come back when I wasn't having to watch out for Felicia.

Just when we had agreed to start for the car, a very fair young man, about eighteen, approached sort of shyly. He was wearing a beautiful suit. His only companion, a man of perhaps twenty-five, was more modestly dressed. The younger man stepped into Felicia's path, brought his heels together, and bowed.

"I beg your pardon, beautiful ladies, gentlemen. Have I the honor of addressing Fraulein Karkarova-Dominguez?"

Yet another variation on my sister's name.

"You do." Felicia inclined her head just as formally.

"I am Ahren Hirsch, son of Mordecai and Rachel. I am from Germany, but I am not one of the followers of the new leader," the boy said. "I am here without my family because they are working to move our assets out of the country and into a place we might be safe during the upcoming war."

I didn't think Felicia had been keeping up with the news out of Europe. I'd only seen the headlines, hadn't read the stories. I figured I had enough trouble right here.

"I see," Felicia said, with concern. Maybe I'd been wrong.

Felicia took a deep breath and kept her eyes directly on the boy. "Who is your companion?"

"I beg your pardon," the younger man said again. "This is my cousin, Hans Goldschmidt."

Felicia looked directly at Hans Goldschmidt and addressed him. "Mr. Goldschmidt, you live here in San Diego?"

There was some significance in the way Felicia spoke, the way she was standing. I looked hard at the man. He was dressed plainly in a gray suit, white shirt, and modest tie. His hair and mustache were a medium brown, but his eyes were mahogany, the only striking thing about him. Average height, average weight, average build. Hans said, "I have lived in this country for the past few years. My family is much reduced. Recently." He lowered his eyes, which had met my sister's.

Felicia stared at him. Hans Goldschmidt's eyes stared at his toes. No one else said anything. Hans looked up. His eyes met Felicia's. He looked like a starving man eyeing a juicy steak.

"Mr. Hirsch, Mr. Goldschmidt, you are sure a war will come?" I said. Somebody had to say something. "I'm Lizbeth Savarov, Felicia's sister."

"Please call me Ahren. Yes, I am sure war is coming," Ahren said. There was anger in his voice, even though his expression didn't change. "Already, things are difficult for any Jew, even Jews who are not devout. And my parents believe we will not be the end of the killing. People besides Jews will be swept up in this net. Anyone Hitler deems not desirable. My parents are moving our family out of Germany, where we have lived for two hundred years, as we speak."

"And you, Mr. Goldschmidt?"

"It is too late for my parents," he said simply.

We were all silent for a moment.

"We are sorry to hear this," my husband said. "I hope we will see you at all the festivities of the week. Do you foresee returning to Europe?"

"I will meet my parents, wherever they are." I gave Ahren high marks for sounding resolute about this. Hans did not say anything.

"How long will you be in San Diego?" Eli said.

"For this week, unless we hear from my parents sooner than I expect. I will go to them when I get a telegram. After all, I am young enough to have another ball season after this one. Surely, within a few days, I will receive a telegraph from my father. If we don't hear anything . . ." Ahren shrugged, and his eyes closed for just a moment.

"We hope to hear," he said simply.

Felicia looked again at Cousin Hans. "And you, Mr. Goldschmidt? Will you remain here?"

Eli and I exchanged a look. Felicia's tone was odd. What the hell was going on?

Since we were all distracted, that was when the attack came.

Felix was standing right by my sister. He made a sound I'd never heard before, something between a growl and a gasp of pain. There was an arrow in his arm. Even in the shock of the moment, I knew it was not like any arrow I'd ever seen.

Magic, I'd expected. Guns, I was always ready for.

Never prepared for an archery attack in San Diego.

I shoved my sister to the ground and stood over her, my gun out and ready, my back to Eli's, who had his hands up. Felix crouched awkwardly across Felicia's back.

"Let me up!" Felicia yelled.

"No! We talked about this." This week, my sister was my cargo, the item I was hired to protect. I was a gunnie. This was my profession.

To my surprise, Ahren and Hans had arrayed themselves around Felicia as well. High marks to them.

Everyone else within sight had scattered.

Just when I wondered if the one arrow was all we would get, another passed between Eli and me and pulled his hat off as it went by.

"Above us," Eli said calmly.

I'd realized this already. We were at the bottom of one of the sculpted hillsides. There were boulders up there. Five archers could be aiming at us. We wouldn't know until we got hit.

An arrow hit the ground right by my foot. "Not hit," I called.

The next arrow bounced off something. And the next.

What the hell?

"Who is doing this? Giving us a shield?" I glanced down at Felicia to see if it was her. She shook her head violently and tried to heave Felix off her. "Don't even *think* about getting up," I said, and my tone made it clear I meant business.

There were no more arrows for two minutes.

"It's over," Felix said. He had blood running down his arm. He held it to the side so it would drip on the ground rather than Felicia. He rose to stand with some difficulty.

"Give it a little more time," I said. I'd been caught once. Not again.

We did.

After five long minutes with no movement or action from the hillside above us, we agreed we could stand down.

CHAPTER FOUR

Our quick, bleeding exit from the Japanese Friendship Garden was marked by staring, exclamations, and open curiosity from the rest of the magical community.

No one rushed up to ask us what had happened . . . none of the suitors who had just been smarming and swarming all over Felicia. (Though to be fair, I did not see Mateo or Clayton among the remaining Listeds.)

Possibly their hesitation was due to Felix's bloody arm, or the fact that I had my gun out (screw the law about no guns in the city), or the rage that rolled off us.

No one offered to help except for Ahren Hirsch and Hans Goldschmidt.

Not only did Ahren and Hans escort us to our car, they went to their own rented vehicle and drove behind us to Felix's house.

We went as fast as we could. Felix could curse like a sailor, and he wasn't holding back.

Felix owned a small house in a humble neighborhood. It had a gravel driveway that ended behind the house. Even with Felix's car parked near the back door already, there was enough space for Eli's car. The rental car pulled into the curb in front of the house. I hurried ahead of Eli and Felix and rang the doorbell to give Lucy a little warning before we all barged in.

Eli's younger sister, wearing an apron, rushed into the small living room. There was an archway at the back of the living room that led to the dining area and then a door to the right into the kitchen. Everything was clean and gleaming.

Lucy slapped a hand over her mouth when she saw Felix's bloody arm. She rallied pretty quick, as befit a Savarov, even one only twenty years old. In no time at all, she'd thrown a towel over the dining table and assembled a basin of hot water, a clean washrag and soap, bandages, and medicine. Then she beckoned Eli into the kitchen, where Felix held his bleeding arm over the sink. Hans, Ahren, Felicia, and I stayed in the living room archway to give them some maneuvering space, but we watched.

"Eli, take out the arrow," Lucy said.

Before Felix could think about it, Eli grasped Felix's arm with one hand and yanked the arrow out with the other. The blood flowed more freely.

Felix clamped his teeth together. He didn't make a sound. The man was not agreeable, but he had courage.

"Dining table," Lucy said. She looked pale but determined. She handed her brother a rag to wrap around Felix's arm, then Eli helped him from the kitchen to a chair. No drips on the floor. Lucy was practical.

Seated at the table, Felix stretched his arm on the towel. Lucy poured antiseptic liquid over Felix's arm. This new product was amazing for preventing infection, but I knew from experience that it stung. Felix turned even whiter.

The rest of us pretended to talk, so we wouldn't witness Felix's pain. While Lucy bound the wound tightly, she was asking Felix questions he wasn't in any shape to answer. Maybe she was just trying to distract him. He snarled at her. She didn't flinch.

Eli had joined us in the living room, still holding the arrow.

"It's very strangely constructed," my husband observed. "Not that I know much about arrows." He went to a window to have a better look and mutely held it out to me. I was the weapons expert.

The arrow was not only very long, but made out of a wood I couldn't name. There was still blood on the business end. Didn't bother me. I ran a finger along the shaft. "I've never seen an arrow like this," I admitted.

"It's Japanese," Hans said.

Felicia turned her head to look at him. It was a slow movement, deliberate. What was up with her?

Hans said, "Japanese arrows are longer because their bows extend more. The bow can be taller than the archer."

"What's this made of?" I asked, holding it out.

Hans took it, but he hardly looked down. "Bamboo, most likely."

"Good to know." Eli glanced from Felicia to Hans, who was looking anywhere but at my sister. He asked me a silent question, his eyes wide. I shrugged. I had no idea what was going on with her.

"Now all we have to do is find out why some unknown Japanese archer wanted to kill Felicia," I said.

"It won't stop bleeding," Lucy called. I could see the bandage she'd wrapped around Felix's arm was turning red. Lucy's mouth was pursed tight as she concentrated on her husband's arm. She was pretty worried. "Maybe there was something on the arrow?" she asked.

Not only had they wanted to pierce us with arrows, but they wanted us to bleed to death afterward.

"Felicia," Felix said. He didn't raise his voice, but he put some force into it. He was in pain.

My sister had a strange expression on her face. She was half-unhappy, half-pleased. She practically stomped into the little dining room. "Lucy, I'll have a try," she offered in a grumpy voice.

Lucy jumped up so Felicia could take her chair. Lucy had no conflict like Felicia did. Lucy was simply relieved someone could help. My sister dropped into the chair with all the grace of a sack of potatoes. She peeled off the soaked bandage.

"I know you don't like to do this," Felix said, doing his best to sound calm and grateful. "But I would be glad if you would."

"It's a misuse of power," Felicia grumped. "I'll have to sleep for at least two hours."

"You don't like it because it requires fine control," Felix retorted, sounding much more like himself.

They glared at each other for a long moment. Though their family connection was very distant, you could see a likeness, just for a moment.

Death grigoris—who excel in taking life—can also give it back, in the form of healing. The process is draining, unless you've recently sucked the life out of something, animal or person. Felicia had complained to me about twenty times that it was difficult and painful, while sucking life *out* was easy and comfortable.

Now my sister put her hands on Felix's bloody, bandaged arm and glared at it. She did not say a spell, as almost all other magic practitioners would have done. In Felicia's opinion, spells and the herb mixtures grigoris used—the reason they always wore the vests—were simply shortcuts. Felicia more or less *thought* at things.

Now she was thinking at Felix's arm.

Slowly, slowly, the bleeding stopped. Felicia dropped Felix's arm and took a few deep breaths before she stood, visibly shaky and pale. I felt a movement behind me. I turned my head to see Ahren and Hans had inched back into the little dining room, their eyes on my sister. Ahren was not a little shocked, but Hans was not a little full of admiration.

That's what a show of power will do. Even power that can be used to take life away.

"That's the most I can do. The rest will have to heal on its own. I need to go back to your house," Felicia told Eli. She was not meeting our visitors' eyes, but she held herself proudly. She did not want the two men to understand how wobbly she was.

Felix clearly needed to rest, Lucy probably wanted to clean up her dining table and take care of her husband, and I wanted to take off the damn heels. I was sure Eli wanted something, too, though I couldn't guess what that was.

It was good that Felix had gotten to the park by streetcar, or we'd have to make arrangements for his car to be retrieved. We didn't need another complication today.

It was obvious that he couldn't attend the massive opening reception tonight. As tough as Felix was, he'd suffered blood loss and the pain of the wound, and he needed to stay home and rest.

"Don't even think about trying to come tonight," Eli told his friend. Felix might have tried to protest this, but Lucy bristled with anger when her husband opened his mouth.

"You won't go, Felix," she said. "Tonight you stay home."

To my surprise, that settled it.

I was glad to see Eli giving Lucy a hug as we left, because she'd coped so well with the emergency. I gave her hand a little squeeze. *Job well done, Lucy.* She beamed.

Felicia was too busy pretending not to be exhausted to do more than give Lucy a limp wave.

We left the house in a group. I couldn't tell how the two strangers felt about the whole incident.

What had we done to upset the Japanese?

What had we done to upset *anybody?*

Felicia was a very young woman attending her first Wizards'

Ball, and she hadn't done anything to warrant being shot. I kind of shook myself when I realized we'd all been standing together in the front yard, all silent.

Eli thought of the right thing to say to the two Germans. "Do you know how to drive to your destination?" he asked. "Do you want directions? If you need, we will be glad to show you the way."

That was a nice offer.

"We only have to drive to the ferry parking lot and leave the car there," Hans said. "We know the way. I've been in San Diego before."

Ahren nodded. "We're staying at the Del Coronado."

Ahren Hirsch's family might be refugees, but they'd sent him to the Wizards' Ball well supplied with money. Even I had heard how swanky the Hotel del Coronado was. The hotel was not only located on Imperial Island (formerly North Island) but on the water. Movie stars stayed there. Apparently, so did wealthy German Jewish refugees.

"I hope we will see you this evening," Hans said. His English was excellent, with much less of an accent than Ahren's.

"We'll be there if nothing prevents us," Eli said. "I hope the incident this afternoon was an isolated one, that we can continue this week in safety."

As if the words had been ripped from her throat, Felicia said, "Thanks for your help in the park. I truly appreciate it."

Her words were the right ones, but her tone was off. Everything she did around these two men was odd. I hoped the German cousins could not tell. I was glad she'd said something, though. We owed them.

At the park, Ahren and Hans could have cut and run, or they could have stood back and let the archers continue to take shots at us. They'd chosen to defend my sister. One of them had been responsible for the shield thrown up around us.

"We were very glad to be of assistance," Ahren said. Ahren and Hans gave us polite bows and were on their way.

Felicia looked after them. I could not read her face.

I was going to have to have a talk with my sister. Maybe not today, because it had been long and uncomfortable and nerve-racking—and it wasn't over yet.

CHAPTER FIVE

I t was about a twenty-minute drive from Felix's humble neigh-borhood to the much swankier one where the Savarov home stood. It had been beautifully restored after the brief siege when the tsar had been visiting and rebels had attempted to take him. We'd all defended him. The front door had been splintered, Felicia's bombs had left craters all over the yard when she and Eli had tossed them from the roof, and the dead were piled high.

Now the lawn looked green and smooth, though it was January. The roof had been reshingled, the windows replaced. The new front door was more handsome than the previous one. And all the blood had soaked into the ground.

We had defended the tsar vigorously. Alexei had been prop-erly grateful, at least in that he'd paid for the repairs and the body removal.

But Alexei hadn't been grateful enough to ask Eli to return to San Diego, to resume his place as a grigori who worked directly for him. Not grateful enough to summon Veronika back to court after the death of her traitor husband.

At least the repairs had been made.

A few months ago Captain Ford McMurtry, aide to the tsarina, had been given the green light to marry Veronika. Maybe soon, when Alexei could think of her more as McMurtry's wife instead of Prince Ivan Savarov's widow, she'd get reinstated to her former social position.

Veronika must have heard the car on the gravel of the drive. She was waiting by the door. Alice was right on her heels, eager to hear about our jaunt in the Japanese Friendship Garden. It was good to see Alice look excited.

Alice, Eli and Lucy's little sister, had been hardest hit by her brother Peter's death. In her letters to us, Veronika had expressed worry about Alice, hoping that something would happen to distract the girl (who was a little older than Felicia, but much younger in most ways) from her grief.

The excitement of the events surrounding the Wizards' Ball had given Alice a lift. Up until San Diego, the festivities had been secret (though in some countries an open secret) because magic was frightening. The people who wielded it did not enjoy the limelight.

But San Diego was doing things differently. The tsar loved his grigoris because Grigori Rasputin's blood (and the blood of Rasputin's descendants) had saved his life. So all magic practitioners were welcome to be themselves in the Holy Russian Empire, formerly known as California and Oregon. Newspaper and magazine articles were full of stories of the visiting families that practiced some form of magic, and their activities in and around San Diego.

I thought it was a big mistake to have a lot of the scheduled events listed in the newspaper, but no one had asked me. Anyway, it kept Alice entertained. Veronika had told me Alice wasn't officially "out," whatever that meant. But Alice was all dreamy about the list of dances and parties and whatnot taking place throughout the week.

Now in her early forties, Veronika was very attractive. She'd been Prince Savarov's second wife, much younger than him. During the yearslong sea voyage with the royal family while they sought refuge, Veronika had had four children. She'd weathered raising those children despite an uncaring husband who already had two uncaring older sons.

Veronika had endured Eli's being thrown in jail for no reason, had survived being a hostage of a renegade grigori in this very house, and had lived through the coup attempt while the tsar was in her home, only to lose her second son.

I had gotten Eli out of jail, saved Veronika and the girls from the renegade, and defended the tsar and the house during the last coup attempt.

That was why Veronika had done her best to act happy when Eli chose to marry me. And she was proving a tremendous help this week, hosting us in her home and loaning us clothes and advice.

I had to give her credit for all this, but we did not like each other. The best we'd achieved was an uneasy truce.

"Did you have a good day?" Veronika asked Eli.

"Felicia, how was the garden?" Alice said eagerly. "Did you meet a lot of men?"

Felicia was halfway up the stairs. "I'll tell you all about it after I get these clothes off," she called. "It was all good but the arrow attack. Felix is okay. Lucy was a rock."

Veronika and Alice turned to us, their eyes wide. Veronika was looking only at me, because obviously if there was trouble, I was the cause.

"I've got to change shoes," I said. "Eli can tell you about it." I went up the stairs as fast as my tired feet could carry me. Damn heels. I was going to have blisters, I just knew it. I plodded up the stairs and across the main landing to continue up a smaller flight of stairs. Every step was slower than the last.

I didn't feel bad at all about leaving Eli to explain to his mother and sister.

Veronika had put us in the attic room again. This third-floor area had been designed to be the maids' room, but there weren't any living in anymore. The current maid, Leah, and the cook came in every morning and left after dinner. Veronika had worked to make the room nicer, and it had much more privacy since it was the only room on this floor besides the attic. And it had its own bathroom, which almost made up for the extra stairs.

I was unpleasantly surprised to realize Felicia was right behind me. She'd managed to change into a robe in record time, and she'd put a net over her hair to keep it smooth.

Okay, she wanted to talk.

She opened her mouth to begin, but I held up a hand.

"Give me a second," I said. I undressed very carefully. I'd have to wear this outfit again. No stains or rips, no arrow holes, no blood. I turned so Felicia could lower the back zipper. While I pulled a frilly robe out of the closet (it had been hanging there when we'd arrived, a gift from my mother-in-law), my sister hung up the dress and coat.

"What's on your mind?" I sat in the armchair by the window, and Felicia perched on the bench at the end of the bed, her knees drawn up and her chin resting on them. I waited. She took a deep breath, glanced around the room. She let the breath out and shook her head.

If she would only get to the point, maybe I'd have time to take a nap.

"Spill the beans. Who is this Hans?"

Felicia's big brown eyes fixed on me. "Dammit, I didn't think I . . ."

"Who?"

She hugged her knees tighter. "During the attack on Segundo Mexia," she said. "While we were trying to get to the Antelope. You were out, remember?"

"Thanks to your aunt," I said. "As if I could forget that." Isabella Dominguez had decided that if I died, Felicia would agree to be guided by her at the parties leading up to the upcoming Wizards' Ball. As Isabella saw it, a marriage advantageous to Felicia would be a marriage advantageous to her. Isabella was also impulsive. She blasted me with a spell. Felicia had stopped her from killing me by gripping her aunt with her own power.

"A man came out of nowhere. He helped me hold Isabella, but he advised me not to kill her. And he checked on you, told me you were alive."

"I remember." Just barely. "He was in disguise. After he made sure I was okay and stopped you from killing Isabella, he vamoosed."

"Why do you say he was in disguise?"

I was taken aback. My memory of the evening was a little woozy, since not only had Isabella knocked me down hard enough that I'd slid across the road, but a few minutes afterward I'd had to fight for my life in my stepfather's hotel. But this I recalled. "He had a bandanna pulled up to his eyes, and he had a cowboy hat on, pulled down," I said. "That's a disguise. It was getting dark, wasn't it?"

"I never saw him. He just . . . came up behind me. He laid his hand on my shoulder. He gave me strength to control Isabella. Which I was doing pretty well, by the way. But it helped."

"So he was a grigori. Some kind of magician, anyway."

"When he went to check on you, he had his back to me."

You could tell she'd relived this in her head many times.

I felt more and more worried. "He must have had some reason for being there, just when the militia was attacking," I said, very carefully. "He must have had just as good a reason for dodging out after he helped you. He never showed you his face. He left in an almighty hurry."

Felicia nodded. She agreed that those things had happened. She did not agree with my interpretation. She looked a little miserable but a lot excited.

"You got fixated on this man who had his hand on your shoulder, though you never saw him and you didn't even talk much?" Not only did this story sound like a bad novel, but I didn't like that Felicia had kept this a secret . . . especially not when we were going all-out to give her this opportunity.

"I've thought about him a lot," she said, talking to her knees. "You see why? He showed up, helped me, and vanished. Just like today."

"Romantic and mysterious." Two words I seldom said, and never with relish. I enjoyed romance and mystery in the odd book I had time to read, but not in real life.

Felicia nodded. "You noticed Hans didn't talk until I said something directly to him?" she said, with great meaning.

"Yes," I said cautiously.

"When he finally said something out loud, I was sure he was the man from that night." She raised her face to look at me directly.

"You going to ask him?"

Felicia shrugged, with a totally unbelievable show of not caring one way or the other. She looked away again. "We may not see him after today. If it was him, he saw me for the first time when bullets were flying, and now he sees me again and gets shot at by arrows. *Japanese* arrows," she added, as if that made the attack much worse.

It was my turn to take a deep breath. "You will recall, right, that the reason you're here is to maybe meet the right young man? That you've waited months for this week. That Eli and I have gone to considerable trouble to make sure you're included in this event, though we were glad to do it. And that you're the strongest Listed woman at this ball."

My sister nodded, doing her best to look miserable and sorry.

But not quite miserable or sorry enough.

She went back to staring at her knees. "Hans has got to be seven or eight years older than me," she said. "He doesn't look rich, like Ahren. That's okay, though. I've never been rich. If he's that guy, he's got power. Just . . . Why is he hiding it? How did he get to be the humble kinsman traveling with the really eligible and cute Ahren? How did he come to be in Segundo Mexia that exact evening?"

I had no answer to any of these questions. My eyelids were feeling increasingly heavy. "Don't get so fixed on Hans that you close doors," I said. "We got to know more about him."

"I agree with you," she said, to my relief. "I can't make a choice this early. I'm not even sure . . . I'm going to go lie down a little." She stood suddenly. "You know the reason I hate healing a little wound?"

"I can't imagine."

"I give a little life back into the wound, to close the little bit of death it caused," Felicia said. "And I get *nothing* back. If I kill something, I get its life, its power, so exciting. Wounds, nothing. Am I not a peach?" Bitter, for sure.

I couldn't think of a single thing to make her feel better. She was what she was. I decided to change the subject. "We need to leave here this evening at six thirty, Eli says."

This evening was the opening reception of the week of the Wizards' Ball. For the first time in its history, the week of matchmaking and togetherness was being held openly and named for what it was.

Tsar Alexei was going to appear to give "opening remarks." The tsarina, Caroline, would be with him.

There would be speechifying from a few members of the organizing committee, a "collation" would be served, and then there'd be singers from the San Diego Opera.

No dancing, very little sitting, no exhibition of magic in any form. Eli had spelled it out for me. We had to be all dressed up for this one. "Evening attire," Eli had drawled in an assumed high-class accent . . . like he wasn't really one of the aristocrats.

Felicia rose to leave. But she had a parting shot.

"Veronika put me in Peter's room," she said over her shoulder. "I think she's punishing me." And then she slipped out the door.

Peter had loved Felicia. But he was dead, and here she was, inviting the attention of other men. Eli had made Felicia's future his business, so Veronika would support his effort. That didn't mean she was happy. Eli's mom was well-bred, but she wasn't above giving a little stab when she could.

Not two minutes later, Eli came in. He began throwing off his clothes, too.

"You're going to bathe?"

"If you are agreeable, I would like to enjoy some husband-and-wife time," Eli said. "There's nothing like having an arrow brush past your back to make you appreciate the things you can enjoy if you're alive."

"I'm agreeable," I said, ditching the idea of a nap. This was something we hadn't done in a while. I missed it. I slid the robe off and stood there in my fancy underwear.

Eli really liked that.

That was the best thirty minutes of my day. Afterward, I finally got in an hour-long snooze.

CHAPTER SIX

I was glittering in one of Veronika's evening gowns. It was clingy and sleeveless, a dark plum color. I had a fur evening jacket to wear over the dress. It would be chilly when we left the island. I was wearing silk evening shoes, the most useless footwear ever invented.

Veronika had located a hairdresser who would come every day this week, though of course Eli and I were paying her. The hairdresser, Abigail, had worked on me after she'd dolled up Felicia. I was wearing some jewelry, also courtesy of Veronika: diamond earbobs and a diamond pendant. I couldn't imagine what my mother and Jackson and their baby, Samuel—my brother!—would think if they could see me now. Samuel would not even know who I was.

I was sure lucky Veronika and I were about the same size. I was also lucky my mother-in-law was really gracious about it, maybe more so because she had no occasion to wear such clothes until she was allowed back at court.

There would be more people at this reception than at any other event of the week. Not only were all the official Wizards' Ball attendees invited, but also many people to whom the royal couple owed hospitality or recognition. It was another "look and walk," but indoors. Another complete change of clothes, a crowd of people I didn't want to know, so many voices talking.

The happiest person in the Savarov house was Alice. Since Felix was down with his wound, Eli had asked his little sister if she'd like to be the fourth person covered by our invitation. She had a rose silk evening dress she'd never gotten to wear. Alice looked real pretty in it, and she was so excited her cheeks were pink.

She and Felicia chattered nonstop in the car on our way to the parking lot at the ferry landing.

This reception was being held in the newly built Imperial Ballroom, attached to the palace on Imperial Island. There was a causeway built on the southern side of the island, but it was for the convenience of the many builders coming to work every day. Eli had told me that sooner or later a causeway would be built across the stretch of water closest to the palace and the other imperial buildings, but that hadn't happened yet. Visitors had to catch the ferry. There were usually two running at heavy traffic times like tonight.

There were guards at each end of the ferry ride. The tsar was the target of assassins, from time to time.

Of course, the deck space was jammed with people in their finest clothes.

I had to say "Pardon me" ten times to stay by Felicia. I had run out of "polite" by the time we crossed the water.

After we'd passed the scrutiny of the heavily armed guards on the island side, we faced a different kind of test. Eli had to present our invitation to the vigilant women forming a ladylike barricade across the road. After our particular lady had looked us over with sharp eyes and read the invitation (which had been addressed to Felicia Karkarova Dominguez, with "Savarov" added in parentheses since the Savarovs were her sponsors), the lady nodded and looked up with a brilliant smile. We were acceptable.

"Prince Ilya, it's good to see you back," she said as she gestured us on our way.

That was reassuring. We hadn't been positive his credentials as Felicia's sponsor would be accepted, though Felicia had received her Listed paperwork.

Eli and I exchanged a quick glance that said a lot of things: relief, mostly, but joy and triumph on Eli's end. He wanted this recognition so bad; I'd never realized how much, until now.

The road forward was also lined with guards. It was possible to move, but at more like a fast shuffle than a stride. At last we reached the ground-level doors to the ballroom, another bottleneck.

We inched closer.

Finally we passed the threshold.

Despite the chilly evening, the vast room was warm from the many bodies packed in. As more and more guests crowded forward, I began to feel constricted. How could I do my job? The arrow attack in a public place in the daytime had proved Felicia had to be protected.

My job was to make sure no one brought her down.

I had only knives on me. I am good with a knife, but firearms are my best thing. I'd gotten away with pulling a gun at Balboa Park, probably because I hadn't actually fired a shot, but I couldn't attempt that here. You couldn't bring guns into the presence of the royal family. There would be no slack at all on that. I would certainly go to jail. I might be executed.

There was a knife in my evening bag. There was a knife in my garter. There was a makeshift pocket sewn into the lining of my evening jacket, and there was a knife in that. If I was able to stand being warm in the jacket, drawing that one was my best bet.

"You look beautiful," Eli said. "I should have told you before."

Though it's always nice to hear this, I have to say it felt strange to get this compliment when I was wearing his mother's clothes. At least Veronika and I had one thing in common: we were both short and slim, but not flat in the chest. The clingy plum dress fit well.

"You look great, too," I said. My husband, his long, light hair slicked back and braided, looked very distinguished in his black tuxedo, with a white vest and shirt and black bow tie. You could see the edge of his neck tattoos. He had new ones on the backs of his hands. He couldn't wear his grigori vest to this reception, the invitation had made clear, but he had a few tiny pockets sewed into the tuxedo jacket lining. Yes, Eli was ready, and he looked good.

He looked best in nothing at all, but I'd call evening wear a good second.

"Felicia is a credit to the school," Eli murmured. "And to us."

Felicia's dress was the rust of an autumn leaf. (I'd seen that once in Britannia. I'd never forgotten it.) Felicia's dark hair was perfect, thanks to Abigail the Hairdresser.

Felicia looked young, attractive, and confident . . . if only there had been enough room around her for anyone to enjoy the view.

Eli had called this the "everyone and their cow" reception, and he hadn't been exaggerating.

After this evening, there'd be many smaller events hosted by the various nationalities and magical systems attending. There'd be dances, dinner parties, picnics, afternoon teas, swimming pool festivities, and so on and so on, held at locations around the city. All the better hotels were booked solid, and some of the lesser-known ones, too. San Diego was booming.

I recognized a few other Listed candidates. I'd studied them as intently as Felicia had. It had seemed important.

I didn't want to waste this evening by letting Felicia be part of the herd.

I set my jaw, jerked my head in a forward motion to Eli, Felicia, and Alice, and began to force a path through the throng to get closer to the gallery. That's where the tsar and tsarina would appear, so

Alexei could deliver the welcome speech without actually getting down into the midst of so many people. I was as nice as I could afford to be in moving us forward . . . which wasn't very. The crowded ferry had taken care of that.

I got the four of us close to the front of the crowd just in time. The big double doors upstairs opened and the tsar and tsarina emerged into the gallery. Everyone applauded. All eyes were on the royal couple.

Alexei was wearing all his medals and ribbons and whatnot. Caroline was shining in silver. Captain Ford McMurtry, Veronika's husband and the tsarina's aide, was right behind her.

I glanced at my companions. Eli looked neutral, which was good, since he definitely had mixed feelings about the royal family. Alice was beaming like a lighthouse, full of delight. Felicia, who had often donated blood to the tsar to cure an episode of his bleeding disease, was smiling because she had to. She was closer to Alexei than any of us, since her blood literally ran in his veins. Her face might be composed and calm, but I could feel the power pulsing out of her.

I also felt something bad coming my way.

I'm not magical. I can't cast a spell. But I have enough grigori blood from my father to know when ill-will is around. Though the huge room was full of people who practiced it, I knew this approaching thing was nearing us.

I slid my hand into the narrow pocket I'd sewn into Veronika's evening jacket (sorry, Veronika) and pulled out a knife. I pressed the button to open it. I stood tight against my sister's right side. Eli was on her left, Alice directly behind. They were all looking up at the royal couple. Everyone was.

Everyone but me and the man who pushed into place beside me. His eyes were locked on Felicia. She was his target. I was only meat in the way. His knife was already in his hand, held down at his side, but when I raised my empty left hand, his eyes met mine. As I'd hoped, he hesitated.

In that second, without even a thought, I stabbed him—low, to keep my hand out of sight of the crowd. He made a shocked noise, not very loud, more of a grunt.

He did look down then, looked at the knife in his stomach, not believing. His layers of clothes were soaking up the blood. I wouldn't get any on me if I moved quickly. I pulled the knife back out, wiped it on his trousers, pressed the button again, and shoved the knife back into its sheath.

I didn't look at him again.

I put my left arm around Felicia and forced her to take three steps forward with me. I caught Eli's eyes, flicked mine toward the man, whose face must have been awful. After he saw that, my husband pushed as hard as I did.

People filled in the space we'd left instantly, like sand filling a hole on the riverbank. The pressure of their bodies kept the would-be assassin standing for a few precious seconds.

Eli and I turned our eyes to the royal couple. Alice's had never left. I wasn't sure about my sister.

Afterward, I could not have told you anything about Tsar Alexei's speech. I was trying to listen to what was happening behind me, without actually turning to look.

A few guests behind us gave shocked little cries. Though their shock was muted—because after all, the tsar was speaking—I had an excuse to glance back. Anyone would. From the little gap where guests had pulled away, I knew the body had finally had enough room to crumple to the floor. I looked forward. No concern of mine.

To my right, a stout uniformed man with many medals raised his arm, beckoning. Two soldiers from the sentries stationed around the edges of the room began plowing through the packed guests to investigate.

Felicia turned her head to look at me. Her dark eyebrows flew up, asking a question. I shook my head.

Lost in happiness, Alice murmured, "This is so wonderful!" She didn't even notice the flutter of action behind us. I smiled at her. Then it was eyes forward.

I was concerned there might be a bit of blood on my dress, but there was no way I could check. I was glad it was a dark fabric. Another quick sideways glance told me the dead man was being supported between two brawny soldiers and removed from the room as rapidly as they could maneuver through the packed people.

Alexei concluded his little speech, but he might as well have been singing "Mary Had a Little Lamb."

My head was full of worries. Could the dead man be traced to me? Who had sent him? Why did he want to kill my sister? Did his family or clan have a prodigy who might shine more if Felicia was not there?

That was a crappy reason to kill my sister.

But I felt the knife going in and coming out, over and over.

If I'd shot the man out in the street while he'd had a gun in his hand, I'd have felt much better . . . though he'd be just as dead.

Or if the guests had panicked and stampeded, down we'd have gone.

All these second thoughts, when as a rule I had none. I told myself this was like being back on a gun crew, hired to defend cargo. I had done this many, many times over the past five years.

But this time the cargo was my sister, I wasn't getting paid, and our situation was not open and clear, but somehow sneaky and unclean.

No matter how it made me feel, I had to carry this task through until Felicia came out the other side.

The applause had died down after the end of the speech, but now Alexei took Caroline's hand and kissed it. The royal couple inclined their heads graciously to the assemblage. There rose a roar from the crowd, and I moved us even closer to the gallery.

Captain McMurtry leaned over to Caroline and said something in her ear. Caroline looked in our direction.

She recognized me and smiled. Once upon a time, I'd saved her life in the same garden we'd visited earlier today. I nodded, which was as close as I could come to a bow, hemmed in as I was.

Caroline's smile went from standard to bright. She deliberately leaned over the railing to wave directly at me and my sister. Of course, that was noticed. Caroline had known it would be.

People turned to look.

Eli might not be in favor with the tsar, but Felicia and I were, at least with his wife. Felicia had saved the tsar's life in more ways than one, and I had saved Caroline's.

My sister somehow executed a lovely curtsy to acknowledge the tsarina.

Points for us.

I ignored the flurry back at the doors to the ballroom, which were being flung open to allow the removal of the body.

Nothing was in my sights but securing the future of my sister.

CHAPTER SEVEN

Caroline's recognition had an unexpected result.

Alice looked impossibly young and fresh and happy in her rose silk dress. I wasn't the only one who thought so.

As per protocol—I had learned that quickly, because Eli was not a patient teacher—I was approached by a couple in their forties. At twenty-one, I was the oldest woman in our party, so I was the point of contact.

The husband, Boris Volkov, explained he was one of the engineers responsible for extending the palace and making the whole island fit for an emperor. His wife, Levdokia, was responsible for the care and feeding of Mr. Volkov and their son, Konstantin, their only child and heir. Konstantin was twenty years old and working with his father every day.

Levdokia told me all this up front and very skillfully, to let me know that Konstantin was an eligible young man with an income and prospects.

Konstantin himself was sturdy and steady. He had dark hair and hazel eyes in an open face.

Levdokia also let me know that Konstantin had a streak of grigori earth talent—not strong enough to warrant going to the Rasputin School, but enough to have been coached by a working earth grigori to use his ability to help in his father's construction work. It had descended to him through Levdokia's mother, she let me know.

Though I'd enjoyed talking to the Volkovs because they seemed down-to-earth people, I was waiting to find out why they'd approached me. I'd assumed their son was interested in Felicia, and she was way out of his weight class. I liked the couple, so I was pleased as punch when Boris Volkov told me, "Konstantin would like to meet the young lady in the rose-colored dress, if that is permitted."

I kept a straight face with some effort. "My sister-in-law, Alice Savarova, is at her first public event. I think she would be pleased to make a new friend." *Alice is gently bred and young.* "Perhaps you know Captain McMurtry, her stepfather?"

"Of course, I know the captain by sight," Boris said, looking relieved at having found a connection. "He has an excellent reputation."

Alice had been listening to a conversation Felicia was having with Mateo Medina Dominguez. "Excuse me," I said, and took Alice's hand to draw her forward. "Alice, meet Mr. and Mrs. Volkov and their son, Konstantin. Mr. Volkov is an engineer on all the new construction on the island, and his son, Konstantin, works with him."

Alice smiled with genuine delight. Someone actually wanted to meet her! Suddenly she looked lovely. Konstantin beamed at her. While I kept up a conversation with the parents, Alice and the young man began to talk. I half-listened to them, and the Volkovs were doing the same, so our own chat was what you would call random.

When Konstantin asked Alice if he could take her to the buffet table to get a drink and some food, Alice looked at me questioningly. That was proper. I was going by the rules if it killed me.

"That would be a good idea," I said. "It's quite warm in here." I was tickled to be in the position of matron.

"May I also get something for you, Princess Savarova? Mama?"

He had good manners. "No, thank you," Levdokia and I said in chorus. The two young people began making their way to the food and drink area. The crowd had loosened up now that the focus was off the gallery. This had turned into another "walk and look."

After a very polite goodbye, and a hope that we would meet again, the Volkovs moved on to talk to another couple. Behind me Eli said, "What was that? Another suitor for Felicia?"

"No, for Alice," I said, turning to enjoy the flash of surprise on his face. "You never thought about Alice and Felicia being about the same age, I guess."

"No, I didn't. She's my baby sister."

"She's older than Felicia. The parents are Boris and Levdokia Volkov."

"Oh, I know of him. Works here on the island? Specializes in earth moving. Where are Alice and the boy?"

I nodded toward one of the refreshment tables lining the sides of the vast room. "He's a man. He's working for his father. The mother made sure I knew Konstantin is in line to inherit the business, when that time comes."

"He looks steady," Eli told me after a long look at the couple. He nodded as if he were fifty years old.

"Think your mother would approve?"

"After the shock of Lucy marrying Felix, Konstantin Volkov would be a godsend. I need to start walking Felicia around, if you will keep your eyes on those two."

Eli could do my sister more good in the social way. He knew everyone and had the rules down.

"I'll watch 'em like a hawk," I said.

Eli took a step closer and bent down. "Who was the man?" he said, very quietly. "What did he want?"

"After Felicia," I said. "Knife."

"Thank you," he said.

"My job."

Off he went with my sister to see and be seen. As I'd promised, I kept my eyes on Konstantin and Alice, who were chattering away. Alice had a glass and a little plate in her hands, and so did the young man. I didn't know what was in the glass, but with my eyes on her nothing would happen. It was good to see the shy Alice blooming.

During the next few minutes, I met a couple more people who just wanted to find out who I was. A Greek magic practitioner, a woman in her forties named Rhea Pappos, stopped first. After we swapped names, I waited to see what she had on her mind.

"Did you see what happened to the man who collapsed?" Rhea asked.

"No. It was sudden, wasn't it? I wonder if he's all right."

"They dragged him by me," Rhea said. She had a heavy accent, but I could understand her. "I am sure he was dead."

"Oh my gosh! Did you know him?"

"I know who he was. He was with the German delegation, but not a Listed candidate."

He'd been too old, at least ten years past the cutoff birthday. But I wasn't supposed to have noticed him. "Maybe he was a chaperone or family member of a candidate?" I said.

Rhea looked at me with an expression I can only call "knowing." I wondered if I'd have to kill her. I hoped not.

"Yes, I think he must have been a family member. Or maybe sent by the German government."

I could feel my brows knitting, and I smoothed out my face. "Governments send guards?"

"A few of them. This year the Germans, the Italians, and the Japanese have sent extra people. Also the British territories. Especially Palestine."

"That's very interesting," I said honestly. I would have to tell Eli.

"Oh my goodness!" Rhea Pappos said quietly. "Someone has spilled wine on your beautiful dress."

Rhea was right about the dark red stain. Just a small one.

"I'm glad you told me," I said, again with honesty. I had been leery of looking down myself. "In this crowd, no telling how that happened." I looked at Rhea directly. "I'm not worried about it."

"Then you are not the worrier I am," Rhea said. She smiled at me. "Watch out for the Germans and the Japanese, especially. This year, they have their own goals to meet. And no discipline." Rhea definitely had no respect for people without discipline.

"Thank you for the warning," I said, and the Greek woman glided away.

Alice and Konstantin had had enough alone time, I judged. I made my way over to my sister-in-law and gently detached her from her admirer. Konstantin seemed like an okay kid, but I wanted him to know Alice had watchful relatives.

Why stop at one success for my sister-in-law? I attached her to Eli and Felicia's progress around the room, so Alice could have even more fun. I sought a place against the wall, where people could be coming at me from only one direction. I finally let myself look down at my dress. There was one blotch. It was quite small. I was glad my dress was a dark color. Rhea Pappos must have the eyes of a hawk.

I had a few moments of peace and quiet, but then I was approached by a man who must have been at least thirty, a magician from some country where the days were hot. He looked incredibly tough. His skin had been darkened by the sun. His hair had been bleached by it. It made his pale eyes show even brighter.

"I hear you're a shooter," he said, with no preamble.

"I am."

The man waited for me to embroider on that, but I was out of embroidery.

"Nice to meet a gal who doesn't talk and talk." He had an accent I'd never heard before. I wasn't curious enough to ask, though.

I waited, hoping he would walk away. But no.

"Do you know much about South Africa?"

"No." But I knew there were lions there, so I was interested. At least a little.

"I am from the Boer community." He had a strong accent, but if I listened carefully I could follow him. "My great-grandfather and -mother immigrated to South Africa from Holland, and they built a lovely farm. Passed it on to their son and his wife. They intended it for their son, my father. Then I would have had it. But the damn British made our lives impossible. We went to war. It lasted for a very long time. We damn near won. They beat us by sheer numbers."

He was waiting on me to comment. "Sheer numbers are pretty important" was all I could think of. He wasn't finished with his story, and he was determined to finish it.

"The British had camps for the Boer women and children. Interment camps. About thirty thousand people died in them. Including my grandmother."

"Where are you going with this?" I said, running out of patience. "If you're courting, I'm already married." I held up the hand with the ring on it. "If you're just aiming to tell me the history of your people, I'd rather hear it some other time." Or never. "This isn't the place."

The South African, who still hadn't introduced himself, gave me a real cold stare. I gave him one right back.

"If you want to know where the lines are being drawn," he said, when I was just about to walk away, "I've told you."

"Right," I said, none the wiser. This time I walked away, shaking my head. This was a crazy night. I didn't know what I'd expected, but it hadn't been this.

Most of these people had a completely social goal. That's what I'd figured. Just words with smiles. I knew now that some people had other goals that came far before courtesy.

All of them seemed to know a lot of things I didn't. That was one of my least-favorite feelings. I'd had it for days now.

After another hour of doing my best not to talk to people, I got Eli's signal that we could leave.

By that time I had a hundred questions, but I couldn't ask them on the ferry. We were surrounded by other guests who'd called it a night. Even Alice and Felicia were quiet, but after we got in the car, they recovered.

The girls talked nonstop the whole way home. I didn't listen. Despite my afternoon nap, I was very tired. Eli seemed pleased, so his promenade with Felicia must have been promising. I wasn't going to ask any questions just now.

Captain McMurtry had not yet made it back from the palace, so Veronika was still awake. Her face lit up when she understood that Alice had met someone, though she immediately clamped down on that so Alice wouldn't see how relieved and surprised she was. Veronika kept a smile on her face even when she understood that Boris Volkov was an engineer on the island, not one of the aristocrats living as close to the tsar as they could manage. After all, the Volkovs had been invited to the reception. That meant they had some standing.

And when Alice told her mother that I had kept an eagle eye on her the whole evening, my mother-in-law gave me an approving nod. (That was a first.) Veronika was much calmer about Felicia's little triumphs and stories, though she listened well enough.

I realized another thing about my mother-in-law. Not only did she maybe blame Peter's death on Felicia and me, she also would have realized that the prospect of a brilliant marriage for Felicia (now that Peter was dead) was much more possible for my slumborn, murderous sister than her highborn and gently bred girl.

I was too tired to feel very ashamed of myself for not having figured this out before.

I plodded slowly up to the attic room. Eli was only a few steps behind me.

While Eli was in the bathroom, I slipped out of the dress. I looked at the bloodstain. I had no idea if it would come out of this material. I couldn't care about that tonight. Maybe ever. I hung it in the closet and hoped the maid, Leah, would think of a way to remove the blood.

I pulled on my nightgown, brushed my teeth, and washed my face, all the time thinking about the dead man's eyes. Eli was pottering around the room, and it didn't take a wife to know there was something on his mind, too.

"He had drawn a knife," I said, pulling the bedspread down. I figured he was about to ask me if my killing the man had been provoked, and I wasn't in any mood to hear that question. Just because I could kill people didn't mean I enjoyed it or did it on a whim.

"I am sure he had," Eli said, and he turned to look me straight in the eyes, so I'd know he meant it. "You did the right thing, the only thing you could do."

"So how come you're bumbling around like a bee in a flower garden?" *But not a happy bee*, I thought.

"I learned a few things tonight that trouble me," Eli said.

No kidding. I never would have known.

"But I can't tell you about them now. Sometime in the next two days I will have to go to a . . . meeting with other grigoris. I hope

I will learn things that will help us guide your sister through this week. If she does seem to favor a particular suitor, this meeting will have a direct bearing on their eligibility."

"And you're going to share this information with her?"

Eli said, "I will if I can. I will have to take oaths before I am allowed in the meeting."

"Will you be able to tell me what happens?"

"I want to, because I don't like to keep secrets from you."

That was rich. Eli always had secrets. Grigori stuff. Maybe if I belonged to a fancy elite group of gunnies I would be the same way? But I didn't think so.

I told him about the Boer . . . who'd been a bore, but a disturbing one. "Do you know what he meant when he told me there were lines being drawn?" I asked, crawling into bed and pulling up the covers.

"I think so," Eli said, getting in on the other side. "He was saying that some of the South African people had a grudge against England and wouldn't side with them in the upcoming war."

About ten questions sprang to mind, but they never made it out of my mouth. The overload of the day piled on top of me all of a sudden. I went to sleep.

CHAPTER EIGHT

When I woke the next morning, Eli had already gone downstairs. I threw on my jeans and a shirt. I'd bathe and get dressed later. I was hungry.

When I walked into the dining room, Ford—I had to stop thinking of him as Captain McMurtry—was telling Veronika about last night from his point of view. She was smiling at him. They were too full of the happiness of being newlyweds for my mother-in-law to be sour about my jeans.

We had known Ford had been accepted by Veronika and that they planned to get married months ago. Eli and I had assumed we'd travel back to San Diego to be present for the ceremony. Instead, a neighbor had come up the hill with a telegram for us. Ford and Eli's mom had gone to city hall. They'd gotten hitched with only Alice and Lucy in attendance.

For a couple of days Eli tried my patience to the limit. He'd fumed. In his mind, he'd become the head of the household upon his father's death. He felt it had been his duty and right to be present at his mother's wedding, with me by his side. He felt this very strongly, as he told me several times.

After a couple of days, I'd talked him around. To me, Veronika's decision was understandable. She was a grown woman, a widow, and didn't need anyone to "give her away." We'd sent them a telegram of congratulations, and Eli had written a long, civil letter. I'd written a note myself.

Looking at my mother-in-law this morning, I could tell how much better life had been treating her . . . with the huge exception of losing Peter.

Ford left for the palace, after giving his wife a fond kiss. The minute he'd gotten out the door, Veronika dashed up to her room. That was strange. I didn't think it was my company she was dodging. She would have been more polite. I shrugged and ate breakfast in blessed silence.

I was wondering about a long list of things.

I wondered where Eli had gone, but I wouldn't have asked Veronika for a hundred dollars and a new gun.

I wondered if Ford knew what had happened to the man who'd "collapsed" at the reception. I figured it wouldn't have been wise to show much interest.

I wondered if he would vouch for the Volkovs. But that was for Veronika to do as Alice's mother.

Eli had left Felicia's schedule for the day on the table. I picked it up with a sigh.

Today I had to chaperone Felicia to a ladies-only midafternoon tea and coffee party at the home of Madame Semyonova's daughter, Tatiana Medvedeva. I didn't know the hostess, but she must have a large house suitable for the occasion. This evening, both Eli and I were going to escort Felicia to a party on Imperial Island, at Hotel Del Coronado. This invitation had arrived the night before by messenger.

Maybe Eli had gone to his secret meeting with the other grigoris. I listened hard, hoping I'd hear the back door open and the sound of his step.

When we were at home in Segundo Mexia, I pretty much knew where Eli was every hour of the day.

As if she'd felt my uneasiness, Veronika came back into the room. She looked pretty pale. Maybe she was ailing. "I forgot to tell you, Lizbeth. Eli left early. He said he was going to check on Felix's arm. I can't believe that happened at Balboa Park." She seemed more startled by the fact that the attack had taken place in a beautiful public park than that someone had shot at Felix.

"Yes, it was pretty alarming." It wasn't necessary to tell her how close an arrow had come to her son. She couldn't do anything about it except worry.

"I better go upstairs," I said instead. "Felicia needs to be up. Oh, what should I wear to a tea and coffee afternoon?"

Naturally, Veronika knew. I thought she seemed to like me better now that she could give me advice all the time. And she didn't seem to mind me borrowing her clothes. It wasn't that I was so proud I had to have a closetful of new outfits. I just hated wearing strange clothes that weren't easy to move in.

"Leah will put a dress and matching purse in your room. Oh, what was that stain on the evening dress? She's trying to get it out."

"Wine," I said. "In a crowd that packed, I couldn't avoid it. I'm sorry."

"Oh, I understand. People drink too much and they get clumsy. You can't be safe from spills."

"And I'm sorry I'm wearing all your clothes," I said, unable to stop myself.

Veronika actually laughed. "I won't be able to wear them for a while."

I assumed she meant she wouldn't be able to go to court, and wouldn't need so many dresses, for a while yet. And then she could get new ones, I hoped. She'd like that.

I knocked on Felicia's door and made sure I heard her stirring before I climbed the final flight to our room.

Though I was concerned about Eli's long absence, it was very pleasant to have some time alone. After I bathed, I was able to settle down with a book Felicia had given me, a mystery by a woman named Ngaio Marsh.

"How do you pronounce that?" I'd asked.

"I have no idea. But no one else does, either, so . . ."

I didn't have to talk to anyone until Leah brought in a dress, shoes, and a purse. I thanked her and stared at the "ensemble" gloomily after she left. Today I would be in black and white.

Lunch was light and quick. I got to lay eyes on Felicia, who had been answering notes, she said.

What kind of notes? From whom? She didn't tell me. I didn't ask, because I had to trust her judgment. The judgment of a sixteen-year-old girl who had never had many friends or opportunities, until the day she had a hundred. Sometimes I felt like shaking her, but I knew underneath her great power she also had control . . . if she felt like exercising it.

Today Abigail worked on me first, while Felicia bathed and dressed. Abigail was young and talkative and a real professional. She slicked and braided my curly hair and wound it in a crown. I looked like a . . . I don't know what. Someone who was not me, and also five years older.

I was relieved when Abigail left me to tend to Felicia. I wrote my mother a letter and took it downstairs to give to Leah to mail. Then I waited for Felicia in the foyer. There was a big mirror there, and I stood in front of it. I saw a stranger for a second, before I knew it was me. I looked better in the black and white than I had in the walking outfit I'd worn to the Japanese Friendship Garden.

Maybe today we'd have better luck. Maybe no one would attack any of us. Maybe I would not have to kill anyone. I made myself smile into the mirror. That was better.

No matter how boring and unpleasant the program was, no matter how much I dreaded it, I had to be cheerful for my sister. This was her time to shine. I had never had such a time, but she would.

Eli came in. He hugged me and gave me a kiss, but it was clear his thoughts were not here with me.

"How's Felix?" I said. I wasn't too worried about the grigori. He'd had some healing, and it had been a flesh wound.

"I think Lucy is enjoying taking care of him," Eli said. "He's feeling well enough to come out with me this afternoon. To the meeting."

Then Eli's thoughts returned to whatever dark place they'd been. He stood in the entrance hall as if he didn't know what to do next, and then he shook his head and walked down the hall. Maybe going to the kitchen.

I didn't like it when Eli was so worried about something, especially something he was unwilling to share with me.

After a moment, Eli returned with a sandwich on a little plate just before Felicia came down the stairs. She was wearing a green dress with white flowers on it. She looked beautiful.

"Are you driving, Eli?" Felicia said.

"I can," I offered.

But Eli looked at the hall clock. All of a sudden he could hardly wait to leave. He insisted on dropping us off at the party. He brought the sandwich with him, wrapped in a napkin. He didn't say a word during the ride to Tatiana Medvedeva's address.

None of this was like Eli.

My husband only got this secretive about grigori stuff. Something was about to happen in the closed world of the society. When he pulled to the curb to let us out, he said, "I hope I'm not late picking you up. I have to take Felix home after the meeting, and I'm not sure how long it will last."

"If you're very late, we can call a cab or catch a streetcar." I had some money in my borrowed purse. "If we're not standing out here, that's what we've done. Don't forget the party at the Del Coronado tonight."

Eli nodded, barely listening. The minute we were on the sidewalk he drove away.

"I am really looking forward to tonight," Felicia said. "The Del Coronado is so famous. And it's a smaller party so I'll get to really talk to people."

I was pretty sure by "people" she meant "Hans." The hosts were a group of Listeds staying at the hotel: Ahren, Mateo Medina Dominguez, and a Swede named Lennart Anderberg. If Ahren was there, Hans would be, too.

Another dress, more shoes, more people I didn't know and would never see again. That's all I could think of.

"I'm sorry I'm dragging you through all these parties," Felicia said.

I felt ashamed she'd read me so easily. "I volunteered, if I remember right," I told her.

That was enough to cheer her up. She might suspect I wasn't happy, but it was okay if she pretended for a while that I was enthusiastic about all this.

We turned to face the Medvedev house. We saw it over the perfectly trimmed hedge. We fell silent.

The house—the mansion—was a few blocks west and north of the school. The lawn was beautiful; it was really more of a garden, flower beds all over. Tatiana Semyonova Medvedeva had made a "good" marriage, as this society meant the term. A very good marriage.

"Does Madame have other children?" I asked Felicia.

"Tatiana is the only one living," she said. "Her other daughter died young from the Spanish flu. She was the one with the talent. I hear Tatiana hasn't got a smidge, but she married a water grigori, and he's made a fortune creating irrigation systems. Tatiana comes to the school at least once a week. She's devoted to Madame."

"She must be, to go to this much trouble to please her," I muttered. We had to go through the opening in the hedge, under an ornate iron arch, and up the walkway to the house. And we had to step smart.

Women were coming from every direction, some from parked cars, some from streetcars, some from cabs, some on foot. Young and old, they were dressed to the teeth.

I sighed heavily and set my jaw. "Do you know any of these flowering plants?" I asked. We were moving slowly toward the front doors. "I know the sage."

"That's lavender," Felicia said, pointing. "And that's agapanthus, we have some at the school. After that, I have no idea."

I wanted to bend down to smell the lavender, but that might embarrass my sister. I could never have a garden like this in Texoma. Water was too scarce, the temperature too hot.

"Fenolla and Katerina will be here," Felicia said. She was bouncy again.

"That will be nice. Your best friends from school." I didn't ask how Felicia knew they'd attend. She used the telephone much more than I did, and when she'd come from the school to take residence at Veronika's for the ball events, she'd started getting little notes from friends every day and writing them back.

Felicia nodded. "We missed them at the Japanese Friendship Garden. Katerina and her brother are both Listed this year. Paul's older than her, but honestly . . . he's not much good as a human being. And not much of a grigori."

Eli had told me that some magic users had come to three, even four, Wizards' Balls, had been Listed each time, and still had found no match. I didn't even try to imagine that. "And Fenolla?" I asked, so Felicia would know I was listening.

"Her father is from England, and her mother is from Sudan. That's in Africa," Felicia added, so kindly that I wanted to spit. "They're both magic practitioners, but from very different schools, of course."

Of *course*.

"Katerina is from Los Angeles, and her family does pretty well there. Least, that's what I hear. Her mother is . . . I don't much like her. Her father is fun, but he hardly ever comes around with Katerina. He's always working. He does something with the movie industry. Set design, I think. He's the grigori; her mom has no magic ability at all. Maybe that's why Paul is such a dud."

Felicia sounded so old as she said this.

I couldn't imagine what it had been like, to transform herself from a slum kid to this powerful, attractive young woman. She'd polished herself all the way, cramming knowledge into her head as fast as she could acquire it. I couldn't see the dusty, hungry kid in her anymore. It made me proud and sad.

We went up the steps to the . . . well, it *was* a mansion. There were lots of women of all ages entering at the same time, so our progress was slow. It was just like trying to enter the reception room last night.

I had plenty of time to look around at the other guests. Some of them were students from the school, bright and young and wearing dresses that were probably very up to date. All the young things were accompanied by at least one older woman—a mother, a sister, a grandmother—also in their most proper outfits.

Though white was the skin color of the majority, there was a scattering of Asian, Black, South American . . . and some I could not identify.

By the time it was our turn to enter the open front door, I was already bored. But my eyes opened wide at the huge flower arrangement on a shining round table in the foyer. I'd never seen so many flowers inside a house. Felicia gave me a sidelong look, and I could tell from the way she bit the inside of her mouth that she was trying not to tell me to stop gawking. I made my face flatten out, and she relaxed.

I knew the drill, having been coached by Veronika, Eli, and everyone else I'd met since I'd gotten to the Holy Russian Empire. First, we had to locate our hostess. That was not too hard, since she was the woman standing with a long line of females waiting to speak to her.

Somewhere in her fifties, Tatiana was still striking, with dark hair and a kind of hawklike face. Her skin was as white as the magnolias I'd seen in Dixie. Did she ever go outside to walk on her beautiful lawn? I couldn't imagine her coming out of Madame, who now resembled a grasshopper more than anything.

We shuffled forward until it was our turn.

Tatiana looked sharply at Felicia after my sister introduced herself.

"You are Isabella's niece," Tatiana said.

That comment put Felicia aback. Not too many people cared to mention the Dominguezes to my sister. "Yes," she said, after a moment. "Dear Aunt Isabella."

"You're a Dominguez." Tatiana sounded as though that was a wonderful thing to be.

My sister's polite smile vanished. Storm clouds gathered across her forehead.

Uh-oh.

"I knew your mother," Tatiana said, smiling. "I stayed with your family when I visited Mexico many years ago."

Felicia froze. She had no memories of her mother at all.

This was not the place for her to hear another woman's memories. But it was Felicia's choice to turn away or stand and listen, and she stayed. "You met my mother," Felicia said, her voice empty. Her face was a blank mask.

"Valentina was a beautiful woman, inside and out, you know."

It really bothered me that this Tatiana was going on like this was a normal conversation, completely not reading my sister's reaction.

"No, I did not know that." Felicia's face was like stone.

I had to do something to get that awful look off her face. People were beginning to notice.

"This isn't a good time or place to talk about something so private," I said, not really trying to sound like a nice person. "Maybe you can meet Felicia *another* day and share memories that Felicia *doesn't* have."

Tatiana gave me a very unfriendly look. "And you are? I didn't quite catch your name a minute ago."

Going for the insult. But I didn't bite. "I'm Princess Lizbeth Rose Savarova, wife of Prince Eli," I said, as sweetly as I could manage. (Not very.) "I'm Felicia's sister."

By then Felicia had recovered a bit. "I'd be interested to hear your memories," Felicia said. "But my sister is right, this is not the right time."

"I'm sorry. I didn't know I was treading on tender ground," Tatiana said, and she did seem to regret her words. "Please enjoy yourselves in my home."

We made way for the next guests—on my part, with huge relief. I could feel Felicia twanging like a bow so without speaking we began to stroll through the large rooms, all decorated with flowers and little tables of what they called finger food and little stations of maids ready to serve tea or coffee.

Two rooms over, we came upon Madame Semyonova, who looked even more like a corpse than she had in the Japanese Friendship Garden. Both of us said respectful things. She remembered Felicia, but not me, which was fine. Callista, the ever-present nurse, gave us a big smile. Callista and Felicia had become fond of each other when Felicia had been in the infirmary for her hurt feet when the Spanish flu had hit San Diego. Felicia had recovered in time to help the swamped Callista with the afflicted children.

Felicia was completely restored to her new self when she spotted Fenolla and Katerina across the wide hallway in a room that looked like a library. "I'm just going to talk to Fen and Kat; you stay here," she said. "You're close enough to watch us like an owl."

"Our girls have ditched us," said a pleasant voice.

I turned to see a very pretty woman.

"I'm Samaah Gregory," she said.

"I'm Lizbeth Savarova, Felicia's big sister. Now I see where Fenolla got her looks."

"Too kind of you. Felicia is a remarkable girl."

"That's one way to put it," I said.

"They are all handfuls at this age, aren't they? I don't know if you've met Irina, Katerina's mother?" Samaah turned to the woman next to her.

Irina was as plain as Samaah was beautiful.

In the next few minutes I learned Irina was also as slow and dull as Samaah was quick and amusing.

Samaah told a funny story about how she'd met her English husband, Matthew, and how surprised she'd been by some of his English customs.

Irina talked about nothing else besides how outstanding her children were, though actually saying little about Katerina. Her son, Paul, was clearly her favorite.

I was bored senseless after two minutes.

When Samaah Gregory saw someone she knew across the room and excused herself, trying hard to conceal her relief, Irina was almost as glad to see her go as Samaah was to leave. Irina made it clear she was uncomfortable talking to a woman who looked so different from herself.

After a couple of minutes alone with me, Irina also invented someone else to talk to and stomped away. I guess I made her uncomfortable, too.

Now that I didn't have to respond to stupid chitchat, I could keep a better eye on my sister. She and her friends weren't in the library any longer, so I began scouting around.

When I got back to the entry door and the receiving line, I spotted a woman I'd figured I'd never see again: Harriet Ritter, an agent of Iron Hand, the best security firm on the continent. She was ushering in an Asian girl with straight black hair, a girl who was even better dressed than Harriet.

Though we weren't always on good terms or even on the same side, today Harriet felt like an old friend. While her charge greeted Madame Semyonova and then Tatiana, Harriet was doing a room scan, same as me. When her eyes met mine, her face brightened.

After I'd finally spotted Felicia, still safely with her buddies, I slipped through the crowd to Harriet's elbow.

"Hi," I said.

"What are you doing here?" she said.

"I got Felicia." I jerked my head in my sister's direction. "Who's your girl?"

Harriet tapped the girl on the shoulder. She turned. I revised her age upward. "Soo-Yung Kim, meet an acquaintance of mine, Lizbeth Rose." The young woman gave Harriet a dark look.

"I'm sorry," Harriet said. "The proper introduction is Kim Soo-Yung."

The girl extended her hand. "I am pleased to meet you," she said. Her English was accented but clear.

"Pleased to meet you too," I said, and we shook for half a second. Soo-Yung had pegged me for a non-magical on the spot.

"Princess Savarova is here with her sister, Felicia Karkarova Dominguez," Harriet told her charge.

"Your sister is one of the Dominguez family?" Soo-Yung was impressed. The most famous witches in Mexico had a worldwide reputation, I had discovered the past couple of days.

"Now there are only two left, Felicia and her aunt," I told the girl.

"I'd like to meet her," Soo-Yung said shyly.

"Of course. Just a word in your ear: better to not ask questions about the family." I took the young woman over to the three girls and introduced her, then returned to Harriet. We had a clear view of our charges. The four were talking a mile a minute.

"You're here in San Diego to work this all week?" Harriet raised her darkened eyebrows.

"I am. Not even getting paid." I smiled for half a second. "You hear that someone shot at Felicia yesterday in the Japanese Friendship Garden?"

"Arrows, I heard. You were there? You sure she was the target?"

"Assuming it. Felix took a hit."

"Felix . . . the little dark wizard I met in Dixie? The one who was such a pain in the butt?"

"The very same. He's married to Eli's little sister." I gave Harriet a very level look. She nodded. Message received. "Turns out, he's distant kin to Felicia. He's been teaching Felicia at the school. She's a death grigori, like Felix."

"Impressive," Harriet said. "That explains a lot."

Harriet Ritter wasn't impressed by much of anything, and my back straightened a bit. I was used to my sister's power, both exciting and dreadful. It was good to be reminded how singular she was. "What about your gal?" I said. "You friends with the family?"

"Her folks sent a kind of nanny with Soo-Yung, but the woman's about a million years old and speaks no English. Maybe. She doesn't trust me enough to level with me. They hired me to be her transportation and protection. We're staying in a boardinghouse. Not exactly fancy, but I don't care. It's easier to keep an eye on the neighborhood."

"Hmmm." I was sure there was more to it than that. Soo-Yung looked wealthy. The wealthy are well taken care of, as a rule. The ancient woman might seem helpless, but I was willing to bet she wasn't. "Soo-Yung's family have a lot of enemies?"

"Yes, absolutely. I had to read up on Korea when I took the job. It's occupied by the Japanese. That's why I was so interested in the attack on your girl. Soo-Yung's father, I gather, is anti-Japanese, so the regime has it in for him."

"No wonder they need you to watch out for her. How old is Soo-Yung?" I asked.

"Twenty," Harriet said. "Hard to tell, isn't it?"

"I'm surprised she was interested in meeting Felicia. At that age, there's a big gap between sixteen and twenty."

"Dominguez is a name everyone in the magical world has heard. It's Soo-Yung's first time here in the Holy Russian Empire, the first time she's been Listed, and her first Wizards' Ball. She needs some friends to help her enjoy it."

"Hmph."

"Your gal is kind of well known."

That was an understatement.

It's bound to happen when you're a death grigori. Also bound to happen when you kill your family to keep them from kidnapping you and selling you to the highest bidder. "Soo-Yung got any followers?"

"Mostly other Asians," Harriet said. "A white boy from upstate California made nice with her yesterday for a few minutes."

"Has a real pretty sister? Anna?"

Harriet nodded.

"Nikolai's a nice kid, but he's not all there in the head. I don't know if he's slow-witted, or something else. Katerina has a brother, too, but he got thrown out of Rasputin for something. That can't be good." I grinned. "Even if Paul was a great human being, which Felicia says he isn't, his mom won't shut up about him, so he's not in my good books."

"That's Katerina Swindoll over there with my girl and yours?"

Harriet had done her homework. "Yep," I said. "And her friend Fenolla Gregory, who is half-Sudanese and half-English. Fenolla likes to pose. She calls herself crazy. She is anything but."

"She's a beauty, isn't she?"

I nodded. "Her mother is here, Samaah, and she's even prettier."

I felt so much better with Harriet here. Another pair of watchful eyes. "By the way, we had trouble with an Asian grigori last summer," I remembered. "He was from an immigrant group living in Brazil, Korean or Chinese. I hope Soo-Yung is not his kin."

"What was his name?"

"Chin-Hao Costa? Something like that."

"I'll ask her. I don't think that's a Korean name, and Soo-Yung's family doesn't have a branch in Brazil."

"He practiced a Korean magic called land-folding. Quick travel."

It had given me the creeps, though I'd been able to save Felicia from the woman who'd taken her.

"Doesn't mean he's a hundred percent Korean. Sounds like he's a blend of Chinese, Korean, and Portuguese."

"It's good they're not connected."

"Understood."

We were quiet for a moment, our eyes on our girls. Fenolla was waving her hands in the air, imitating something buzzy, and Katerina was laughing along with Soo-Yung. Felicia was smiling and shaking her head.

"I really hate this," I said, surprising myself. I waved my hand to indicate the crowded room full of dressed-up women.

Harriet was the only person I could tell.

"It's not what I thought I'd be doing when I joined Iron Hand," Harriet agreed. "And it's a far cry from one of your gun crews."

For the first time in what felt like days, I smiled from my heart, rather than with my face. "What did you think you'd be doing, when Iron Hand hired you?"

"Running from gators in Dixie. Getting you out of a trainwreck." If the train station in Ciudad Juárez was my worst memory, the train wreck in Dixie was the second worst. "Anything but chaperoning a little Korean magician in San Diego while she's trying to find a suitable husband."

I laughed. It felt like a long time since I'd done that, too. I wanted to ask Harriet if she'd gotten a new partner—either at work or in life—but I forbore. Her last partner had been lynched in Dixie. I'd seen him swinging from a tree.

I didn't ever want to see another hanging, if I could help it.

As if she'd read my mind, Harriet said, "I'm getting married in a month."

"That's good news. Who's the lucky person?"

"Bob Webster. He's an Iron Hand negotiator."

"What's that mean?" I didn't mind confessing ignorance to Harriet.

"If you've had a relative kidnapped, or you've had a picture stolen, and the thieves want to sell either one back to you, Bob makes it happen."

"I'll bet that's not as calm or orderly as it sounds."

"Pretty tense occupation, as he tells it."

"You going to keep working?"

"As long as I can. No kids, unless God plays a trick on us."

I nodded. I'd lost one baby early in pregnancy.

Eli had had a hard time telling me how that had made him feel. His dad had not encouraged sharing feelings. Most men, in my bit of experience, aren't good at that. I'd like to be pregnant again. Now that I had my little half brother, Samuel, he was filling the hole in my life. For the moment.

"How's your prince?" Harriet said, coming right in on the tail of my thoughts. "Liking Texoma?"

I sighed heavily. "Yes and no. He's a lot more relaxed. But I'm not sure he wants to be."

"Too bad. Whoops, she's on the move. Talk to you later."

Harriet coasted off, maneuvering among the women like a shark in a minnow tank. Soo-Yung had gone to one of the refreshment tables. I stood some more. I waited.

After what seemed like hours, Felicia signaled she thought it was time to go. I was ready to leave, of course, though it had been real pleasant having Harriet to talk to, someone who understood my life.

We did our duty, telling Tatiana how much we'd enjoyed the afternoon and saying goodbye to Madame Semyonova, who was almost asleep in her chair. I nodded to Harriet, who was with Soo-Yung. They were also in line to say their goodbyes. As we made our way down the porch steps, I was so relieved I almost broke into a sprint.

The front yard seemed so much quieter, even with the traffic occasionally going by. I could swing my arms without hitting anyone. The relief was huge.

My sister wasn't reading my mood. She just *kept on talking.* Where was the dangerous grigori who loved explosions? Normally Felicia was an eagle. This week she was a butterfly.

After tolerating this as long as I could, I said, "Have you put any thought into who could have fired the arrows at you?"

An *angry* butterfly. "I'm having a good time! I'm meeting people who aren't scared of me! They actually want to know me! They might want to marry me!" Her lips pressed together in a furious line.

My timing had been crummy. I admitted it to myself. "I'm sorry for bringing the 'kill Felicia' part of this week up. But it's a very important part."

She scowled. "I know that. But I want to have a good week with fun people. Just for *a while.*"

"I understand. But you have to be alive to do that."

"I may have had a talk with Felix and Eli," she said sullenly. "Three days ago. While you were unpacking."

Before I could ask her what that talk had been about, I spotted the Savarov car parked at the curb. Eli was in the driver's seat. He was staring into space.

I took a deep breath. "It would have been good if you'd had a talk with me, too," I said. "I'm here. In this city. To make sure you live to plan a great future. With someone who can keep you safe and make you happy." *And I'm hating every minute of it.*

It was Felicia's turn to take a deep breath. "I'm sorry, Lizbeth."

Alert. "Look to your left. Know this person?" A brown-skinned girl was approaching, her arms outspread, a smile on her face, closing in at top speed. My knife was in my hand and I dropped my purse to the sidewalk.

"No! I don't know her!" Felicia's hands flew up in defense.

I stepped in front of my sister, knife in my right hand, just as I heard Eli throw open the car door. I couldn't spare a moment to look at him.

The girl said very rapidly, "Felicia, don't you know me? It's Maria! We grew up together." The smile did not falter.

"I don't know you," Felicia called from behind me.

The girl pretended to be hurt and angry. At least she stopped advancing. "I just wanted to give you a hug," she said, in Mexican-accented English. "I'm wounded."

She would be, in about five seconds.

The scattering of departing guests around us were moving away in a great hurry. Smart.

The girl looked desperate when we didn't soften our stance.

She lunged forward. There was something in her hand.

Eli attacked. I was glad because I did not want to stab anyone else, especially with so many people watching. Not this girl, whose eyes were widening in panic as she realized she had lost: the moment, the opportunity, her life. Eli's spell knocked her down. She sprawled on the grass.

With all the agitation running through the women around me, not to mention me and my sister, it took me a moment to realize "Maria" was still alive. She was pinned to the ground, not moving her arms and legs . . . but her eyes were blinking.

"Thanks, brother-in-law," Felicia called. "Maybe we can find out who sent her."

"Maybe," Eli said, with a little smile. He got within a foot of me. His eyes met mine. "I know you don't like to use the knife. I'm sorry about last night."

It was done. I shrugged.

"Last night?" Felicia said, even angrier. "What happened? I *knew* something happened."

"Later," I said. "Let's get this gal loaded into the car and take her to Felix."

Harriet stepped forward to help Eli raise "Maria" and drag her to the car, the toes of her new shoes scuffing against the pavement. Harriet's charge, Soo-Yung, watched with a calm face.

I looked at all the faces in the crowd around us, the knife still in my hand. I could throw it if I had to. No one approached us or said a word.

"Maybe I did know her?" Felicia muttered. She was second-guessing.

"You probably know twenty girls named Maria from Mexico," I said. "But she's not one of them."

This girl, whoever she was, was smart enough to be terrified. Thanks to a quick gesture by my husband, she was also mute.

After she'd helped deposit our "Maria" in the car, Harriet and Soo-Yung went directly to a car that was double-parked beside Eli's, a man sitting in the driver's seat. The car left immediately. Harriet was getting her charge out of the range of the consequences, if there were any.

The grigori "police" got to the scene very quickly. This was a new organization, and one the San Diego police were glad to welcome. The last thing a regular police officer wanted to be called on was a grigori-on-grigori crime.

The younger enforcer was named Casimir, a lanky young man who had sandy hair, freckles, and a great eagerness to meet Felicia. My sister actually managed to shed some tears so Casimir could console her. Casimir did not suspect the tears were from rage.

The other grigori, Sandrina, had known Eli since he was a boy on the boats. She was gray-haired, walked with a limp, and was about as tough as an old boot.

While Casimir made doubly sure that my sister was completely and totally unharmed, Sandrina asked us all the pertinent questions. I gave honest answers: lucky for me.

As we were driving to Felix's house to leave Maria there, Eli told me that Sandrina was a truth-teller. "I thought all grigoris had a talent for earth, air, fire, or water," I said. "Where does the truth-telling fit?"

"Same place being a death-dealer fits. Somewhere in between. You can be an air grigori like me and Peter, and also be a truth-teller."

"You could have let me know that." And so could have my sister.

"I knew you weren't going to lie. No point, when the truth was in our favor."

Though "Maria" deserved whatever was coming to her, I felt at least a little bad leaving anyone in Felix's hands.

I'd helped Eli march a struggling (but silent) Maria up Felix's back steps and held her while Eli knocked on the door.

Felix himself had looked oddly grim and silent when he'd opened it. He'd also been surprised. "Back again so soon?" he said.

"This girl tried to get close to Felicia outside the Medvedev house. Though this Maria claimed she knew Felicia, she doesn't. This is what she had in her hand. Since she's not a grigori or a witch, that I can tell, this must be some spell designed to do harm."

Eli handed Felix a small cloth bundle the size of a lemon. That was what Maria had been holding when she'd rushed toward us.

"What is it?" Felix said, turning it over in his hands.

"I haven't got a clue, and I doubt this Maria will, either."

"Don't you think the grigori police should take charge of this?"

I was very, very surprised. I could see Eli look at Felix, with some doubt in his face. He said, "Sandrina came from the grigori police, but I thought you would rather I brought her here."

"Sandrina" was all Felix said, but I knew we had him, then. Felix had always excelled at what he called "interrogation." He looked past Eli to see me holding Maria's arm, saw the girl struggling to speak. It was like someone had turned on a light switch inside Felix.

"And here I was, bored and worried and with no outlet for that," he said. "Perfect timing. Lucy is out."

I didn't like to think about Felix interrogating "Maria." I'd been present when Eli had gotten information out of someone in Dixie, and I hadn't liked it any better then. At least Eli hadn't relished the process. It was a necessity, not a pleasure.

Felix really enjoyed it.

After we returned to the house, all of us silent, Felicia pelted straight up to her room, probably to begin getting ready for the next event. Or to write a few dozen notes.

Eli and I went up to our bedroom. I shed the tea-party dress. I hung it up carefully. No stains of any kind. It was five o'clock, and I could have gone to bed already, I was that tired. But there was another party at the Del Coronado that night.

I hoped Eli wasn't getting any husband-and-wife ideas because I was not in the mood.

"This is one of the things I don't understand," Eli said. He sat on the bed. His elbows were on his knees, his hair falling in light brown waves around his face. "Why pick such a public place for this attack?"

"The girl's a throwaway," I said. "Whoever gave her the spell didn't care if she died along with Felicia."

"But why kill Felicia?" Eli looked up at me. "Why? She hasn't done anything to anyone. She's in the market like all these other kids are in the market. Granted, she's the . . . princess of the season. But there are other girls who have great talent, too. Those two friends of Felicia's, for example. They're worthy of respect."

"Felicia is prettier." I hated that, even as I said it.

"True, but when you're talking value . . . the other girls come from families with more money. Fenolla's father would be a great wizard if he didn't live in England where it's forbidden, and her mother is from Sudan, which has an interesting magical tradition. They seem to be very well-to-do. He uses his magic in investing. The Swindolls have money, and Katerina's father works in Hollywood. Though several people have told me the brother is something of a problem."

I pulled on my jeans and a plaid shirt I'd had forever. My mother-in-law most likely would use it as a rag, but what the hell. I sat on the floor and began to stretch. I was not getting the movement I was used to. I would try to go for a walk before dinner, if I had the time.

Eli went to the sink to wash his face I tried not to glare at his back. It wasn't his fault that I was here in San Diego, missing home, missing my mother and stepfather and baby brother.

"Felicia says she had a talk with you and Felix when we first got here, without me. I want to know what she said."

I could see Eli's back heave as he sighed. "I can't tell you now. But I hope I can tell you soon."

"So I'm charged with keeping her safe, but I can't know about this mysterious conversation?"

"Not just yet. In fact, the meeting today bore directly on it. And I'm sworn on that one. But as soon as I can, I will tell you." He turned around to face me, a towel in his hands. "And you will be sorry to know."

Of course, that didn't worry me at all. Of course not.

I wasn't used to being the person who was groping around in the dark.

But that was what I was in San Diego.

CHAPTER NINE

Felicia was on cloud nine while she was getting ready for this evening's party at the Del Coronado. The dress hanging on the wardrobe door was a deep orange. With her light brown skin and dark hair, Felicia would look lovely. Casimir, the grigori she'd met this afternoon, had told her he'd be there, too. But I knew the big attraction was seeing Hans, which was a sure thing. Felicia was as full of what-might-be as any girl could ever hope.

Eli and I had planned some more that afternoon, in our short time together and alone. We hadn't had much of that lately when we weren't asleep.

"I'm going to be a little late," I told Felicia. "I'll catch a cab. You and Eli will have the car."

If I'd supposed my sister would be curious about my mysterious errand, or worried about what it might be, I'd have been disappointed. Felicia hardly listened. She said, "Okay," to acknowledge that I'd spoken, while not taking her eyes from the mirror on the dressing table.

Her hair was being done again. I wondered how many other heads this Abigail, a scary young woman with bright red lips and shingled hair, had been attending to all day. She might make enough this week to last her through the year. I'd decided I didn't need her this evening, and my own hair was falling in its natural curls to just below my jawline. I was wearing a black evening dress. There wasn't much at the top, and it fell in beautiful lines, and it fit.

"You look pretty," Felicia said, to my surprise.

"Thank you. That dress is going to be a great one on you," I said.

"Thanks. I'll see you at the party, then."

Maybe she knew there couldn't be any pleasant reason for me to be late, and she didn't want her bubble burst.

Felicia and Eli left at seven o'clock, because it would take a while to reach the hotel on Imperial Island. There would be other parties at the Del Coronado, and the ferry would be a crush.

Eli patted my shoulder as he left. He had been brought up to keep what he felt to himself, but he tried, sometimes, to let me know he understood when I had to do something I really did not want to do.

When they'd been gone for ten minutes, I was sure they wouldn't return for some forgotten item. I grabbed the fancy black stole Veronika had loaned me. I paused in the doorway to the living room. "I'm going out," I said. Veronika and Alice looked up from their books. Veronika just nodded. Alice said, "Have a good time, and tell me all about it tomorrow!"

"I will," I promised. I made myself smile.

I wouldn't.

I'd telephoned Felix earlier. His car was parked down the block where he'd said it would be. Lucy was in the driver's seat. "Felix is waiting for us at home," she said. "He was afraid driving might pull his arm. It's almost healed."

"Lucy," I said. "You've picked up a new skill."

Lucy looked proud and happy. "I go to the store and pick my own groceries," she said. "I take our dry cleaning to Wong's."

"You do your own cooking?"

She nodded. "I do. I bought a cookbook. I'm learning so many new things."

So even a marriage without sex could work if people were getting other needs met. Lucy seemed quite pleased with her current life.

When we reached their little house, Lucy parked behind it on the gravel apron. Since it was her house, we entered through the back door leading into the kitchen.

"I'm home," she called.

"In here," Felix answered.

We threaded our way through the little dining room into the living room. Felix was sitting on the couch having a drink. He was glad to see us, from his smile. "Maria" was tied to a straight chair in the middle of the floor, by her elbows and ankles. Lucy ignored her.

"How's the wound?" I asked Felix.

The grigori grunted. Mr. Manners. "Not back to normal, but much better. I knew it wouldn't take long to heal if Felicia put her hands on it. And Lucy has been a great help."

Lucy gave her husband a pat on his good shoulder and without further comment went into the guest bedroom and shut the door. They'd made it into a reading and hobby room. I could not imagine what hobbies Felix had. Lucy liked to sew. Felix had bought her a sewing machine for a wedding present. I heard the whirr of the machine as she started it up.

"Maria" wasn't bleeding and she was conscious. This was better than I had expected. I sat down opposite the prisoner.

I figured Maria was eighteen at the most. She had black hair, brown eyes, and brown skin. No surprise there. Someone, I assumed Felix, had removed her shoes, which were good ones, brand new. Her bare feet were evenly brown. This girl had been shoeless in the sun for a good long while.

Since Maria's elbows were secured to the chair, I bent from one side to the other to have a good look at her hands. As I expected, they were rough and the fingernails were not filed. In fact, they weren't very clean. Maria's teeth were crooked. She had a scar on her neck. I'd seen a lot of scars. This one spoke of a very serious attempt to kill her.

So, a poverty-level upbringing and a dangerous life.

Maria was wearing a dress that was brand new, just like the shoes. (That was how she'd managed to blend in almost long enough to reach Felicia.)

Last, I looked into Maria's eyes. However tough the girl was, she was pretty antsy now. She didn't like me looking her over, not speaking.

I said in my slow Spanish, "Who gave you the dress?" That was why I was here instead of Eli. He could speak only a little Spanish, and Felix spoke none. He'd called the Savarov house to ask me for help.

Maria answered so rapidly I couldn't understand every word. I got the gist of it, though. "A woman was standing outside the Spanish Mission for Women on Camilla Street when Maria came out after a free meal," I told Felix. "This woman offered Maria a job and a new dress and shoes."

"What did this woman look like?" Felix asked. I translated and told him what Maria said.

"She was in her forties. Her hair was all gray, but she had few wrinkles." I listened a little more. "She had money. She took Maria to a department store and bought her this dress and these shoes."

Felix raised his eyebrows. "Where was this?"

"What store?" I asked, in Spanish and then in English so Felix could follow.

Maria looked confused.

"The name of the store?"

"Walker Scott," the girl said clearly.

Even I had heard of Walker Scott. Veronika bought things there. The black dress I was wearing had come from Walker Scott.

"It was a white building, many floors," Maria told me. For a moment the girl looked as awestruck as she'd been to enter that store. "So many pretty things," she said quietly.

I relayed that to Felix.

"Walker Scott's at Fifth and Broadway," Felix said quietly. "About four blocks from the Mission. Short distance, big difference."

"This woman gave you these clothes and told you to kill my sister?" I said in Spanish.

"She did not tell me to kill your sister." Maria did not meet my eyes. "I swear," she said, nodding vigorously, as if that would make me believe her. "This lady said that she was testing the defenses around the girl, and she needed to make sure the girl's bodyguards were reacting quickly."

"You believed that."

"Who knows what witches will do? She gave me enough money to eat for a week, and the clothes. At the moment I didn't care," Maria said, giving every sign of frankness.

I told Felix all of this.

"But Maria had this spell," Felix said. "I called an acquaintance of mine who specializes in analyzing spells. In her opinion, if Maria had hit Felicia with the little pouch in her hand, it would have exploded. A pretty drastic way to test Felicia's defenses."

That changed everything. I had felt some pity for the girl, but it faded in that second. Maria well knew there was nothing innocent in the pouch, and she hadn't truly believed the woman's story from the get-go.

I switched languages again. "Did the woman give you the little pouch? Tell you to hit the girl with it?"

Maria nodded. Tears began to trickle down her face. "I was supposed to tap her on the chest with it. But I couldn't do it," she said. "I couldn't. The girl was so young and beautiful, and you were so frightening. I didn't even see the grigori until his spell hit me."

Her only words I believed were in the last sentence. She hadn't known Eli was waiting for us. I looked to the side, to Felix, while I told him what Maria had said. He grimaced. He would have said he was only impatient, but I knew better. It irritated Felix to need my help. Felix knew death, and he knew interrogation, but he didn't know Spanish.

"Make sure she's telling the truth," he said.

"Do you have sisters, Maria?" I was going for the best threat I could think of.

"I do. Three."

"The girl you tried to kill is my sister."

"Oh, please, don't harm them for what I did!" And for the first time, I believed her absolutely.

Tears and snot ran down her face.

"She understands Felicia is my sister, and she has sisters who must be in this area, too," I explained to Felix. I couldn't stand looking at her face.

"Felix, loose her bonds," I said in English. "But if she rises from the chair, kill her."

Felix understood that clearly enough. I thought Maria did, too.

He untied the girl's elbows while I went to the kitchen. But he stood to her side with his hands at the ready, a pinch of something from his vest between the forefinger and thumb of both hands. He made sure Maria could see that.

I fetched a wet rag and a towel from the kitchen and offered them to Maria. She took them from me just as carefully. But she worked on her face for an awful long time, clearly stalling.

I'd given her something. I'd expect something in return.

That was the way acquaintanceship, as opposed to friendship, worked.

When our expressions made it plain that she couldn't put it off any longer, Maria looked at me and kind of sighed, resigned. Clearly she believed I wasn't that great, but I was better than Felix.

"Maria, who paid you to kill my sister?"

"I *didn't really* try to kill her!" Maria said, as if her life hung on that point.

"I have to know who paid you to do this."

"She threatened me and my family," Maria said, stalling again. "She didn't tell me her name."

"You threatened mine." I wasn't budging, couldn't. "And she did tell you a name."

"Will you help me get back home if I tell you?"

"Won't do me any good to have you around." I shrugged.

Maria leaned forward. Felix tensed up.

"*Alemana*," she whispered. "That was what she was."

A German had hired this girl to attack my sister. I hoped Felix hadn't understood the word in Spanish. I tried to keep still. I took a long, silent breath.

"No *Rusa?*" I said. *Not Russian?*

Maria looked at me like I was a dummy. "*Alemana.*"

I remembered the young German woman who'd tried to talk to Felicia in the Japanese Friendship Garden. But I had to be sure.

I got up and went to the bedroom door. I knocked softly.

"Yes?" Lucy opened the door. She looked very surprised.

"Do you speak Spanish?"

"A little."

"I need to you to speak to this woman."

"What shall I say?"

"Ask her if she wants to earn some money in a strange way."

"All in Spanish?"

I nodded.

Lucy worked it out in her head for a second or two. "Okay." She went into the living room. Felix gave us an unreadable look. Sure wasn't loving Lucy being there.

Lucy said in Spanish, "Do you need to make some money? The way may seem strange to you."

Maria looked past Lucy to meet my eyes. She shook her head. "*Rusa, no Alemana.*"

"Thank you," Felix said to his wife, careful not to use her name. "You've been very helpful."

Lucy retreated to the spare bedroom with a smile on her face.

"So now I can go?" Maria asked.

Felix had no intention of letting Maria walk out of here alive. I knew that. I had to ask questions while I could.

"This woman approached you outside the Spanish Mission for Women?" I didn't sit, so she'd think it was almost over. "Tell me again what she looked like?"

"Gray haired, like I said. But that may not have been her own hair. Her face was not much lined."

"What clothes was she wearing?"

Maria shrugged. "The kind of suit a wealthy woman wears to go out."

"Did she make arrangements to meet with you again? To get the results of this so-called security test?"

This was the question Maria had been asking herself, I could tell.

"No," she said slowly. "She did not. I was sure she would be there, to see the results."

"And did you see her?"

"No," Maria said. "I did not." The girl knew what that meant. She gave up hope.

Felix killed her then, without touching her. After the job was done, he sat with his eyes closed, radiating vitality. The expression on his face was one I'd only seen on men after good sex. I didn't move or speak until he'd calmed down. He flexed the arm that had been wounded; he smiled. Good as new.

I helped him carry the body to the trunk of his car.

While he went back inside to tell Lucy he'd be gone for a while, I searched Maria. The car was in Felix's backyard, and it was dark, so I wasn't being watched. I used the small flashlight from the glove compartment. I was sure Maria had been searched more than once throughout the course of the day, but I had to be sure.

I came up with nothing.

She had a very small amount of money on her, a token for a meal at the Mission, and a crumpled letter from one of her sisters, who lived in Encinitas. I made myself read it in case it was in code or had some bit of information I needed, but it was just a letter from a barely literate woman to her younger sister, who was trying to make a living in the Holy Russian Empire.

Her name really was Maria.

Felix and I were silent on the drive to the bay. We drove south to be sure we didn't see any patrols. We worked our way to the water by an old cannery or warehouse, about to fall down. I was terrified the whole time something would happen to my black dress, so I took a lot of care. Felix made frequent comments about that.

After we'd gotten rid of Maria, Felix dropped me off at the ferry landing. Again, we hardly spoke. That was fine with me.

I didn't like the things I'd done. Nothing was clear; nothing was simple.

It was a relief to get on the ferry by myself. I went to the ladies' room and checked my dress in the harsh light. It looked fine.

I got a taxi to the Del Coronado. It was on the other side of Imperial Island. I arrived looking very proper, despite my body disposal stint. From the music and bustle, there were several parties going on throughout the hotel grounds. The uniformed man at the door directed me to the correct room for the Medina/Hirsch/Anderberg party.

I'd missed the dinner, but the dancing had begun.

I spotted Eli right away. His light brown hair was braided back, and he was in his evening clothes. Ordinarily, my husband looked a little gawky, a little awkward, in his everyday gear. But not tonight. When our eyes met, he let me know he thought I looked pretty good in the black dress, too. It had been a while since he looked at me like that.

Eli knew I'd want to know where my sister was, and he nodded at the dance floor. She was partnered with Clayton Dashwood. I relaxed. Clayton had been by far the most pleasant of the men and women who'd shown up to get an early look at my sister. And he hadn't tried to kill me or abduct Felicia. Maybe my standards of pleasant weren't that high.

It was a pretty lively dance number. Though I wasn't surprised that Felicia could dance (my sister could do anything), I was a little taken aback that she and Clayton were so in sync. They looked good together. Ahren Hirsch was dancing with Katerina Swindoll, Felicia's friend. They were not as quick on their feet, but they were smiling. Fenolla was standing close to the drinks station, talking to a young man I didn't know. I should have remembered him from studying everyone Listed, but I was too tired to recall his name.

When the dance ended, Felicia smiled at Clayton Dashwood and went to speak to Eli. He pointed to me, and she tracked me down to give me a little wave. She began working her way around the room. She was making her way to me, I thought, but Felicia stopped halfway to talk to a young man and stuck there. Hans Goldschmidt.

For the life of me, I didn't know how I felt. Did it even make any difference?

"The sister," Clayton Dashwood said. Somehow, he was standing right in front of me.

"That's me," I said, trying to sound bright. "The sister. Lizbeth."

"I talked to your husband earlier."

I noticed again that his brown eyes were more a mahogany. Clayton was a handsome man. "Camilla is here, too. I think she's having a pretty good time. She found a guy from Canada who loves to ride and raises Arabians."

"How about you?" I said. "Has your evening been successful?"

"I think my suit for Felicia might be a failure." Clayton inclined his head toward Felicia and Hans. He gave me a wry look.

"You don't seem real heartbroken," I observed.

"Let me get you a drink," he offered. Clayton didn't seem heartbroken, but he might have been a tad relieved.

"That would be nice." I hadn't realized how thirsty I was until he said the word "drink."

Clayton put his hand on the small of my back, very lightly, I guess in case I got lost on my way to the drinks table. "What would you like?" he said.

"Not alcohol," I said. "Anything else."

"I'm not a drinker myself," he told me. "Drinking runs in my family. I'm going to dodge that bullet."

"I'm real glad to hear that," I told him. I'm always impressed by people who see trouble coming and try to head it off.

Clayton had a funny expression on his face. He was surprised, and quite pleased. Huh. He got me a glass of soda with ice. I was glad to take a sip. This chitchat was not going the way I'd expected.

"I'm going to ask you a delicate question," Clayton said. He was real serious.

"Go ahead." Another surprise from this Britannian.

"Your husband is clearly a grigori. Did he go to a meeting today?"

I'd been looking around the room to find out where Felicia had gotten to, but now Clayton had all my attention. "Eli's a busy guy," I said carefully. "I don't know where he goes. Or what he goes there to do. Maybe he went to a meeting."

"So that's a yes," Clayton said, doing some direct looking of his own. "I'm very anxious to know what went on. I believe Britannia's about to go to war, and I'd like to know why."

"You read the papers, I guess. What do you think?"

"I think this Adolf Hitler is a terrible man," Clayton said. "But that war will be in Europe. It's not likely to get to this soil, even if Japan allies with Germany, which maybe has already happened. It would be our mother country that draws Britannia into it. Half the English government is determined to fight. The other half is just whistling in the dark, hoping everything will be all right. I wonder what your husband thinks will happen, if he went to an important meeting today."

"I would like to know the answer to that, too," I said. And I'd never meant anything more. "I hope we'll both have that answer soon."

"Will you undertake to tell me that answer, if you learn it before I do?"

"I want to say yes, but I can't. I have to see what . . . secrecy is laid on me when I hear the answer."

We stood in silence for a moment, looking at each other.

"How many knives do you have on you?" Clayton said. He was not looking so serious anymore. In fact, he was smiling.

I had to count in my head. "Four," I said.

"I really like you," he said. "You're one of a kind."

I'd give Clayton a dance, if I weren't married. But I was. Both those ideas were surprises.

"I better check in with my better half," I said. "I'll see you around, I expect."

"I believe you'll see me tomorrow at the teahouse close to Balboa Park." Clayton smiled back and wandered off.

I watched Felicia—still talking to Hans—for a minute, and when I turned, Eli was standing beside me.

"What did Mr. Rich Guy want?" he said, and he sounded more serious than I liked.

"Wanted to know why the grigoris met today," I said.

Eli stared at me. "Really."

"Really. He's worried Britannia will have to go to war because England will. He wants to know why."

"He's scared of the fight?" There was contempt in my husband's voice.

"Eli, anyone with a lick of sense is scared of war." I had to stop myself from throwing up my hands. Instead, I took a deep breath and said, "I want to hear about that meeting and why it's got you so spooked. And we better do something about Hans and Felicia, because Clayton was wondering if she was already spoken for."

Eli looked at the couple, still talking, still very wrapped up in each other. "You're right." I couldn't tell exactly how he felt about Felicia having this thing for Hans. And it really, really bothered me that I didn't know why Hans, a German Jew, had been in Texoma at such a critical moment last summer.

Eli kind of shook himself, and his face got stern.

"Don't march over there in a straight line and try to shake your finger at her," I said.

He smiled at me for a brief, happy moment. "I know she'd put her back to the wall," he said. "I can live with us doing all this for nothing, if her mind is made up, but they don't really know each other. What if he hadn't come to the Ball Week? What if he'd been detained, as he might well have been? Would she have set her sights on someone else?"

"Good questions. I don't know the answers. She's sixteen."

Eli worked his way through the crowd, trying to be indirect. He said something polite to Hans, with that "I'm not really feeling this" look. Then Eli and Felicia moved away from the German. Felicia was doing her best not to scowl. I only hoped not too many people were watching.

The band started playing a new tune, and Mateo Medina popped up in front of Felicia like a jack-in-the-box to claim a dance. She accepted with at least a decent show of enthusiasm.

And the evening wore on. I didn't see much of Eli for a couple of hours. He was renewing his acquaintance with some of his former pals and colleagues.

We let ourselves into the Savarov house about one o'clock in the morning, and we weren't the last to leave the Del Coronado by any means. Felicia almost ran up to her room as if she couldn't wait to be alone. Eli was parking the car in the former stable behind the house because he was sure it was going to rain.

I had a few precious minutes to myself. I didn't think I'd ever had an evening where I wore evening clothes, helped dispose of a body, and went to a dance. And listened to so many voices, none saying anything I wanted to hear. My body was tired, and so was my head.

Though I wanted to collapse on the bed, I hung up my dress and took a bath—as if I could wash the evening off me.

Eli still wasn't upstairs when I was ready to go to sleep. I wondered why, but I was too tired to go looking for him. Finally in my nightgown, I pulled the covers over me. I stared up at the ceiling, and I could not see my way forward. If someone had suddenly appeared in the bedroom and handed me a dime to go home, I would have gotten up and gone to the railway station.

Instead, I fell asleep. I woke during the night and knew Eli was next to me. In the faint light coming through the window, I looked at his face. He was in deep sleep, his face relaxed and young.

My heart clenched. I did not think this would end well. And I could do nothing to stop it.

I'd never been more unhappy in my life, even when Eli had been in prison here in San Diego. At least then, I'd known I could do my damnedest to get him out. And I had.

I'd done bad things then, too. But I'd known what I was fighting for, and against. I struggled in my head, in that moment, looking at my sleeping husband.

I'd volunteered for this. No one was making me. Without my vigilance, my sister might not live to make the decision that would change the course of her life.

It was not the first time I'd gone through all these thoughts, and it wouldn't be the last.

Nothing for it but to keep the bit between my teeth.

After this week, I could go home to Segundo Mexia. I would see my new half brother. I would go hunting, I would cook my own food in my own kitchen. Eli would come back with me. He'd resume taking the small jobs the local people paid him for, and we'd be pretty happy.

Maybe.

Maybe he wouldn't come back. If Eli decided to stay in San Diego permanently, if the tsar said he could come back to court, I thought Eli would be delighted to resume the life he'd had before his father's decisions had almost ruined it. And if he assumed I'd stay here with him?

I couldn't live here.

I put my hand, so lightly, on Eli's bare shoulder. My heart ached. Had I ever been sure we'd stay together?

I lay there in silence until I smelled coffee. Then I pulled on my normal clothes and went downstairs. I wanted coffee, and I needed food. And I had to look at our schedule for the day.

CHAPTER TEN

Alice was alone in the dining room. She looked at me with concern. "Are you well, Lizbeth?" she asked, her brows puckering together.

"I just had a late night," I said. "Lots of people smoking, lots of noise. What are you up to today?"

Alice looked down at her plate, very pink and shy and smiling. "Konstantin and his mother are coming to call this afternoon."

That brought a smile to my face and heart. "What time?"

"Four o'clock, after he gets off work."

"Your mother is pleased?"

Alice's smile grew. "She is. I had worried, since he's not of noble blood . . ."

"Neither is Felix," I said.

"Mama was *not* happy about that, but Lucy was fixed on it and Felix said the right things. For once." Alice scrunched up her nose like a rabbit, and I had to laugh. "And Lucy seems happy."

"She does," I agreed. "I can't imagine living with Felix, but they seem to suit each other."

"He's difficult," Alice said, which was an understatement. "I am sure Konstantin is not scary like Felix."

"Alice, be open to noticing things you don't like, as well as things you do. No two people can live together without having a set-to now and then. There are going to be differences."

That was as close as I could come to—not *warning* her, but *alerting* her, that marriage was not all a bed of roses, no matter how much you cared about your partner.

I loved Eli, but some days I both loved him and wanted to sock him in the jaw.

Alice considered my words seriously. "I'll remember that," she said. "Mama was forced to marry my father, you know. He was older and had the two boys, who were not . . . agreeable. But he was a prince, and a grigori, and her parents were in poor health and wanted to see her settled before they died. It was not a good marriage, and he was not a good man. He brought shame on her and us."

I had never known Alice to be so serious. This was obviously something she'd thought about at length.

"I'm sure your mother is glad to have you and Lucy and Eli," I said.

"I believe she loves us dearly. But she should not have been made to marry a man she detested, much less have children by him."

I had never heard Eli's thoughts about his parents' marriage. Alice's were sad and interesting.

"There are faults you can live with, and faults you can't," I said. "I hope Konstantin has faults you can live with. His parents seem like very good people."

"They do, and they seem to like me," Alice said. She looked happy again.

I felt better after our chat. My spirits rose. *I can do this*, I thought. *It'll be over before too long. Just a few more days.*

I was able to smile when Eli trailed downstairs, clean and alert. He seemed pretty pleased with the night before. Too many people passed (the housemaid, the cook, Veronika herself) through the dining room for me to tell him what I had been doing while he was squiring Felicia around. I wanted to let him know what Maria had told us. It would have to wait until later, when I couldn't be overheard. And that would be a good time for him to tell me about the big meeting of the day before. If he would. If he could.

We went over the schedule for the day.

Eli told me he had an afternoon meeting with his grigori superiors, though he didn't say exactly who would be there, why he was doing it, or where this meeting would be. I got the feeling this was a smaller secret meeting to discuss the big secret meeting.

"So you'll have Felicia by yourself," he said. There was a question in his voice.

But I could hardly complain about it. She was my sister, after all. Eli and his family were doing more to help her than I'd ever expected.

Felicia slouched into the dining room in a dressing gown and helped herself to some bacon and eggs. Then toast. After the food and some coffee, she was bright-eyed and bushy-tailed.

She and Alice talked about the night before for a few minutes, and then Alice went upstairs to plan her outfit for the very important visit this afternoon. Eli excused himself to fill up the car since I would need it.

"Here's what's on your schedule," I told Felicia, passing her the sheet of paper.

"This afternoon I have tea at a real teahouse, English style," she said. "I am so looking forward to that."

She really was. I tried to look forward to it, too. With pleasure. "Three o'clock," I said. "We need to leave here at two thirty."

"Fenolla, Katerina, and Soo-Yung will be there." Felicia picked up the schedule. "Fenolla's mom reserved a table for eight at Mrs.

Forrester's English Teahouse. Four Listed men coming . . . Clayton, he's nice. I saw you talking to him last night."

"Camilla's not invited?"

"Fenolla's mom and dad did the inviting. I think Camilla had another engagement. She and this man from Canada are hitting it off."

"Who are the other men?"

"Mateo." She looked at a little notebook she'd started to carry with her. She was making notes on people. "A guy from some Arab country named Hasani El Masry, haven't met him yet. A Korean boy named Park Joon-Ho. There'll be a table for the adults, too. You and Miss Harriet and Matthew Gregory and Katerina's mom."

At least I'd have Harriet to talk to. Ahren was not invited, so Hans wouldn't be around. I was aiming to get Hans on his own to ask him some pointed questions. That wouldn't happen today.

"What are you looking so crabby for?" Felicia said. She was irritated that I wasn't delighted with the schedule. "Have you ever had an English tea? I sure never thought I'd be doing that. And all these people are perfectly respectable! A teahouse is not a dangerous place."

Meaning, there was nothing dangerous or suspicious about the event. But there was, I realized. Mateo and Clayton had made overtures to my sister already. So why were Samaah and Matthew Gregory inviting them to an event meant to feature their own daughter?

For that matter, why ask Felicia?

Maybe just because Felicia and Fenolla and Katerina were friends. Maybe Fenolla didn't have many. The few times I'd talked to the girl, I'd found her levelheaded and smart, a good companion for my sister. But people were very strange about Fenolla's dad being white and her mom being black.

I was not so sure about Katerina. I hadn't really talked to her much, and I hadn't been impressed by her mother, Irina. The questionable older brother worried me. But people couldn't help who their families were.

I had to tiptoe around my sister. It was so easy to set her off these days. Even now she was looking at me narrowly, like she was sure I was thinking bad thoughts about her friends.

I made myself sit up straight, to look cheerful and lively. I had to pay attention to the road right below my feet, while being alert to the upcoming cliffs. I would wear another dress today, and the heels, and I would be pleasant. And I'd keep my eyes open. That was my job.

Since Felicia had gotten up late and eaten such a large breakfast and had her hair done afterward, she didn't want lunch before we started for the tearoom. At least it wouldn't be a long drive. I'd looked at the map and made a list of turns so Felicia could navigate.

I gave Eli a quick kiss as we went out the back door to where the car was parked. Eli headed for the front door. He meant to catch a streetcar to his meeting.

I had remembered to wish Alice good luck with the Volkovs' visit. I almost envied Alice. She could be sure Konstantin and his parents didn't want to kill her.

"Did you have a good time last night?" I asked Felicia. I was sure I was on the right route. I could spare a little attention. "You looked as though you were."

"It was so much fun," Felicia said. From the corner of my eye, I could see her beaming. "The food was good, and I danced and danced."

"With Hans?"

"Oh," she said airily, "a time or two. And Ahren. And Mateo. Clayton. A couple of other men. Why were you so late?"

"I had an errand to run."

When she didn't ask me any more questions, I knew butterfly Felicia was at the forefront that day. She was full of the upcoming tea party. "Fenolla told me that an English tea has little sandwiches and cake and lots of other special food. We'll all sit and be served. It's very fancy. Other than that, I don't know. This restaurant has been open for over thirty years. It's in an old house."

"I'm looking forward to it," I said. I was hungry. "We're on the right street; look sharp."

The address was that of a two-story house that must have been built in the 1800s. It was painted dark green with white trim and planted around with bushes. The house had been a private home once upon a time. It was still pretending to be one.

The only thing that gave it away was a very small sign that read MRS. FORRESTER'S ENGLISH TEAHOUSE. You had to turn down a side street, since the house sat on a large corner lot, to turn and park behind the building. There were very few other cars there.

"Mr. Gregory reserved the whole building," Felicia told me. "We're a little early, so there may be other customers here. Don't you think that's kind of grand to have the whole building?"

"Yes, I didn't expect that," I said, which was all I could think of to say.

The back door was marked EMPLOYEES ONLY, so we followed the paved walkway around to the front. I was glad of my light coat. As Eli had predicted, it had rained a little before dawn. The bushes and the grass still shone with the moisture. The sky was still cloudy. A gray day. I wasn't surprised that the outside tables on the porch were covered with canvas.

Inside, it was homey, if your home was very pleasant. There were fresh flowers on each table, and the tablecloths were white and stiff with starch. The waitresses wore black uniforms with white aprons and caps.

"That's the way they do it in England," Felicia whispered.

That's the way they did it if they were rich.

The forks and knives and spoons were real silver. I bet those waitresses kept sharp eyes on the guests, especially the table of noisy young people seated by the west window. Their tea was in the winding-up phase from the used dishes on the table and the crumpled napkins by each plate.

We were not the first ones of our party to arrive. Fenolla Gregory, as hostess, was surrounded with other Listeds. Clayton Dashwood was the oldest and Felicia the youngest.

I cast an eye over the other young women and was relieved to see that Felicia was dressed well and appropriately. *Thank you, Veronika.*

As soon as Felicia saw her friends, she took off. I joined the other chaperones/what have you, who were standing at a respectful distance.

I introduced myself to Fenolla's father, a fair, handsome man in his forties, who wore glasses and a calm expression. He was an English wizard, so he had to practice in secret when he was in his home country. (If he had lived here, he'd have been a grigori named Gregory.) Harriet Ritter came in right after us with Soo-Yung, both smartly dressed and smiling. A really old woman hobbled in behind them, wearing a garment I'd never seen before. It was all white, except for the ribbons tying the blouse where it wrapped across her chest. The old woman was tiny and bent over.

"So this is the lady who came from Korea with Soo-Yung?" I said, amazed.

"She insisted on coming. The outfit she's wearing is a *hanbok*. Traditional."

"I like it," I said. There was a short blouse on top and a full, floor-length skirt so she had plenty of room to move. She could have concealed an army under there. I said as much, and Harriet nodded.

"I think there are pants below the skirt. She really, really wanted Soo-Yung to wear her own hanbok, but Soo-Yung insisted on wearing Western clothes."

I gave the old lady a little bow, pointed to myself, and said, "Lizbeth Savarova."

The old lady returned the bow, made no attempt to repeat my name. "Kim Bo-Ra," she muttered, tapping her chest. After sliding her eyes over to Harriet and shaking her head (didn't need a translator to explain that to me), the old lady went back to watching Soo-Yung, who was talking away with the other young people. Soo-Yung was very aware of the old lady but was pretending not to notice her.

I felt a little sorry for both of them.

Katerina's mother, Irina, entered with her daughter. Irina Swindoll was higher strung than she'd seemed the time I'd met her before. Thick and stolid, she was dressed in an ugly shade of green. Irina didn't even try to be polite to the old lady, she was stiff and distant with Harriet, and would have been the same with me if I hadn't been married to Eli.

Hired hands she could ignore. The wife of a prince she could not.

Katerina looked just as eager to get away from Irina as Felicia had been to get away from me. She joined the other Listeds and melted right into the group. Clayton Dashwood, Hasani El Masry, and Park Joon-Ho were all in their early twenties, older than the girls and Mateo, but they all seemed to be blending well.

I looked around and realized (with a little surprise and envy) that the young men must have come on their own. I would have thought they'd have needed as much watching as (or more than) the girls. I guess that wasn't the way it worked, at least at daytime events.

"Samaah sends her apologies," Matthew said. "Something came up, and she was detained."

Irina started to be offended, but she left off when the rest of us told Matthew we were sorry and we'd miss her.

There was a big gust of laughter from the only table still occupied.

"I understood you'd reserved the whole place, Matthew?" Irina Swindoll said, in kind of a snooty way. "Oh, Paul is with them. What a surprise!" She looked like a different woman, all bright and happy. The loud young people were instantly all right with her.

I would have sworn she already knew her son was present.

One of the young men did look a lot like Irina. He was the loudest and the rowdiest. He was not the one who picked up the check. He waved at his mother when he saw her looking.

By then I'd recognized a few at that table from the biographies and photographs that had been sent to all the people Listed. Some of them had looks or money, but little power (like Paul, probably). Some of them had power but no money and no one to back them, as Eli and his mother were backing my sister. Some of them had no money, little power, and weren't attractive.

All of them, male and female, had to be completely aware of their status. Maybe that was why they were being stupid in public.

"That group is paying their bill now," Matthew Gregory said calmly. "I noticed Paul. The last time I saw him he was called Mikhail. You gave him an American name."

"He picked it himself," Irina said, as proudly as though that had been a real feat.

"I hope he's having a good Wizards' Ball." In a quiet way, Matthew was as good-looking as his wife, Samaah. No wonder Fenolla was so pretty. At Tatiana's tea, Samaah had told me they'd sent Fenolla to school in the Holy Russian Empire so she could learn everything she needed to, openly. When she returned to live in England—if she did—she would have to use her talent out of view of anyone.

(I had spent a few odd moments this past autumn hoping Felicia wouldn't fall for some English magic practitioner. She'd be terrible at keeping her talent concealed, as the English had to. Seems like I hadn't needed to worry, since I had yet to meet an English magician except for Matthew.)

An imposing gray-haired lady in a muted purple dress came out of a doorway at the rear of the dining room. This had to be Mrs. Forrester. She went to the rowdy table, and as she stood waiting for their attention, they remembered their manners. I was impressed. With a small smile, she talked to them quietly. The oldest boy (really a young man) nodded. He offered his payment to a hovering waitress (no one would dare hand money directly to Mrs. Forrester) and they all stood to leave. A couple of them exchanged a wave or a word with members of our party. Paul gave a kiss on the cheek to his mother and a careless wave to his sister. Katerina lifted a hand half-heartedly.

After that was done, Mrs. Forrester glided over to Matthew Gregory while two waitresses began to clear the party's table. One was gray-haired and stout, one was younger and thin. They were both very efficient.

"Good day, Mr. Gregory," Mrs. Forrester said. She had an English accent, though not as strong as Matthew's. "We are ready to seat you now. The table for eight is for the younger people, the table over here for you four . . . five, I see." Bo-Ra was a surprise. Mrs. Forrester told the younger waitress to set another place and bring another chair, and the girl hopped to obey.

"Mrs. Forrester owns the place outright," Harriet said quietly. "When her husband's mother died, she had to find a way to earn her own living, since she was a widow. So she used the house and her baking skills." Trust Harriet to have found that out. The young people took seats at their table while the extra place was being set at ours. There was a name card at each seat for the table for eight.

Since Fenolla's father was paying for this party, I guessed he'd picked the seating order. Another thing I'd never thought of.

Clayton and Mateo were on either side of my sister. That was good. She might yet change her mind, but that was a pretty dim hope. Clayton was seven years older than Felicia, but he seemed like a nice guy in a very stable situation. Mateo was younger, but he was also attractive and talkative, and his family was wealthy and close-knit. I hadn't seen anything bad in either one on short acquaintance. I didn't pay much attention to the other kids, but I did notice that Soo-Yung was sitting by her countryman.

Harriet, the ancient Korean lady, Katerina's mother, Fenolla's father, and I shared a table on the other side of the room. We were within sight but not hearing, which suited the Listeds. Matthew didn't want to seem like he was eavesdropping, I guess.

When our waitress came, Matthew ordered a full tea for our table, and we all smiled like that was wonderful. Turned out it *was* wonderful. We not only got two kinds of tea along with everything that could be added to them, but a big tray with lots of layers, different food on every single one: little sandwiches, pastries, preserved fruit, cake, and what Harriet, who was sitting to my left, said were scones. Which turned out to be like biscuits. There were all kinds of things to slather on the scones, too.

For the first time in what felt like days, I was really happy and interested.

Kim Bo-Ra was to my right, and I made a plate for her. She gave me a nod of thanks—or anyway, a nod. She was not paying our table conversation any attention. She held her head cocked, as if she were listening to someone far away.

"Far-hearing," Harriet whispered from my left. "Soo-Yung told me."

I had never heard of that as a grigori gift. I was really impressed. I remembered the only other person of Korean background I'd met before this week: Chin-Hao Costa, from Brazil. He had been able to travel far distances by a process called "land folding." Different magic traditions had different gifts, which kind of made sense.

I didn't know what conversation Bo-Ra was listening in on, but it had to be more interesting than ours.

Irina decided to tell us what Katerina's older brother, Paul (formerly Mikhail), had been doing for the past few days. It was just as boring as it had been at Tatiana Medvedeva's tea.

Felicia had told me the teachers wouldn't talk about why Paul had gotten expelled from Rasputin. But he was doing well at his college. "He's got to be smart to study chemistry and electronics," Felicia said. "But everyone knows Paul has a wild side. Anna went to dinner with him once, without telling her parents. They would have had a fit. He had a lot of conversation, but she didn't think he had a future."

That was not the opinion of Irina Swindoll. She was like a radio station that only broadcasted "Paul."

I envied Bo-Ra her ability to listen to another conversation. Since she didn't admit to speaking English, she could get away with tuning Irina out. Matthew, Harriet, and I were obliged to pretend we were interested.

"Paul had a great academic career at Rasputin," Irina told us. "But he found the studies not to his liking." Irina shrugged her heavy shoulders as if to say, *You know what young men are like*. "His talents lay elsewhere, he decided. So he transferred to a conventional college, where he's much happier, and his grades are so good!"

"It can be hard to pick the right path to follow, among so many choices," Matthew said. Tactful. I hadn't been able to come up with anything to say.

The little wrinkle in Harriet's brow told me she was deleting Paul from Soo-Yung's eligible list. Irina would be an awful mother-in-law.

At least I got to eat my fill while Irina kept droning on and on.

The silence fell like a brick when none of us could pretend any longer that we gave a tinker's damn about Paul. Even Irina could tell the topic was done.

Katerina was at the table across the room, in clear sight. Katerina was smart, nice-looking, interesting enough to be Felicia's friend. Not once did Irina say anything good about her daughter.

As I swallowed the last bite of cake, I found Matthew looking at me with his brows raised. I guessed it was my turn to move the conversation along. "Do you live here in San Diego?" he asked, to prompt me. Since he was English, everything he said sounded polite.

"No, I'm from Segundo Mexia in Texoma," I said, which didn't appear to surprise anyone. "My husband and I are in town to . . . attend . . . Felicia through the week."

Matthew asked me a few questions about my hometown, though he couldn't have been really interested in a small town in a poor country. Harriet lived in the Boston area, in Britannia, and she had some funny stories to tell about it.

I glanced over at the other table.

Everything seemed fine. The young magicians had enjoyed the food and the tea, and the talk had never slowed down.

Felicia laughed a lot, Fenolla listened to Hasani El Masry in a serious way, and Katerina was talking to Mateo with a big smile on her face. She was happier than I'd ever seen her, for sure.

Matthew, who had finished eating before the rest of us, was watching his daughter with a little smile.

"Fenolla is a lovely girl," I said. I meant it.

Matthew beamed at me. "She's got her mother's beauty," he said. "A bit inclined to be too serious about herself, though."

"Not everyone is a laugh-out-loud kind of person."

He nodded to acknowledge that. "Your sister is an impressive young woman."

"She's scary, all right." I could translate that from polite-talk.

Matthew laughed out loud. "She's unique."

Irina leaned across the table, her eyes wide and avid. "Is it true she killed her own grandfather?"

There was a moment of silence you could have cut with a knife. The smile dropped from my face. Matthew looked appalled.

"This is not something to discuss here," Harriet said. Even Bo-Ra cocked her head.

It finally dawned on Irina that she'd stepped over a line. *Dashed* over a line, stomping her feet while she did it. "I'm sorry," she said, very flustered. "I've just heard so many stories . . ."

Could she be that stupid? I looked at her without blinking for a long moment. She looked frightened.

Yes, she could be that stupid.

And guilty. She looked guilty. Huh.

"We should have wonderful weather the rest of the week," Matthew said smoothly. Harriet agreed instantly and said that we'd been lucky so far and she was hoping that kept up.

The young people at the other table began laughing very loudly, and I turned my head to see that Mateo was making a spoon spin around in midair.

I was at his side in the blink of an eye. "Not in a public place," I said quietly. "Not with civilians present." The waitresses were staring at the spoon with wide eyes. Though everyone in the Holy Russian Empire knew about grigoris and were supposed to revere them, grigoris were told to keep their magic practice "discreet."

Mateo's smile vanished and he let the spoon fall to the table. All the kids looked at me with a resentment . . . including Felicia.

Too bad. There were rules. I'd learned them. No public magic unless there was an emergency. An afternoon tea was not a dangerous situation.

I was wrong about that.

The two boys I didn't know, Hasani and Joon-Ho, simply stared at me. They did not appreciate a woman's cautioning them.

Mateo had better manners. "My apologies, Princess. There are so few people here, I forgot to be careful," he said.

I nodded and returned to my seat. I couldn't stand Felicia's mortified expression.

Harriet muttered, "The little sneaks! They know better, or they ought to."

"Fenolla should have forced the spoon down," Matthew said, and he meant it. "She is the hostess. She knows the rules."

"It's hard to mind the rules when you're young and having a good time," I said, just to say something. I was still brooding over Felicia not stopping Mateo, and then acting all huffy when I did.

Irina glanced at her watch. "Excuse me, please," she said, and rose to go through the doorway marked RESTROOMS. She took her purse with her. It was like she had an appointment in the bathroom.

Bo-Ra punched my shoulder. "We go," she hissed. I didn't move, I was so startled at this sudden English and the command in her voice.

I am a short woman, but the ancient Korean lady only came to my shoulder. She pulled me out of my chair, grabbed hold of my arm, and started yanking me toward the kids' table.

The door to the hall was closing behind Irina.

"Matthew, did you invite Paul to this party?" I said, ignoring Bo-Ra's violent tugging on my arm.

Matthew gave me a sharp look, decided I had a reason. "Fenolla wanted to, since she thought it would please Katerina. I had reservations because I had heard he was wild, but I agreed. Then Irina called last night to say Paul couldn't come, to my relief. I was surprised to see him here with this other group. He must not have cared for our company. Fenolla asked Clayton Dashwood instead."

I opened my mouth, closed it. Bo-Ra tugged even harder, and we started across the room.

"What's happening?" Harriet called.

I jerked my head toward the kids' table. "Bo-Ra thinks something is wrong here, and I do, too. Get ready to leave, please, Matthew."

To give him great credit, Matthew called to one of the waitresses to bring him the check and hastily handed her cash to cover it. Harriet had already grabbed her bag and mine, ready to go.

We'd reached the table, and the young ones were looking up, even more annoyed at my second visit.

Bo-Ra pointed under the table, yanking my arm down in a violent way. "See," she said. "See."

I squatted, raised the long white tablecloth. *Oh, shit.*

"Get up," I told the kids. "Out the door, now, *now*!" I yelled the last word.

They all stared at me like bumps on a log. Only Felicia pushed back her chair and stood.

Matthew was there suddenly. He bent to look under the table, too. He stood. He said in a very sharp voice, "Do not exclaim or ask questions. Rise and leave through the front door. Quickly." Matthew didn't look like an aristocrat anymore. He looked hard as nails and all business.

Everyone was moving by then, the girls grabbing up their handbags. Felicia hesitated, maybe thinking she should stay and help me do whatever I was going to do. To Clayton's credit, he laid his hand on Felicia's shoulder and said, "Right now!" He pushed my sister toward the door.

Felicia was abruptly no longer the butterfly, but the eagle. She called back to Katerina, "Up and out, Kat." Fenolla and Mateo were just ahead of my sister.

Hasani and Joon-Ho had beat everyone out the door.

Matthew Gregory had stepped around them to hold the front door open. Bo-Ra ran out of steam all of a sudden. We were more or less hobbling fast. *She could hear the bomb ticking*, I thought. *She's saved our lives.* Then I realized, *Not quite yet.*

"Where's Mother?" Katerina called over her shoulder.

"She's outside," I lied, so the girl would move. Katerina began to slow down. I think she meant to help me with Bo-Ra. *"Run,"* I said, in the voice I used when I had to be obeyed. It worked.

Matthew, still holding the door, called to the two waitresses who were standing and staring at our sudden exit. "Ladies, there is a bomb!" he called. "You need to run out this door right now."

The older waitress half turned as though she would go fetch the owner, but at the last moment she wheeled to move toward the door, grabbing the other woman's hand and dragging her along.

The two waitresses broke into a trot and passed me. I was half carrying Bo-Ra, who had a death grip on my arm.

After what seemed like an hour, I got her out the door. Matthew let go. The door swung shut. Then Bo-Ra and I were across the porch. The older waitress slowed down. I had to shove her, hard. From the street, Felicia screamed my name.

Then we were down the steps into the front yard, still pushing for the street. I felt like I was walking through glue.

Matthew, who'd been in front of me, turned to face the teahouse, and his hands began to make a series of movements, very precise and full of angles. "Hurry," he said, not looking at us but at the building. The two waitresses pounded past him.

I tried to do the same, but Bo-Ra sagged against me and I could not let her go. I knew it was important to get past Matthew, just from the strain on his face. I did my very best, but I didn't make it.

CHAPTER ELEVEN

A giant fist hit me in the back. I staggered into the older waitress just ahead of me. She fell hard onto the paved walkway to the street. Bo-Ra and I landed on top of her. Though a sharp pain in my back took almost all my attention, I managed to slide sideways off the woman so she could breathe.

There was some screaming (Katerina, who'd realized she couldn't see her mother), and some cursing (Clayton Dashwood and Matthew Gregory).

I ought to get up. I ought to draw my knife in case we were attacked out here. For some reason, I couldn't get myself on my feet. I wondered if Bo-Ra was alive, and Matthew Gregory, and the waitress. I was lying on the grass beside the paved walkway, just inside the hedge. After another second or two, I knew I was hurt bad. That held most of my attention, but just on the edges of it I smelled a chemical reek and dust, which was settling on me. My clothes felt wet. On my front, I was sure the wetness was the rain-soaked grass. But on my back . . . I was pretty sure that was my blood.

There was yelling above my head. The voice was familiar. I might have relaxed, if I hadn't been hurting so badly. Felicia was standing over me, absolutely her eagle self. I did not have to fear, now that she was with me. I wondered in a fuzzy way what I'd been thinking, to believe I could protect Felicia. She was capable of defending herself in the most savage way. I was proud of my sister. Then her face was in front of my eyes. My sister was lying on the grass, too, so she could look into my face.

"You hurt?" I asked, trying to keep my voice steady.

"You're the one who's hurt," she said. "Your back has a huge piece of wood stuck in it."

So that was the pain. "Shit," I said, for once not minding my language. "Is it deep?"

"Don't know, but it's sticking straight up like a spear."

"I'm bleeding?"

"Like a stuck pig," Felicia told me.

"How are the others?"

"Don't care," Felicia said.

I gave her a look.

"Oh, okay! Everyone is fine, even that little old woman who heard the bomb. She may have a broken arm, though. You're all that matters."

That was lovely to hear, though it wasn't true.

"Irina knew it was going to happen," I said, because that was important. I had to be sure someone else knew, in case I died. "Katerina didn't, pretty sure. There was a bomb under the table. The whole time. Bo-Ra heard it."

Felicia's face twisted into a snarl. *There* was my sister! "I'll get to the bottom of this," she said, and I felt sorry for whoever waited at the bottom.

"Matthew's responsibility," I said, though I didn't sound firm like I wanted to. I sounded wobbly, like I was going to pass out.

But I didn't. I wished I had when the ambulance men slid me onto a stretcher on my side, told me to hold on, and lifted me. I made a sound through my teeth that sounded more like a growl than anything else.

"Hurting, huh?" the taller man said, sounding cheerful.

I wanted him to have this piece of wood in his own back.

"Just doing his job," Felicia muttered in my ear. "Just doing his job."

I could see her hand, swinging close to my face as she walked. By the stiffness of her gait, she was very angry, which didn't surprise me at all.

"Eli?" I said.

"I'll call his mom's as soon as I know where they're taking you," she said.

"Mercy," said the tall man. "It's closest."

I did not want to go to a hospital. I hated the way they smelled, the way they were chock-full of suffering, the way the doctors treated the patients. And some of the nurses, too.

But I wasn't exactly in any shape to stop this from happening, and if Felicia stuck to me I might get good treatment. I wouldn't ask her to do it herself; she'd already brought me back from death once before, and she needed her strength to defend herself. But I knew my sister would keep a close eye on me.

The pain got worse because of the bobbing of the stretcher. I could only close my eyes and bite my lip.

They stuck me in the back of a vehicle. I was resting on a shelf built for the stretcher. I was on my side because of the wood in my back, which was still in place. The men got in the front seats, while my sister crawled in beside me. The vehicle started with a lurch, and I groaned.

"She still alive?" one of the men called.

"Yes," Felicia said. "Get us there."

"Hold your horses, sister," the driver said. "We'll get her there as fast as we can."

"I'll watch you," Felicia promised me. "I'll get Eli. This is a regular hospital. They wouldn't take you to the grigori one."

"All right," I said, because I didn't dare nod. That would make the pain worse.

"How far?" I said, after the ambulance went around a curve. I'd always considered myself pretty tough, but this was getting to me.

"Northwest of the park, the man says." That was all Felicia knew.

We went to a special ambulance entrance. I could see the sign as we went by. The men carried me in, jostling and bumping all the way. I almost threw up. I realized, in a hazy way, that this was a bigger hospital than I'd ever been in, and I heard voices all around me, but I quit trying to listen and understand. All the energy I had was focused on fighting the pain.

Shallow breaths. No talking.

I heard Felicia while I was carried into a big room and the two men sort of eased me sideways onto a bed so they could take their stretcher with them. I was now on my stomach.

"She's still bleeding," Felicia was saying to a nurse. "The doctor needs to come right now." I pretended to be unconscious while Felicia told the woman my full legal name and my husband's. The nurse's tone altered after that.

Maybe I wasn't just pretending to be unconscious, because I'd lost some seconds (maybe even minutes) when I was aware again. I heard Felicia tell me she was going to find a telephone, but then I lost some more time. Next thing I knew, a man in a white coat was standing by the bed telling a nurse what a mess my back was and inquiring how I'd happened to be close to an explosion.

"The teahouse on Spruce Street," Felicia said, from behind his back. "Lizbeth, Eli's on his way. I caught him at the house."

Good, I thought, in a kind of fuzzy way. *He's back from his meeting. I hope we can pay for this.*

"Please tell your sister I'm going to take this piece of wood out. This is going to hurt," the doctor said.

Maybe he thought I couldn't speak English. "I can hear you," I said, aware that my words were coming out funny. "You said it's going to hurt."

He was right.

Getting the giant splinter out was easy (at least for the doctor). Just one terrible yank and it was done. But the hole had to be cleaned, then stitched, then bandaged. The doctor talked the whole damn time. He told me how lucky I was that it hadn't gone in half an inch deeper or half an inch to the left, he told me my spine was okay, probably. He told me he was making sure I didn't have any splinters or debris in the wound to fester. He told me he'd never heard of anyone blowing up a teahouse.

Maybe he hoped his conversation would distract me from the pain.

He was wrong.

Felicia took my hand during the stitching and bandaging. It didn't help, but it made her feel better, I guess. Then they wheeled me into a room and shifted me to another bed. I felt tears running down my face to soak the sheets.

I lost a little time just then. The next time I opened my eyes, I felt a familiar presence, and I knew my husband had entered the hospital. I knew he was angry. I just didn't know who the target was.

Turns out he was mad every which way.

I was glad he talked to Felicia first. But while she was telling him what had happened, as far as she knew it, he fumbled for my hand. He held it throughout.

"She got us all out just in time," Felicia said, and I thought she was crying a little. "If it hadn't been for Lizbeth and Bo-Ra, we'd all have been blown to smithereens."

Eli took a very deep breath. I could almost hear him making himself calm down. "Tell me," he said.

While the doctor finished working on me, my sister told him what had happened at the teahouse, in a sort of indirect way since the doctor and nurse were in the room.

I squeezed his hand. "Irina Swindoll," I whispered. "She left the room right before we found the bomb. I think she knew."

"Felicia was just telling me about her," he said, trying to sound tender instead of angry. He almost made it.

"Don't leave me here," I said.

Eli crouched down to look me in the eyes. "I won't leave you here. I'll take you home," he said. He knew how much I hated hospitals.

"Thanks," I whispered.

"This good doctor will give you a prescription for pain medicine," Eli assured me. "Won't you?" He was looking up at the doctor now.

"Yes," the doctor said. "This could have been a very serious wound if it had gone deeper. She will have to be careful for a week or two."

That wasn't possible, not if I was going to fulfill my duty to Felicia. I started to say something, but Eli's eyes were on me again. He shook his head, very slightly. I kept my mouth shut.

I figured he was planning to get me healed.

The problem with that was . . . it was too easy. I shouldn't get used to being healed so quick. I would start taking bigger risks if I thought there would be only a light price to pay for sticking my neck out. I already had. My sister had brought me back from the dead.

I knew myself well enough to foresee this.

But I was in San Diego to protect my sister. I couldn't do that lying in a bed on my stomach.

I'd been faced with a lot of bad choices in the past couple of years, and here was another one. I was sick and tired of bad choices.

The doctor gave me a shot. I felt the drug moving through my body inch by inch, almost. And then there was no pain. I was terrified.

"What was in that shot?" Felicia said.

"Morphine," the nurse said.

I might not be feeling the pain, but I did feel fear. Felicia bent over me, just like Eli had. "Don't let them give me any more," I whispered.

"Didn't it work?" Her face was anxious.

"Yes," I said. "But you can get addicted."

"Okay." She must have turned to Eli. "No more morphine. It scares her."

"We'll get some Anacin on the way home."

"Anything but this," I whispered.

And then I went to the land in between. I wasn't asleep and I wasn't awake but floating somewhere. I didn't hurt, but I knew the pain was only wearing a mask.

Then I realized I was in a wheelchair, with a pillow behind my back, and Felicia was pushing it to an exit door. Eli was waiting in the car outside. I wondered how he'd gotten the car from the teahouse to the hospital, but I didn't care enough to ask.

I had to stand to get in the car. I needed a lot of help, from both Felicia and Eli, and movement was very unpleasant—but not painful, not yet. My sister held me up while Eli ran around the car to open the back door to help her ease me in. Together they got me settled on my side on the back seat, my legs drawn up.

I slept while Eli drove to the Savarov house, but I woke when they had to get me inside without the wheelchair. And then up the stairs to our room. I thought the climb would kill me. Then there was our bed, and Eli was taking off my clothes, bloody and ruined. That outfit would never be worn again by anyone. Sorry, Veronika.

Rather than try and get a nightgown over my head, Eli just let me be naked, and pulled the covers over me. I was still on my side. But the other side. That was a change.

"Can you hear me?" he asked. "Do you understand?"

"I do."

"I'm going to get some pain reliever from the pharmacy. Felicia and I will go do that. Leah will watch you."

"Find out how Bo-Ra is?"

"I'll try." He touched my face gently. "Explosions seem to follow you around," he said, on his way out of the room.

I thought about that for half a minute. He was right. I didn't cause them, but they happened. Felicia . . . my sister liked explosions . . . she didn't care for seeing the results, but she loved causing them. Made her feel powerful.

And I slept again.

When I woke up, Leah was sitting by the bed reading a book I'd gotten at a secondhand store. When she glanced up and saw my eyes were open, she said, "I'm glad to see you moving. I began to think I needed to take your pulse, Princess."

"Where is Eli?" He'd said they were going to get something for pain. But I could tell night had fallen.

"He called to say he'd taken your sister straight to a party tonight. He said to tell you not to worry. He'll be back soon, he said."

But when I woke up in the night, Eli wasn't there. A woman I didn't know was asleep in the chair, a lamp turned low by her elbow.

"Who are you?" I asked.

Her eyes flew open. "I'm so sorry, I fell asleep. You were so quiet. What can I do for you?"

"You can tell me who you are." Though it seemed like I knew her. Her hair was red.

"I know Felicia from the school."

"I've met you."

"I was Callista Roper. I'm the head of the infirmary at Rasputin. These days, I'm Callista O'Day, and I mostly watch Madame Semyonova."

"You were at the garden, the first day of Ball Week. And at the big fancy tea."

"I was. And now I'm here watching you, and I'm betting you need to get to the bathroom. Here's the good news. I can carry you there."

"I can walk," I said, but I didn't sound sure, even to myself.

"Malarkey," Callista said. "It's my bit of magic, and very handy if you're a nurse."

She was wearing a grigori vest, a very simple one, and she pulled a pinch of stuff from the main pocket, sprinkled it over me, said a few words, and scooped me up. Before I could get over being surprised, she'd deposited me gently on the toilet and turned her back.

Life was much better and more comfortable a few seconds later. Callista took me to the basin to wash my hands and face, and then lifted me again to take me back to the bed. She gave me Anacin to swallow. Grateful for that. As I lay back, I realized I'd been cleaned up and was wearing a nightgown. I was grateful for that, too.

"Thanks so much. You married Tom O'Day?" I said. "He used to be on duty in the school's lobby. He's the only grigori from Texoma, where I live."

Callista nodded, grinning. "He is. That's his claim to fame."

"You just got married?"

"Not a month ago."

"Congratulations. Felicia told me last year that all the girls at school had a crush on him. But he wasn't having any of it."

She grinned even more widely.

"My Tom, he's not vain, and he's a very practical man."

I had to like this woman, who was surely younger than me but so practical herself. I tried to shift around a little and sharp pain told me to stop. "Hell," I said. "Shouldn't have done that."

"The Anacin will be working soon," Callista said. I drifted back to sleep.

She was right. It didn't wipe the pain right out, like morphine, but the pills made it more manageable.

The next time I woke up, Eli was in bed beside me and it was broad daylight. Our corner room had windows on two sides, west and north. From the way the sun streamed through the glass, I figured it was about noon.

With great care, I swung my legs over the edge of the mattress and pushed myself up. I was sitting!

"How are you?" Eli asked behind me.

"Not too bad," I said. "But I'm scared to turn around to look at you."

"I don't mind looking at your back," he said, and I could hear the smile in his voice.

"How does it look today?"

"A lot better. It's healing. But you can't do anything extra today."

"Extra? Like walking and bending over and so on?"

"Yes, extra like that."

"You weren't here last night."

"You got along with Callista?"

I nodded. That didn't feel so good. "I like her. You know she married Tom O'Day?"

"She was a little kid when I was in Rasputin. It's hard to believe she's old enough to get married, and that Tom saw the good in her. He's a secretive man."

Since Eli wasn't telling me where he and Felicia had been and what they'd been doing, I knew that it was something he didn't want to talk about right now. "Did you get enough sleep to take Felicia where she needs to go today?"

"I did. It's all safe stuff."

"I thought afternoon tea would be safe."

He had no answer for that. The silence stretched out. Then Eli said, "Why do you think someone is trying to kill Felicia?" It sounded like he was trying to open a conversation. That wasn't the real question.

"I don't think someone is trying to kill her. I *know* someone is trying to kill her. Can you come around so I can see you?"

I felt the bed move, and a moment later he was sitting in the chair facing me.

That was better. "Are you asking me, or are you going to tell me? I think you know why Felicia is a target. And I don't think it's because she's the prettiest, or the strongest, grigori of this season."

"There's always a front-runner at every Wizards' Ball, a young woman or man more powerful, more beautiful, richer, or all three. Never before has anyone tried to kill the lucky girl. Or man." He was still waiting on me to come up with the right answer. I was tired of playing this game.

"You tell me. Why is Felicia such a threat that she has to die?"

"There's something deeper behind this. I'm going to tell you some secrets."

"All right, shoot."

"That means go ahead?"

I nodded, very carefully. I was still learning what would make the wound in my back throb. "I guess this was the subject of your many meetings?"

"Yes. Not Felicia specifically, but the state of the world."

He lost me there. All I cared about was Felicia.

"This war that is brewing in Europe." Eli was looking at me, and he was very serious.

"The one Ahren and Hans were talking about. What is happening in Germany."

"This man, Hitler, is determined to eradicate the Jews. You know that Ahren and Hans are Jews. You know what 'eradicate' means?"

I had never heard the word before, but it wasn't hard to figure out. "Why?"

"He has made the Jews his scapegoats. His followers blame the Jews for everything that has gone wrong in their country," Eli said. "He teaches that if they are all done away with, Germany will be the better for it."

I wrestled with that. "Doesn't make any sense."

"It's someone to blame. Sometimes it's Catholics, sometimes it's homosexuals, sometimes it's Roma, or immigrants, or Masons. Or grigoris."

"Okay. So?"

"Adolf Hitler is very much interested in the occult. He is a believer in magic and magic practitioners of whatever school. In fact, he is fascinated by them."

I nodded very slightly.

"He is marshalling a large company of wizards, grigoris, witches, sorcerers, all kinds of magical folk. Any of them who believe his creed and will come to his aid. He rewards them lavishly."

"So?"

"He would be glad to have Felicia on his side, because she's a death grigori."

"She hasn't mentioned being approached."

"I don't think she has been, not officially. But they've put out feelers. And she has been seen to be friendly with Ahren and Hans. She has not encouraged the attentions of the German wizards here to court her."

I could only remember that one encounter in the Japanese Friendship Garden, but Felicia talked to many people at the parties. "So if she's not Hitler's friend, she's his enemy?"

"Exactly. He doesn't want anyone else to have her on their team if she will not join his. The Japanese are Hitler's allies. They are currently occupying Korea. The Koreans hate their oppressors."

I pondered this twist in the tale. "There were two Korean kids at the teahouse. And Bo-Ra. Were they the targets?"

"Maybe their deaths would have been a bonus. But I think Felicia was the real target. The Japanese shot at us in the garden, and there were no Koreans with us."

"But she's just one girl." It was too bad that the thing that made her so desirable was the thing that might get her killed. It was *mean.*

"She's one girl who killed a whole troop of soldiers in less time than it's taken me to tell you all this."

"Oh," I said. "Well, she did do that."

It was hard not to shudder at the memory.

"So the Germans, or maybe the Japanese, fired the arrows in the Friendship Garden, and got the bomb planted at the teahouse. And they may keep trying."

"I think so. Felicia wasn't sure what alerted you to the bomb, and I haven't asked. What made you suspect there was something wrong?" Eli said.

"Bo-Ra. She has far-hearing. I guess she heard the bomb ticking."

"No one else heard it?"

"No," I said. "The kids didn't hear it. They were making a lot of noise. And at our table . . . I told you about Katerina's mom. She kept talking about her son, Paul, and how wonderful he is. She blabs about him like he is the second coming, like Katerina is nothing. But we wouldn't have heard that tick at our distance, even if everything had been silent. Bo-Ra saved all of us."

"Don't worry about Irina," Eli said. "Don't worry about anything."

"I don't see how she did it herself," I said. "She and Katerina didn't get there until after we did."

The silence drew out.

"But Paul was there," I said slowly. I didn't want to believe this. "Paul turned down the invitation to have tea with our people, but he was there with a group of other Listeds."

Eli nodded. "Felicia told me about their less-than-stellar behavior."

"You think Paul planted the bomb. And Irina knew about it. She got out in time and . . ." *She walked out and left all of us to die, including her own daughter.*

I had been feeling empty. Now I began to fill with anger.

"All the kids sitting at that table," I said. "With their legs underneath. They all would have bled out if they'd been there when the bomb went off. Or they would have lost their legs."

It was hard to breathe normally.

"There's more I need to tell you, but you're tired," Eli said. His face became even more serious. "Lizbeth, never doubt that I rely on you."

"I don't," I said. "I just wonder if you feel I am worth giving up the life you had before you met me." I almost sucked in my breath to draw those words back. I hadn't meant to say them out loud, for fear of the answer.

Eli's face hardened in tense lines. "Do you think I want to be back at court, trusted by the tsar, making money for my family?"

"Yes, I do." I was cutting my own throat.

"Some days I miss the way my life used to be," he said, with every appearance of honesty. "It was a good life, and I made enough money to help my mother and sisters. But when I met you in Texoma, and Paulina and I hired you to lead us to Ciudad Juárez, I knew I'd met my match."

I wanted to say "Really?," but I knew that would sound like I needed more sweet talk. (Which would have been nice.) He'd said the right words, and he'd seemed to mean them. That would have to do at this moment. I wasn't up to further talk. But Eli wasn't finished.

"In return, I wonder," he said slowly, "if you miss your straightforward life."

That was smart of him. I'd been wondering the same thing. If I'd been hired to protect something, I protected it. If people tried to take it away, I shot them.

I didn't feel bad about that, because that was my job. Everyone who came against me knew the risk they were taking.

I wouldn't last more than a few years. Gunnies rarely made old bones. And it took me away from Eli after we married. But it was a job I did well, and I could support myself. Every time I left now, I wondered if it would be the last. That wondering was what brought me down, and one day it might slow me up enough to cost my life.

"I do miss the life I led by myself," I said. "But I would miss you more."

Maybe we both could have added, "For now."

CHAPTER TWELVE

E li said a few healing spells over me, and I'd been whispering them every time I'd been awake. By the next morning, though I wasn't completely fixed, I was better enough to resume my duties with Felicia.

I hadn't seen much of my sister. She was keeping her social schedule and only came up to our room to look me up and down, before bubbling over about dancing with this man or eating lunch or dinner with that one. And then she was gone before I could ask many questions.

Almost like she was withholding something from me.

Alice had kept me company the night before while Eli took my sister to her evening party. When Alice came into our room looking all glowy, I remembered what had been happening in Alice's life . . . something much more important to her than Felicia and I almost getting blown up.

"How did the Volkovs' visit go?" I asked. I'd said exactly the right thing because Alice actually laughed out loud.

"So well," she said. "His mama was very . . . She did everything right and impressed my mother so much. My mother, you know, she's . . ."

I knew. "I understand," I said. Veronika wanted every association of her family's to be aristocratic. So far, she'd been disappointed.

Lucy had married a death grigori, Eli had married a gunnie from Texoma, and when Peter had passed away he'd been pretty fixed on Felicia.

Konstantin Volkov probably looked pretty good by comparison. His family was well-to-do and employed on the royal island. Mr. Volkov owned his own business. Though he and his son had to work for a living, it was honorable work and the tsar was his employer.

Konstantin himself was pleasant looking, well educated, and intelligent enough to appreciate Alice.

Yes, he had to look pretty good.

"Not that she doesn't love you and Felix," Alice said, falling all over her words in confusion.

"I know how your mother feels."

Alice was willing to take that at face value. "Anyway," she said, "Konstantin's manners were perfect, and he sat by me, and said I would have to come see their house! It's on the island!"

"Oh, that will be so interesting," I said, almost at random. I mentally shook myself. I had to do better, for Alice's sake. "You'll charm them out of the trees, I know. His mother and father were very friendly."

Alice's hands were clenched together in her lap. That told me how excited she was by the promise of this new connection. She must have wondered if she would ever marry, because of her father's traitor status. Even with the new respectability of being Captain McMurtry's stepdaughter, Alice hadn't gotten out much or made many friends.

"It would be wonderful if I . . ." Alice began, and then stopped. She looked at me with a face I could only describe as embarrassed.

"What?" I asked. I was beginning to feel sleepy.

"Did you know," she said, very slowly, "that there is going to be a new arrival in the family?"

"Oh, Alice, tell me you're not pregnant," I said, all traces of sleep leaving my body.

"I?" Alice stared at me. "How could I be? I'm not married!"

I had nothing to say to that. "Then who?"

"My mother is going to have a baby," Alice whispered, her cheeks red.

I sat up so fast my back twinged. "Oh, that is big news," I said, just managing to calm my voice. "She told you?"

"I heard her being sick in the morning. Leah was telling her, 'That'll be the way of it, from now on till the baby's born,' in this gloomy voice."

We stared at each other.

"I hope the pregnancy goes well and the baby is healthy. Won't it be nice to have a little brother or sister?"

"No," Alice said, with a lot of conviction. "I'm too old for that. I need to have my own husband and my own babies. Maybe I'm a little young for marriage, but it would be very nice to be engaged and to know I was getting out of this house before Mother gets all wrapped up in another child. I want to have my own place. Like Lucy does."

"Alice, you amaze me," I told her honestly. "I won't say anything to your mother until she decides to tell me."

"Please don't." Alice suddenly sounded about twelve, rather than sixteen.

"I won't." I couldn't imagine bringing it up to Veronika. *Mother-in-law, I hear you've been having morning sickness. Anything your son should know?*

When I'd miscarried, the two weeks after had been the saddest weeks of my life.

After Alice left, I had a stern talk with myself. I would not be one of those women who begrudged happiness to other women who had babies. I was in my very early twenties, and Eli was not yet thirty. We had plenty of time to have a family. Many women had at least one miscarriage and went on to have healthy infants.

It was a talk I'd had with myself a score of times. But I never seemed to believe it.

Veronika was old to be having another baby.

It was dangerous to bring a child into the world when you had to be at least . . . forty-four? I shuddered. Childbirth was tough enough when you were young and strong. I'd been with Chrissie, my neighbor, for her first two deliveries. I'd kept her company till the midwife arrived and held her hand as the babies came.

My own mother's labor had been hard. Mom was thirty-six, and it had taken over a day for her to have Samuel. I'd done my best to be strong and calm, but inside I'd been cringing with sympathy. Angry about it, too. Why were women condemned to such pain? I knew such a question was pointless, but still . . . the world would be a better place if every man had to have at least one baby.

Veronika would not welcome sympathy from me, and she had the right to tell her son when she chose.

I was so jangled after all this thinking that when I got up to go to the bathroom, I stayed up. I put a pillow on a chair and sat with my back against it, chanting the healing spell I'd learned from Eli. Maybe I was fooling myself, but I did think I felt a little better after a hundred repetitions. Besides the actual wound, I'd been black and blue all over.

After I got tired of chanting, I got up stiffly to go back into the bathroom. I took a sink bath and washed my hair. I had to rest for a few minutes after that.

Moving very slowly and carefully, I struggled into my undergarments and a robe. I didn't know tonight's schedule, so I didn't know what kind of clothes to put on. Better if I waited until I'd eaten. Fortunately for me, Leah came up to check on me at Veronika's behest.

Now that I knew Veronika trusted her, I gave Leah a longer look. Leah's hair was dark brown, and her eyebrows were ferocious. I figured she was ten years older than me, and they hadn't been easy years. She was strong and sturdy, and her eyes were bright and alert. Veronika didn't require Leah to wear a maid's uniform, but the pinafore that covered the front of her dress was a big clue.

"Do you have time to bring me some food? I'm trying to put off going down the stairs until tonight."

"You got blown up," she told me.

"I sure did."

"Bet that was a surprise."

"It was."

"Who done that to you?"

"I don't know." I knew who had done it, but I didn't know why. She gave a sharp nod. "You find out then and take care of 'em."

"That's my plan," I said.

"You want cheese and crackers, or a sandwich, or some little cakes?"

"All of those, and some water."

"Coming right up." Leah left the room. In less than ten minutes she returned with a loaded tray. She put it down on the table by my chair, gave me another sharp nod, and took her leave.

Now that I saw the food, I was really hungry. I tucked my napkin across my robe, picked up a fork, and piled in. I gave a good account of myself before I had to quit eating. Then, still sitting up, I fell asleep, to be awakened by my husband coming in to rouse me for the night's activities.

The good times just kept on rolling.

A few hours later, I was at a dinner dance at a big hotel on the mainland. I was wearing an evening gown of Lucy's this time because it covered my back, which was still bandaged. It didn't fit too badly, and I had heard from Alice that Lucy had only worn it once. It was modest, since Lucy had been only fifteen when she'd gotten it, and it was Nile green, according to Alice. It had pockets, so I could carry my knives.

So far I hadn't had to kill anyone this evening, but that hung in the balance. The woman talking to me was fraying my nerves.

She'd led by asking if I'd been at the opening reception. When I'd said I had, she'd asked if I'd seen the man being killed.

"I knew someone died, since I saw them carrying him out," I said.

"Well, turns out he was a German named Dietrich Gruber," she said.

She was from Philadelphia, in Britannia, but that was all I could remember. Her name had been swallowed in the noise of the dance band. Her son was at this party, she'd said.

I'd seen Katerina dancing. The girl looked pretty distracted. Irina was nowhere in sight. Nor Paul. Which was good, for them. I wondered where they were. I wondered very much.

"A German," I repeated.

"Yes, but not Listed this year," the woman chattered on. "He was a general escort for the German group." Who was she? Suddenly it seemed more important I should remember.

"I'm sorry, I missed your name," I said, as politely as I could.

She laughed. "I'm Penny Featherstone. I'm here with my son, Jason." She pointed at a tall, gawky fellow in his late teens. He was dressed very well, but that didn't disguise his rounded shoulders and narrow chest.

"It's his first Wizards' Ball season?"

"No, his second," she admitted. That meant he was older than he looked. "Jason is a wonderful, kind son, but he's a bit shy. Who is your horse in this race?"

That was an honest way to put it. "My sister," I said. "Felicia Karkarova Dominguez."

Her face went from polite inquiry to gaping astonishment. "The girl who killed her family?"

Oh, for God's sake. "Yes, Penny. That girl."

"Oh, golly. I'm so sorry for my blunder."

Good recovery. "After all, they were trying to abduct her to sell her to the highest bidder."

"Then good for her," Penny said stoutly. "My husband was a bastard, too." All of a sudden, I liked Penny better.

"I'd love to introduce your sister to my son," she said hopefully.

"Then I will do my best to make that happen," I said. "Getting back to Dietrich Gruber. Have you heard any rumors about why he was killed?"

"According to my friend, he had a knife *and* a vial of acid in his shirt pocket," said Penny. "Evidently, he'd planned to do someone awful harm."

Acid. I couldn't even think about acid tossed at my sister's face or I'd throw up. Still wasn't completely sure I wouldn't. "I wonder who stopped that from happening," I said, and pulled my lips into a smile. "I'll fetch my sister." I owed Penny.

Felicia was fine with being retrieved from the company of a boy from some country in the Far East whose broken English made conversation very uphill. She excused herself politely, and was just as polite when she met Jason Featherstone, who seemed really overwhelmed at meeting Felicia.

"I say, you're quite the belle of the ball!" Jason said.

Felicia was charmed. "You're so sweet."

"Would you like to have a dance?" Jason offered, terrified by his own courage.

"Of course!" My sister gave Jason her hand and he swept her onto the dance floor.

Penny and I watched as Jason did a decent job of maneuvering Felicia around. I felt like patting Penny's shoulder and saying "He's doing so well," as I would for a three-year-old. Penny glowed. "There's hope for the boy," she said. "Look at him! Who would have thought it?"

"He should meet Fenolla Gregory," I said. "Her father, Matthew, is from England, and Fenolla goes to the Rasputin School. If she goes back to England, she won't be able to practice her art openly. If she stays here, she will."

"None of that 'keep your light hidden' in Britannia," Penny said briskly. "Can you point out the young lady?"

I did. Penny may have looked a bit thoughtful when she saw Fenolla's color, but she was agreeable to being introduced. I had done my good deed for the evening.

Eli was making the rounds, as usual. When he came back to my side, he said, "There are some people my age still looking this year."

"They should come to Texoma and hire a gunnie."

"That's what I tell them," he said, with one of his rare smiles.

It was my turn to glow.

"You can go do something else," Eli offered. "I'll watch."

So I set off around the crowded room. I nodded and smiled to people I had met. I tried to look pleasant when I was close to people I had not. I greeted Harriet, who still had a bruise on her face from the explosion but seemed otherwise hale. Her charge was dancing with Clayton Dashwood, but they didn't seem to be enjoying each other's company.

Konstantin and his parents weren't here, since he wasn't officially entered in the Wizards' Ball events. I would have enjoyed talking to them. Instead, I wandered, hoping to meet someone who could tell me more about the man I'd killed at the opening ceremony.

Then I bumped into Felix. His part of guarding Felicia seemed to be scowling at everyone in the room. We leaned against a wall together.

I told him what Penny Featherstone had related to me about Dietrich Gruber. Felix and Eli had talked about it the day after it happened, so Felix was fully informed. They'd known his identity and hadn't told me. It had slipped their minds, Felix said. "There's been so much happening." I couldn't deny that.

"Why was Felicia wasting time with that gawky boy?" Felix muttered.

"It didn't hurt Felicia to dance with Jason Featherstone," I told him. "And see, it made a difference to the boy." There Jason was, right now, dancing with Fenolla Gregory, who seemed to be enjoying herself.

"We had another meeting yesterday," Felix said, out of the blue. I was instantly on the alert.

"Another one?"

Felix nodded. Lucy had made an attempt to smooth his hair, but at this point in the evening it was a mess.

"The first meeting a couple of days ago was to hear the vision of a seer." I would have thought he was joking, but Felix sounded very serious.

I kept my mouth shut. I hated Felix knowing that Eli hadn't told me something. "Didn't know there was such a thing," I said finally.

"I'm assuming Eli didn't tell you what the old man said. But I think you need to know. I think Eli may have told Felicia. Which is the last thing in the world he should have done. The girl's not subtle."

I waited. I wasn't sure, for a moment, if I really did want to know. I gritted my teeth. I had to listen to this. Knowledge was valuable. Felix stepped from my side to face me, turning his back to the room. No one would read his lips.

"The old man said that in the next few years, most of the Jews in Europe will be murdered. Buried in mass graves. Men, women, and children. Literally millions of people."

I heard these terrible words while people were laughing and wine was flowing. Girls in their pretty dresses, men in their evening best, surrounded me. And I was listening to these *terrible words*. "How? By what means?" I managed to ask.

"Old Walter said the Germans would kill them all. And gypsies. And homosexuals. And anyone who harbored them. With poison gas. Batches at a time."

I would have liked to sit down, but there weren't any chairs in sight.

Felix, relentless, kept on going. "Millions, he said, and he repeated it."

That was on a scale so large I couldn't grasp it. "But won't the German people rise up to prevent it?"

"No. Nor will anyone else."

I turned on my heel and walked away, my legs shaking. I had to put space between myself and Felix.

But he followed me.

He took hold of my shoulder and turned me to face him. From the corner of my eye, I could see a few people take notice.

"Let go of me. People are looking," I hissed. At home I would not have cared who saw this, and I would have punched Felix in the face. Here, that was a bad thing. It would reflect poorly on Felicia.

Felix was smart enough to drop his hand and straighten his back, but his face did not relax enough. "What does this mean to you?" he said in what I could only call an angry whisper. "What have you heard?"

"Heard? What do you mean? I only *heard* what you just said." Now I was not only angry, I was also confused.

Eli boomed, "You two! Squabbling again!" I looked up to see his face, smiling cheerfully as he shook his head in mock disgust. This was so unlike Eli that it shocked me back into my senses.

"You know your brother-in-law," I said, forcing myself to smile back. "He loves to spring jokes on me at the wrong moment."

"Felix, I've warned you about teasing Lizbeth," Eli said in a more moderate voice, since people were already turning away. "You really have a poor sense of timing."

"Eli, why don't we dance? We can still watch Felicia as we take a turn around the floor."

Eli looked as though I'd proposed he dress in a clown costume. But after an awful little pause, he said, "Of course. I'd be honored to dance with my wife."

I gave Felix a little look that told him where he could stick his awful stories and put my left hand on Eli's shoulder as I saw other women doing. (At some of the dances they were doing the more modern and exciting things, but this evening was completely traditional.) Eli took my right outstretched hand and off we went. I had been pretty sure he could dance, and I had known I could follow. We didn't do too badly.

"I'm sorry, I didn't even ask if you wanted to dance. You always surprise me. What did that ass Felix say to you?" he said, under cover of the music.

"It should not be talked about here."

"Felix," he muttered, in no fond tone.

"Yes, *Felix*," I said. After a moment, I found myself able to enjoy dancing with my husband. I had a gratifying glimpse of Felicia's astonished face as we swept by her and Clayton Dashwood.

Even Eli seemed pleased with our little excursion on the dance floor. His smile was not forced but genuine, as we resumed watching Felicia after the music ended. Eli even held my hand for a few seconds.

Mateo Medina Dominguez partnered with Felicia next and led her into dinner afterward. Eli and I split up to sit by separate people of interest, me by Mateo's uncle Agustin, since I could speak Spanish, and Eli by Clayton Dashwood's twin, Camilla, who was being pursued hotly by the Canadian horseman. Eli wouldn't have to talk much, since the Canadian was really wrapped up in her.

Agustin avoided all mention of Felicia's family, though I took care to let him know that she'd had no contact with them growing up, when they could have helped her out of a terrible situation. He gave a grave nod as he absorbed this information, which was probably common knowledge by now. He took equal care to let me know his acquaintance with Felicia's grandfather had been slight, and he (the uncle) had not liked or trusted Francisco when he'd met him.

Agustin kind of slid a lot of questions into our conversation, and I answered them all honestly. If Mateo was sincerely interested in marrying Felicia, the Medinas should know that Felicia intended to complete her grigori training . . . and that she certainly knew how to take care of herself, having grown up poor as dirt, with very spotty supervision.

"I understand you brought her out of her situation in Mexico?" Agustin said.

"Eli and I."

"It's true there was a gun battle?"

"It's true."

"And you prevailed?"

I had had another dream the night before about that day in Mexico, the hot sun on the train platform, the long, dangerous trek back to Texoma alone.

"It was a near thing," I said, aware I'd been quiet too long. "What do you see as Mateo's future?"

A good diversion. Like most good uncles, Agustin enjoyed talking about his nephew. Mateo would one day be a leader of the clan Medina, and Agustin's house close to the beach would be Mateo's, since Agustin had no living children. "Though, of course, if Mateo marries," Agustin said, "he would have his own home, a smaller cottage, with only two servants, immediately. They are right behind the bigger houses. One can still see the water."

Agustin was warning me that that would be a hardship, but one a young couple must be expected to undergo. Mateo and his wife had to be prepared to live a simple life for a while. They could not expect luxury right away. In Agustin's view, the Medina family was being stern.

That life—a small cottage on the beach of Baja California, with only two servants—would be luxury to Felicia.

"That beautiful lady across from us and to the right . . . is that Felicia's aunt?" Agustin was trying to sound casual.

I had to look for a minute before I spotted her.

The "beautiful lady" was indeed Isabella, who was having an animated conversation with a grigori around her own age. I didn't know him, but the tattoos and vest pegged him.

"Yes, that's Isabella Dominguez."

"Hmmmm." Agustin looked very interested. "I have heard she is very strong magically."

"That's true, too," I said.

"I'll have to meet her later," he murmured, and then properly turned his attention to his left-hand neighbor.

Eli had instructed me that I should talk to both my dinner companions, as if I never would have thought of that myself. I turned to the man on my right to start a conversation. He was stout, in his sixties, and food was more interesting to him than polite chatter. He answered my opening questions with as few words as he could and asked me none in return. I felt I could ignore him after that.

That left me free to glance at the parallel table. Mateo and Felicia were having a good conversation, at least if all the smiling was any evidence. Farther down my table, Eli was listening to Camilla Dashwood with polite attention. Fenolla was sitting by Jason Featherstone. My good deed had paid off.

I looked for Felix, and eventually I found him. He was sitting by the German woman who'd introduced herself to Felicia at the Japanese Friendship Garden. Felix was sitting on her right, and on her left was a man who looked—to me—Japanese.

Felix never did anything by accident. What was his purpose?

The meal dragged on forever. What had been described as "a light supper" was anything but.

When the host and hostess, a Canadian couple from Vancouver, rose, everyone else got up, too, which suited me fine.

To my surprise, Clayton Dashwood sought me out and asked me to dance. When I made sure Felix was close by Felicia, I accepted.

"Your husband sat by my sister at dinner," Clayton said. He was a man who smiled often and easily. He was smiling now.

I didn't know what to say. Clayton might believe that had been a sign in favor of his courtship, Eli seeking out his sister.

"Yes," I said, smiling back. That seemed safe enough.

"She took quite a shine to him."

"I feel that way myself."

Clayton laughed.

I needed to change the subject since I might say the wrong thing. "Britannia didn't follow the example of England in barring the practice of magic," I said. I was genuinely curious.

"We have enough autonomy for that. It's legal in Canada and Australia, too, mostly so the natives of those places can practice their religion freely."

Another item to add to the list of things I hadn't known.

"Tell me about your home in Virginia."

"There are a lot of Dashwoods. We're scattered all over the state. My sister and I live on a large farm in Cumberland County. Richmond, the capital, is the closest city."

"Your parents?"

"My father is gone, but my mother is still living. She's quite a character. Everyone calls her Birdy."

"What do you raise on this farm?" I asked next, when I figured I was following his steps well enough.

"Mostly grains. Camilla and I don't have to actually get out in the field to plant or reap. We have a lot of families working for us."

Black families. "And they're free to come and go as they please?"

"Of course they are. But most of them, their families have lived on our land a long time. We pay them fair wages, and they own the houses they live in. So they stay. Are you suggesting we still have slaves?" Clayton sounded indignant.

"I spent time in Dixie, where people are slaves in all but name."

"Cumberland County is better than that," Clayton said firmly.

"I'm sorry to have given offense," I said, and I meant it. "So, the Dashwoods have many family reunions?"

Clayton brightened. I believed Clayton was hoping my questions meant he had a chance with Felicia. I liked this man. I believed Felicia could do much worse. Mateo was so young. I didn't know if he was completely his own man yet. I didn't even think about Hans Goldschmidt. There were too many questions.

"Camilla's never married? Is she the older twin?"

"By three minutes. She married a Preston a few years ago, but they never got along. They called it quits after two years. She came home to live."

"Too bad."

"They just didn't share any interests," Clayton told me, whirling me around the whole time. This was a man who could do a lot of things at once. "Camilla loves the land, throws magic at it when she can, and loves to ride and fish and hunt. John Preston was more of a stay-in-the-house person."

I felt a twinge inside. Did Eli and I really share interests? I made myself ignore it. "And you? Are you more one or the other?"

The music ended and we stepped to the edge of the crowd.

"I like to be out on the land," he admitted. "But I do read in the evenings, and I practice my magic every day. It's a big help in farming, especially with the weather, and Camilla's power is real . . . up and down."

Clayton had told us his family needed to find mates with very strong magic. Felicia certainly had plenty and to spare. Might not be the kind he needed, though. I had a picture of Felicia strolling through fields making millet grow . . . but Felicia was more likely to throw bombs at the invading crop pests, whatever those would be. I knew very little about farming, since Texoma ran more to ranching. Farming depended heavily on things outside the farmer's control. Seemed like that would be a better choice for an earth or air mage, like Eli.

When the band struck up again, he led me out onto the floor and we began dancing as if we'd discussed it.

I must have been staring at his face while I thought about what he'd said, because Clayton looked uncomfortable. I hadn't intended that. "It sounds like a beautiful place," I said. "Is there running water?"

"Of course," he said, surprised. "We're not far from a river, and we have two wells."

"That much water," I said, envious.

Clayton smiled. "I forgot you're from Texoma. Must be a pretty dry place."

"Very dry," I said.

When this song was over, we gave each other a goodbye smile. Clayton excused himself to claim a dance with some other girl. I got back to the business of watching my sister. But the first person I saw was Felix, skulking by the wall. He caught my eye and gave me a jerk of the head to summon me. He was the last person in the world I wanted to talk to, after his ill-timed revelations. But he jerked his head again, more urgently.

Well, shit. Okay.

I wandered over to him, doing my best to look casual. "What's happening?" I said in a low voice.

"The German and Japanese together," he said. "They're conspiring against Felicia. They're also targeting some of the other Listeds."

This sounded so weird and creepy that I almost laughed. "How on earth do you know that? They'd hardly tell you."

"I acquired a mind-reading spell," Felix said. He said this in a straightforward way, but I could tell there was something real shifty about it.

I hadn't known such a thing was possible . . . or for sale. I thought magic had to come from spells you'd learned, or from the well of magic inside you, or from the use of potions. That's what I understood.

"You bought it?" I said. I could feel my lips press together in disgust.

"Yes, from someone who can power them, a Frenchman," Felix said impatiently. "It's quite rare."

"That's wrong," I said, before I could think twice.

"Says you. You shoot people for a living."

My temper was at the end of its tether. "I hate the idea you can buy a way to read someone's inner thoughts," I said, just in case I hadn't made myself clear.

"I've acquired valuable information to protect Felicia," Felix said. I couldn't argue with that.

"That's why I sat between two people I despise. Now we know who's trying to kill your sister. We can stop them."

"How's that going to work?"

"We have to kill them," he said.

I took a very deep breath. This was a bad place for an argument, and it was the second one Felix and I had had this evening. Why couldn't he have told this to Eli? Did he believe I was more likely to agree this was a good plan?

"What the hell is driving you?" I said, working hard to keep my voice low and even. "This comes from someplace besides keeping Felicia safe."

"My mother was a Jew."

I couldn't say anything for a minute. Half of me couldn't believe Felix cared about anyone's religion, even his mother's. Half of me wondered how he'd kept it under wraps for so long if it was so important to him. Eli had to have known this. He'd grown up in the flotilla with Felix. "All right. How do the Japanese come in?"

"They're allied with the Germans. The Germans will take Belgium and France and then try to take England. The seer said so."

I couldn't think of what to say.

"Don't stand there with your mouth hanging open," Felix snapped.

"So they're trying to kill my sister because?"

"Because Eli forbade them to approach her and offer her marriage. After we'd heard the seer."

I thought the top of my head was going to fly off. I stared a moment longer at Felix, and then I spun on my heel and walked away. I went right out a side door and stood on the terrace. I could hear the music faintly, and the sound of the crowd, but muffled, because my anger filled my head like buzzing bees.

I could not leave. If I was going to be of any use to my sister, I had to stay. I had to talk to Eli about this. I had to resist my strong urge to do him harm.

The air was cool and fresh, and I breathed it in in huge gulps. When my nerves and my thoughts quit humming, I had a lot of other ideas. If England was going to be the target of the Germans, where did that leave Britannia? Would all Britannian men be called up, in event of war? Canadians, Australians?

Worst thought of all: Did Clayton Dashwood want Felicia because he knew this, knew what an asset she would be in wartime?

Eli came out of the door behind me. I knew it was him without looking.

"Don't talk to me right now," I said. "I mean it. Not a word. Just go back inside."

And for a wonder, he did.

I didn't manage to be social for the rest of the evening, but I did work at looking at least not unpleasant and staying in the room. Uphill battle. I watched Felicia like a hawk. She danced, smiled, talked, and laughed. I saw the German woman dancing with a man from . . . Italy? Maybe? The Japanese man did not dance. But he circulated. He better not circulate any closer to my sister, or I'd step in. There were conduct rules at the Wizards' Ball, rules about aggressive acts and the penalties for them. I'd already broken them at the opening ceremony.

I would do that again if I needed to. Rules be damned.

After what seemed like four more hours, but was only one, the evening began to wind down. We all retrieved our wraps and coats. We needed the extra warmth. The temperature had dropped at least twenty degrees. At least we didn't have to deal with a ferry. We did have to wait for our car to be brought around, and we stood in silence. Eli, Felix, and I did our best not to look at one another. Eli must have talked to Felix; he now understood why I was angry. Felix didn't like to talk to me anyway. Nothing new there.

Felicia wanted to chat about her evening, but when she took the temperature around us, she fell silent, too.

Eli dropped Felix off and began the drive to the Savarov house.

"Are you two going to tell me what's wrong?" Felicia asked from the back seat.

"No," we said in unison.

"We have to talk to each other first," Eli said.

"Okay." Felicia sounded very guarded. As well she might be. It must be like having Mom and Dad fighting.

If Peter had not died, this whole long procedure would be unnecessary. Felicia had been fond enough of Peter to marry him, maybe. We could have done without the dresses and the dances and the long meals.

This was me being ridiculous. Felicia had been on track to let Peter down. Then we'd have had a spurned Peter to deal with, as well as all these new suitors. Though at least Peter would be alive, and oh, how I wished he was.

And what about Felicia's secret affection for Hans Goldschmidt? Did he return it? Was he in any position to offer Felicia *anything*?

What if we did everything right this week and Felicia didn't cotton to anyone? Would we have to wait another three years and do this over? In three years, what would the world be like if this war happened? Would there even be another Wizards' Ball?

The house was silent and mostly dark. Veronika, Ford, and Alice had turned in. We parked in back and went into the house, still wrapped in silence.

Felicia paused at her bedroom door to say, "Thanks for all you're doing. I know this isn't the way you want to be spending your time, Eli. Or you, Lizbeth. I want you to know I appreciate your doing it."

"I'd do anything for you," I said.

And I had, already.

I began the last flight of stairs. I don't know what Eli said to Felicia. I heard his voice. I'd made it clear I was done with him for tonight.

I guess he slept in Lucy's old room; wisely, he didn't come to bed with me. We'd been married a little over a year. We had never slept apart if we'd been in the same town.

I felt it sharply. But tonight his absence was a relief.

CHAPTER THIRTEEN

The next morning, I pretended to be asleep when Eli crept into the room to get fresh clothes. He'd already bathed; I could smell the soap. I was still tired after a restless night. It wasn't hard to keep my breathing slow and my body relaxed.

Eli left just as quietly to dress somewhere else. He was as loath to have the big fight we were going to have as I was. But it had to be gotten through. I bathed and dressed and went down for breakfast, to find that Eli had already left the table. Felicia was there and gave me a doubtful look . . . the first time she'd ever looked at me so.

"What happened last night?" my sister asked directly.

"So many things."

"Make a start."

"Felix bought a mind-reading spell from some magician. He used it last night."

"Mind reading," Felicia said. She looked unhappy. "To read my mind?"

"No, some of the people at the party. But I don't see how he could pick and choose what he heard. The last place I want Felix is in my head. Anyway. He *heard* a German and a Japanese, and he's sure they're the ones plotting to kill you."

"*Kill* me," she repeated. "They want to kill me? Why?"

I explained to her. The upcoming war. The probable use of grigoris in the war. Her power to kill. And to top it all off, the fact that my husband had put a target on her back by telling the two parties they could not approach her.

"Ahhh . . ." Felicia had a strange look on her face. "After I talked with Hans at the Del Coronado, I knew a bit about the way the war is shaping up. Not all you've just told me, but a little."

I looked at her, stunned. "So you asked Eli to do that," I said. "And you didn't tell me. You too."

I had never seen Felicia look guilty, but she did now. And she ought to.

I got up from the table and left. I went back up to the third floor, got my guns out of the wardrobe, and lay a towel over the small table in our room. I got out my Colt 45s and all my cleaning things, the Hoppe's and the rags and thin brushes. I fetched a stool from the bathroom, since the chair was not right for this work.

I took the Colts apart. I lay the pieces out. I began to take care of the tools of my trade: I could clean them without thinking about it, but today I paid attention to each little task. It was one that gave me pleasure.

There was a storm inside me. What the hell? Did no one trust me? Why was everyone I most cared about keeping secrets from me? Whereas Felix, whom I had never liked, was all too willing to tell me things I should have known already. Things I really didn't want to hear, by the way.

Part of my brain focused on little task after little task, making the guns clean and beautiful. Part of me imagined packing my bag and calling a cab to go to the train station.

That was a very satisfying daydream.

Leaving behind Eli and Felicia seemed like a grand idea. My husband didn't think I needed to know what was going on around me, for no reason I could see. My sister, for whom I had rearranged my life, had so little regard for me that she didn't share a major decision.

Why would she do that?

Because she had already made up her mind. She had fixed on this Hans Goldschmidt. Everything else was just pretense.

She could have simply told me.

I don't know if I'd ever felt as low as I did that morning, in that bedroom, in my mother-in-law's house.

Oh, wait, I had. When Eli and Peter had taken off following the militia that had come into Segundo Mexia, without telling me. When Felicia and I had had to rescue them from that militia. When Eli'd gone to San Diego the previous summer, without telling me why he was going.

My hands grew still as I simply looked out the window and thought.

Even when my first gun crew had died, all in one night, one of them my lover, one my best friend, I'd had a clear purpose. Now I had none.

I'd come to protect and support my sister through a grigori rite of passage, one you only got to experience if you were very lucky and your family had enough money. I'd done it gladly . . . to discover she was throwing it away behind my back.

Was I looking at this wrong? At the moment, I didn't think so.

There was a knock at the door, but I didn't say anything. The next knock had more muscle behind it. "Go away," I said, hoping whoever it was would take me at my word.

No such luck.

Both Eli and Felicia shuffled into the room. I could tell by the sound of their shoes. If they were waiting for me to say something, they'd wait till pigs flew.

"Lizbeth, you're sulking," Eli said.

Something in me snapped. Probably my last straw. "Am I? Is that what I'm doing? Please tell me, because *I* sure as hell don't know." I resumed cleaning. My guns had never let me down.

Felicia, who was smarter about people than Eli, said, "I'm sorry we didn't talk about it."

"Why? Since you both don't tell me anything else. I have no idea why I went to all this trouble. Borrowing Veronika's clothes. Wearing shoes I hate. Getting shot at by arrows. Getting blown up. Killing a man in the middle of a crowd. Waiting to be arrested, if someone saw me stab him. When this turns out to be a *game* to you." I put the first gun down and turned to face them. My face was made of stone. My heart felt like that, too.

Eli finally understood this was not going to go away.

Felicia finally understood that for the first time, I was seriously angry with her.

"Just leave," I said, suddenly feeling very tired. "Go away. When you're ready to be honest with me, I'll listen, but you better make it snappy. Otherwise, I'm on the train home."

Wisely, they left.

I finished cleaning my guns. I wished I had brought my Winchester so I could clean that, too, but you couldn't come into the Holy Russian Empire carrying a rifle. At least I hadn't been able to figure out a way.

I stowed all my cleaning stuff and lay my guns carefully on a shelf in the armoire. I sat in the easy chair in the corner, and after a while I moved it closer to the north window overlooking the backyard. I could see the north-south sidewalk marking the end of the block, two yards over to my right. I watched cars on that street, I watched people walking (some with dogs), I watched the yard crew come in to tidy up the flower beds. I watched Leah hanging up laundry on the clothesline between the house and the garage. A man wearing a starched white bib apron walked up to her. Leah seemed surprised to see him. They exchanged a few words, and he handed her a piece of paper. She finished pegging up the clothes, and she brought the paper inside. Huh.

Was someone sending my sister a love note? Requesting a meeting? I felt something, finally. Curiosity.

I heard footsteps coming up the stairs. I assumed either Eli or Felicia was coming to try to mend fences again, but it was Leah who came to the door.

She knocked.

I said, "Come on in."

"Barney, he works down the street, he said a man paid him to bring you this." An envelope was in her hand.

"Down the street where?"

"At the corner grocery. Barney brings the deliveries around."

I'd been in the grocery during the insurrection, when the people running the store and my sister had been taken hostage by the rebels. Touch and go.

"Did he say who this man was? What he looked like?"

Leah shook her head. "He gave Barney a good tip." She lingered, enjoying the novelty of the event, but I was waiting for her to leave before I read this mysterious message. "In case you were wondering, Miss Felicia went into her room crying," she said.

I nodded. "Thanks for bringing this to me."

She left then. I kind of liked Leah. She was doing her best to enjoy a job that must be full of drudgery.

I tore open the envelope.

"I know this is irregular," the note began. "Since you are Felicia's older sister, I need to tell you some things about my past."

Even more promising.

I hope you are free to meet me in the park across the street from the grocery store. I will understand if you can't come, but if you are home and not engaged, maybe you will agree to talk to me.

It was signed "Hans Goldschmidt."

I held it in my hand and tapped the paper against the window. I pretended to think about this.

Of course, I'd go.

I had some pants I'd brought with me, purchased the last time I'd been in San Diego. I pulled them on, and a blouse and a jacket, and I tucked a gun into the waistband in back. It was good I'd lost some weight, though I hadn't much to spare.

Leaving the house without anyone knowing? That took some figuring. With my shoes in my hand, I eased down the attic steps, and then took the servants' stairway to the back of the house. Mrs. O'Clanahan, the cook (hired when McMurtry married Veronika), was in the kitchen. She was chopping an onion, and she looked up with teary eyes to see who'd come into her kingdom. I nodded at her as I went out the kitchen door, and she nodded back, and that was that.

I sat on the steps to pull on my shoes. Then I went around back of the former carriage house (now the garage) at the rear of the yard, now home to two cars, McMurtry's and Veronika's. Walking on the rear property line, I cut across the yard of the two houses next door to reach the sidewalk. Then I walked to the corner grocery. Across the street lay the little park I remembered from my previous visits.

At this hour of the afternoon, the park was almost empty. Two children were playing on a seesaw, a uniformed nanny watching them while she knitted. No one else was in the park but Hans Goldschmidt, sitting on a bench. He jumped to his feet when he saw me.

I studied him. This was the mystery man who had helped Felicia bring me back to life. This was the man whose voice she had recognized after so many months. This was the man who had somehow impressed her so strongly that she gave only the slightest attention to the several other men who wanted to marry her. Men who were richer, handsomer, and . . . not involved in sneaky stuff. Men who didn't pop up in the middle of an attack in Segundo Mexia, Texoma, and then vanish.

Whatever it was Felicia saw in him, I didn't.

I shook my head. I didn't understand.

Hans took that headshake for dismissal. His face fell. But after just a split second, Hans's back stiffened. Determination filled his face. "We must talk, please, Princess Savarova."

I sighed, up from my toes through my heart. Talking. Never my best thing. Lately, this seemed to be all anyone wanted to do. I took a seat on the bench, patted the wood beside me. "So talk."

Hans sat beside me, keeping a respectful distance. He was angled toward me. He was stretched tighter than a Japanese bow.

I wondered if I had enough money to catch a cab to the train station. I discarded the idea. I had to stick this out.

"Princess, I know you love your sister, and she loves you. That was evident in Segundo Mexia."

Felicia had been right. He was the grigori who had helped her.

"Why were you there?" That was the big question, as I saw it.

Hans drew a deep breath. "I had been tracking your sister."

My hands tightened into fists. I could draw my gun and kill him now. I broke down the movements I needed to do that.

"I admit this with reluctance. I am not supposed to tell you or anyone."

I raised my eyebrows. "Keep on talking, fella."

"We had heard of Felicia."

"Who is 'we'?"

"The Jewish magicians organizing to fight back. Hitler intends to kill us all."

I nodded. I knew that already. I knew some things he would hate to hear, assuming he hadn't been at the sitting with the grigori seer. I thought Eli would have mentioned Hans's presence. Maybe not, the way things were going between us. *Maybe he just told Felicia*, I thought. I pressed my lips together.

"What does my sister have to do with that? She's not Jewish. She's not German. She's sixteen years old."

"This is all true. But she has the power, and she is not afraid to use it. Most magically gifted people have—constraints. Drilled into them by society and their instructors. She does not."

"So what do you want her for? To kill your enemies? Why is this her fight?"

"Because—you have to forgive me, if I offend you—"

No, I don't.

"Felicia enjoys using her skill and power. She grows every time she does. There is no one like her, with the possible exception of her aunt, Isabella."

"So ask Isabella. At least she's a grown-up woman."

"As you could tell that night in Segundo Mexia, Isabella was willing to kill you to have Felicia for herself. Isabella didn't understand that if she killed you, Felicia would never agree to be her . . . anything. Isabella cares only about Isabella."

I didn't believe that was completely true. But right now, that was beside the point. "You're willing to ruin Felicia's life—in fact, you're willing to put her in extreme danger in a war that isn't hers."

Hans closed his eyes, really squinched them tight. He gave a great impression of a man in a lot of anguish. "This was the mission I was given. I am truly Ahren's cousin, and I love the boy. But me escorting him? That is my pretend reason to be in San Diego. I am here to try to add people to my cause. Even Tsar Alexei I have talked to."

"What did the tsar say?"

"He said he would talk to his advisers about it. There are Jews in his court, though as everywhere, there are others who think any Jew is scum."

There are always people who will look down on you, because they have to be better than *someone*. I had experience with that first-hand. Hans was bitter about it. I was not. "Why did you want to meet with me?"

"Because you love your sister, and she loves you. In the middle of a skirmish, she had to hold off her aunt, an experienced witch, to make sure you were alive. When she should have been running for cover."

"You said you were there following her?"

"Yes."

"You helped her hold Isabella, so Isabella couldn't try to kill me again."

"I couldn't stop myself. It wasn't smart. But I did it. I was supposed to have a look at Isabella, too. I did not like what I saw."

Hans was not asking for my gratitude. He hadn't done it on my account. He had done it because he admired my sister.

"What do you want from me?"

"A chance to explain all this to Felicia."

"What do you need to explain? She's already on your side. She already told the Germans and the Japanese she didn't want to hear any offers from them. Putting a big target smack-dab on her back."

"She did?" Hans looked stunned. With happiness. "There are things I have to tell her, things I can't talk about at parties with people all around trying to hear what we say to each other."

"So you're asking to talk to her privately."

"Yes. I know it's not . . . proper."

I had no idea if it was or not. Hans believed it wasn't, which was the big thing. "Felicia can easily defend herself if you behave in a way she does not like."

For the first time, he smiled. "I certainly believe that."

"All right," I said, and stood.

Hans stood, too, but looked at me with some confusion. "When can this be done?" he said finally.

"Right now. Let's go."

Hans's eyes went wide. He was thunderstruck.

We walked to the Savarov house together. Hans didn't say anything the whole way. He kept darting glances at me, as if he expected me to change my mind.

There was no point putting this off. The sooner the better. Hans would talk to Felicia. Felicia would make up her mind for good, assuming she hadn't already. I thought she had. I could not keep this from happening. Next time Hans wouldn't ask. He would make an opportunity for this important talk. He would not back down or give up.

I went in the front door without knocking. I was part of the household.

So I startled my mother-in-law, and I surprised Eli, and I shocked Felicia. They were all standing in the foyer in an intense little group.

"Where have you been?" Veronika said. She was loaded for bear.

"Back down," I told her. "I got other fish to fry." Her mouth fell open.

"Felicia, here's Hans," I said.

My sister had the strangest expression on her face. I couldn't tell if she was happy or sad. She was something big, though. "Hans wants to talk to you alone, and I agreed. But Eli and I will be right outside the door."

Eli had a quick recovery. He nodded.

"If Veronika doesn't mind . . . the living room would be best."

Veronika was still staring at me as if I'd grown another head. Finally, she nodded.

"Great," I said. "You two, in you go. Hans, you got half an hour. Then we're coming in."

Felicia kept glancing at Hans as if she couldn't keep her eyes off him. I swear my sister looked shy. That was a new emotion for her. She started for the doorway and Hans followed, like she was a magnet and he was a nail. Would they even manage to talk to each other?

Veronika went upstairs slowly. I expected any minute she'd come back to ream me out. But she kept on going, and she murmured a few words to Alice, who'd opened her bedroom door when she heard voices.

Alice looked disappointed when she saw Eli and me. Maybe she'd been hoping for Konstantin. *Sorry, Alice. Just us.*

That left Eli and me alone in the hall. To say the situation was very uneasy was to give it a mild name. He'd look at me, then away.

We had thirty minutes, too.

I should have made it fifteen.

"How did you come to meet with Hans?" Eli said, when the silence had gotten even more painful.

"He wrote me a note. Leah brought it to me. I sneaked out and talked to him. Nothing left to do but let them talk to each other. That's what people do when they're in love." I tried very hard not to put a foot down on those words.

Eli flinched. "Yes," he said. "Yes. I should have."

"And you didn't because?"

"I knew you were on edge. You don't like being here, you don't like doing the things we had to do, you don't like going to the events we have to attend."

And I'd thought I was being so strong and calm about it all.

"After the Japanese Friendship Garden incident—I don't know if it was the day after or two days—I was approached by a German man, Fritz Weber, and a Japanese man, Hikaru Nakamura. Instead of taking the opportunity to meet Felicia themselves, they wanted to ask my permission first, which seemed odd. After all, this whole event is designed to allow young people to meet each other in a natural way. They were both older than I'd like, older than me. Closer to thirty." Eli paused to pick his words.

"It seemed peculiar enough to make me uneasy," he continued. "I decided to talk to Felicia about it. She'd heard a little about the upcoming trouble in Europe, and she wanted no part of being on the side of the Germans or the Japanese. The men were both too old to interest her, anyway. She did not want to meet them. I wrote them each a note, couched in as polite terms as I could."

"After she'd gotten shot at with Japanese arrows. After a German came to stab her at the opening ceremony. With acid in his pocket as a backup."

Eli nodded. "I'm not sure Felicia put that all together, but I did."

"And you didn't tell me? Though I killed the man at the reception?"

"I didn't tell you."

"Why? Am I not here to protect my sister?"

"You are, as am I. And Felix."

"You thought it was safe for me to be ignorant?"

"I thought . . . I don't know what I thought. I thought it was a complicated situation. I thought they would leave Felicia alone, after two failed attempts to kill her. I thought maybe if she publicly favored some suitor who didn't threaten them, like Mateo or Clayton, they would see Felicia was not likely to enter the war at all. I didn't know about Hans, though I could tell when she met Ahren and Hans she was touched by Ahren's story. I didn't know it was Hans that had made an impression on her. He hardly said anything. How did you know Felicia favored him?"

"She told me in confidence that she thought she had met him before. He just confirmed that, by the way. He impressed her then, though they didn't exchange names. He was in Segundo Mexia that night." I didn't need to specify which night. The night Peter died. "Hans tells me he was there tracking her down, to see if she was everything she was reported to be. And he saw her up against Isabella, winning, which is important, since Isabella was also on his list of grigoris to . . . test, or something. Hans was just as smitten as she was, but he also figured she was the right woman to recruit. I got no objection to him, though it makes me feel tired . . . and useless . . . that we went to all this effort, and she was already taken."

"You didn't tell me Felicia knew him."

"It was a confidence. I couldn't. I hoped she would tell you herself. And she didn't say anything else about him, not a word. It was all about other men. I see now that was just a cover."

"I can see how she would not want to tell us she was actually interested in a man whose name she didn't know, whose face she hadn't seen. Felicia can be very practical."

We still weren't looking at each other too directly. I could feel the tension in the air slacken a bit, like a string with a certain amount of give in it.

I said, very carefully, "Hans seems like a good man. But Felicia would be drawn into this war that's brewing. Felix told me about the seer. I wish you had told me."

Eli looked both depressed and exhausted. He looked at me directly. It felt like a long time since he'd done that. "It made me sick with horror to think of this thing coming. All those people dying, not only the slaughter of the Jews, but all the soldiers on both sides.

To think we may all have to choose a side. As young as Felicia is, the mere fact that people are trying to *make* her choose a side, to fight in a war for them . . ."

I gave up the hopes I had held for Felicia's future: that she'd be safe, that she would never be hungry or desperate again.

"I hardly think there's anything she'd like better than to fight in a war," I said.

Finally, I'd made my husband laugh.

CHAPTER FOURTEEN

We were looking at the hall clock when the door to the living room opened.

Thirty minutes, on the nose.

Hans stepped out first and held the door for Felicia. She had discarded the weird, shy look that had been so unlike her. Now she was blazing. For one of the few moments since I'd arrived in San Diego, my sister looked like the Felicia I'd known.

Felicia had decided to go with the adventure. I'd known she would, all along. I let out a deep breath and forced my lips into a smile. I could only hope she would not be killed by someone faster, someone more powerful, or someone luckier.

Hans was as lit up as Felicia. His face was full of happiness, excitement. Hope. For the first time I could see what my sister had seen, had heard in his voice. This was a brave man.

This brave man was my sister's fiancé, I discovered in the next thirty seconds.

Eli and I stood together and let the tide wash over us.

"I will try to finish at the school," Felicia said rapidly. "I know that's important, to learn as much as I can before I start practicing full-time." She was so quick to tell us this, she must have felt I'd be very upset if she didn't complete her studies.

Eli drew breath to say something, but I put my hand on his arm.

"I don't care if you do or not," I said, which was mostly true. "But I think if you two don't get married right away, you'll have time to grow up some more. And if you gain more control over your power, so much the better."

Eli said, "I agree."

"Also, Hans needs to figure out where you two will live," I suggested. "What with the upcoming . . . troubles." I didn't want to say the word "war." It was too terrible. "Hans has a lot to take care of, and a lot to plan, since I guess any day Ahren may hear from his folks."

"He has heard," Hans said. "This morning. That is another reason I needed to talk to you. In pleading my personal suit, I am afraid I pushed Ahren's needs to the back. His parents have found a house in England, in the countryside outside London. They have secured their financial situation. They are safe for the moment . . . unless England is invaded."

"What about your own family?" Eli asked.

I wondered why Hans hadn't led with that detail.

"As I told you, my parents are already dead," Hans said simply. "They had a fine jewelry store in Hamburg. Last November, Hitler's stooges broke every window in the store, stole all the jewelry they could find, and killed my father when he would not open the safe."

We froze. That was about the worst thing I'd ever heard. "And your mother?" I said.

"My father had stayed in the store overnight, because he thought he could protect it. He thought his neighbors would help him. When my mother didn't hear from him the next morning, she made her way to the store and found everything broken and destroyed, including Father."

Hans took a deep breath and looked up, his eyes going from one of us to the other. I could see this was the first time Felicia was hearing the whole story. Tears rolled down her cheeks. I had never seen my sister cry before. She leaned against Hans, and he put his arm around her.

After a moment, he said, "Mother knew how to get in the safe. She was brave enough to do it. She hid the jewelry in her clothes. She left out the back door and crept home, staying out of the way of people as much as she could. Even our own people. She met our rabbi in the street and told him what had happened, and he insisted on walking her home. She knew that would actually put her in more danger, but he insisted."

I realized I was holding my breath.

"She was right. He stopped to speak to another Jewish man. She simply kept on walking. The rabbi and the other man were arrested, and she could hear the commotion behind her, and the screams, but she kept on walking. She did not look from one side to another before she got home. She hurried inside and locked every window and door. Mother evaluated the jewelry and loose stones she had managed to save. She put them all in a padded box and wrapped it. She wrote me a letter, and one to my sister, Liesl, too. She went to the post office, one quite far from our neighborhood, because she thought it was safer. There she mailed the letters to me and Liesl, telling us what had happened, and she mailed the box to her brother-in-law in Switzerland, where he had opened another branch of our store. She knew my uncle would keep the jewelry or its monetary value for us. We have heard from him. He received the box. So I am not penniless, if I can get to Switzerland, thanks to my mother. On her way home, she was accosted in the street by a group of thugs and got shoved to the ground. She hit her head on the curb and died in the hospital. Her friend Esther saw it happen."

There was a long moment of silence. "Where is your sister?" I asked.

"Liesl is in Hamburg, still. She has a husband and a son, very small, only three." Hans almost smiled as he mentioned his nephew. "Her husband is not Jewish, which my parents thought was a terrible disgrace, but it may save Liesl's life. And the boy's. Or it may not."

I wondered if the seer's vision had to come true. Could it be prevented? If enough people rose up and fought against this political party in Germany? If someone shot its leader? I would have to ask Eli or Felix, but only when we were alone.

"So you plan to finish school unless war breaks out," Eli said, returning the conversation to something less fraught.

"Yes," Felicia said. She was still leaning against Hans. "I will finish. Hans has to take Ahren to England. Then he'll try to cross to Switzerland to open a bank account. If Liesl has to run, she'll have something to live on, too. Thanks to her mother."

"And her father," I said, remembering the man who would not give up the code to the safe.

"If war does break out, what then?" Eli said. I had been too scared to ask, because I was sure I already knew the answer.

"Then I'll join Hans, and we'll fight," Felicia said. "I know that's why the other side wanted me, to use me as a weapon. Maybe to kill Jews, and anyone else who rises up against them. England will fight or be occupied. France and Belgium, too. Maybe Britannia and Australia and India will have to join the fight to support Britain."

I hadn't been aware my sister even knew where those countries were, much less their alliances. I was surprised I did.

I wondered if any of those places would have a chance to fight before they were overrun. Evidently this man in Germany had been planning this for a long time. He would have built up his army and store of munitions and all kinds of weapons. He would have magicians on his side, of whatever background. Because he believed.

England had always forbidden the practice of magic, and pub-licly treated those with magical power as dangerous enemies of the state. I wondered what the wizards and witches of England, Ireland, and Scotland would do.

"I got to say something that you don't want to hear," I said.

Hans and Felicia put on their worry faces.

"You have to keep this a secret. Your engagement to Hans, your plans, his plans, everything."

Eli was already nodding. "I agree," he said.

"I don't," Felicia all but wailed.

"You can't say a word," I said, and I was dead serious. "Hans has to leave for Europe with Ahren. He has to spend time over there getting his finances straight. You need to stay here and go to school like you had planned. If you announce you're marrying Hans, they'll try to track him and stop him. Or they'll go all out to kill you. I can't stay here forever." I wasn't going to speak for Eli.

"There's some protection at the school, but this Hitler and his followers may not respect the fact that the school is a safe area for the students."

Hans and Felicia looked at each other.

"We can be married when I return to get you," Hans said. "The most important thing is that we are pledged to each other and have that to look forward to."

Hans seemed completely sincere.

My sister thought about crying again. Her face puckered up. To my relief, she recalled she was supposed to be mature enough to marry. "You're right," she said. "The most important thing is that we know we belong to each other."

Eli and I exchanged a quick glance. I felt like I'd never been as young as Felicia. Maybe he was thinking the same.

"Hans, what's your age?" I said.

"I am twenty-two." His back straightened. "And now I am the head of my family. What remains of it."

Actually, he and I were almost the same age. Hans was younger in experience, but after what happened to his folks, he was catching up fast. I couldn't imagine the sense of betrayal he must feel. He'd grown up in Hamburg, he probably loved his country, and look what his country had done to him.

Felicia was all excited and in love. What would happen if Hans returned to Europe and was killed? What if some German agent got to him before he could get out again? What if he never came back? Felicia would have a broken heart before she was seventeen. She would mourn Hans more deeply than she ever had Peter.

"Hans, when do you leave?" Eli asked, bringing us down to the practical level. "What can we do to help you?"

"I have been booking our passage on an airplane to get us to New York."

"You're going to *fly*?" Felicia said, excited and terrified.

"You're going to fly?" Eli said, envious.

"How long will that take?" I was beyond startled.

"All day," Hans said. "But it will save time. We talked about flying over the Atlantic, too, but there are not that many flights. We will go by ocean liner instead, which should take us four to five days."

My husband's face tightened. Though Eli had been born at sea, the boat he'd grown up on had not been nearly as fancy as a real ocean liner. He'd just been glad it never sank. Other refugees in the tsar's flotilla had not been as lucky. He had told me once he never wanted to be on a boat again.

"So as soon as you can go, you'll be on an airplane flying across the country," Felicia said.

"And you will have to pretend," Hans told her very tenderly. "When all we want to do is tell people."

I had to hand it to Hans: he made this sound like a huge sacrifice.

Poor Felicia! She'd have to dress up and flirt with handsome men and eat good food and drink wonderful drinks, trailed by her faithful (and tired) watchdogs. While her beloved flew in the sky across the continent in a big tin can with wings.

My little sister gazed up at Hans as though his was the face of God.

"I will be back as soon as I can, Felicia," he said. "I promise you that."

I wondered if Hans had told her he'd been following her to see if she was worth recruiting for his cause.

"What if you had decided I wasn't worth the trouble?" Felicia said.

Okay, he'd told her.

"That wasn't possible, once I'd felt your power and seen you in action," Hans said gallantly.

If Felicia had been able to blush, she would have.

There's no telling how long we would have stood there watching them make goo-goo eyes at each other. To my relief, the doorbell rang, and Leah rushed past us to answer it. Konstantin's mother and father had come to call. Apparently Veronika had invited them to drop in. And down the stairs Veronika came, smiling and gracious as though she hadn't known a major crisis was taking place in her foyer.

It was lucky the Volkovs hadn't come ten minutes before.

After some hasty introductions, and giving the excuse of pressing business, Hans departed. It wasn't how he'd wanted to say goodbye to his new fiancée, anyone could see. But it cut short any more drama.

The good side to the Volkovs' arrival was that Felicia had to start pretending right away. She was real convincing as a social girl greeting the parents of a young man interested in Alice. I couldn't tell whether this was all news to Felicia or not. She'd been pretty absorbed in herself, but she was fond of Eli's younger sister.

Alice herself came down the stairs smiling and shy. She looked very pretty in a navy-and-maroon dress. Konstantin beamed. Alice beamed back.

"Love is everywhere," I muttered. Eli gave me a quick smile. I didn't smile back.

I talked to Levdokia and Boris, talked about the weather and the effect all the balls and parties were having on the construction schedule on Imperial Island, and stayed for a few moments while Veronika asked Leah to serve coffee. The small plates for the cookies and tiny sandwiches were already in place.

I certainly was not wearing the right clothes, as a tiny glance from Veronika confirmed, but if the Volkovs were serious they'd learn sooner or later that I wasn't a proper princess.

After we'd each downed a cup of coffee, Eli and I gave our excuses. Felicia left the room with us and bounded up the stairs to go to her room and shut the door. That was a good idea. She could decide whether to be happy with her engagement or miserable that Hans was leaving for who knows how long.

To my surprise, Eli didn't suggest I go up to change into city-appropriate clothes. Instead, he walked rapidly through the dining room to the kitchen. He was intent on something, I could tell by the set of his shoulders.

"We're going to see Felix and Lucy," he said over his shoulder.

"How come?"

"We have to tell Felix about this."

"Why?"

"Because he needs to know," Eli said impatiently.

I couldn't see why, but I figured I'd go along. Better than staying here and thinking dark thoughts. I would have understood if (for example) Felix had lied to me, because we didn't like each other. When it was Eli and Felicia, that was pretty painful. I supposed I'd get over it.

Eli drove us to Felix's house and parked in the driveway. We could see Felix's battered car sticking out, just at the back of the house. Eli barely knocked on the front door before he put his hand on the knob and began to open it. His sister's face, pale and tear-stained, appeared in the narrow opening. "This isn't a good time," she said.

Eli was so surprised it was almost funny. "Why not?"

"We are having a talk," Lucy said with some dignity. "We need to have some privacy to finish it."

"They might as well come in," Felix called from the depths of the house.

Lucy was definitely angry about that, and I didn't blame her. She shot a mean look over her shoulder and stood aside to let us pass. I tugged on Eli's sleeve to tell him we should go away. He pulled away from my grasp.

"What the *hell*," I whispered to Lucy.

"Yes, what the *hell*," she said. She shrugged. "My brother doesn't seem to have any tact in leaving us alone to discuss our problems. You might as well come in, too."

I didn't have a choice unless I wrestled the car keys away from Eli and drove off. I stepped inside.

Felix was sitting in the small living room, and he was fairly popping with . . . some strong feeling. Maybe several. Lucy, besides being angry, was looking as though she faced some terrible doom. Kind of stunned and confused. She took an armchair rather than sit by Felix and slumped in it. There was a balled-up handkerchief on the little table beside her.

I looked from one of them to the other. Eli waited for them to tell us what was agitating them. When neither of them spoke, he said, "You both seem to be upset."

That was a whopping understatement. Lucy actually laughed in a sarcastic kind of way.

Felix did not look at Eli directly. Since gazing at Eli was his favorite thing to do, I found that strange. He looked kind of furtively at his Lucy. "I guess we have to tell them," he muttered. She looked down at her hands like something was written on the backs.

Eli and I exchanged a glance, our eyebrows raised almost to our hairlines. We were baffled.

After another few seconds of nothing, Lucy raised her head and glared at us. "I am pregnant," she said, her voice hard, daring us to say any of the things that might have occurred to us.

My jaw fell. I snapped it shut. Eli did the same thing. I did not like myself when my first thought was, *Everyone but me. Even people who never wanted a baby.*

I started to say something, because someone had to. But I thought twice.

Unfortunately, Eli decided to say, "You are pregnant by Felix?" I put my hand over my eyes.

"Who *else*?" Lucy's rage rolled over us.

I glanced at Felix. He was kind of hunched over. I couldn't tell if he was just embarrassed at having had sex with a woman, or angry with her for being pregnant, or . . . something else.

"How far along are you?" I said.

"I don't know," Lucy said. "I don't know anything about having a baby, since I never thought I would have one."

"How many of your monthlies have you missed?" Time to be blunt.

"Three," she muttered, looking down again.

This was like pulling hens' teeth. She didn't want to know what would happen now, but she had to learn.

"You're in your fourth month," I said. When she didn't scream, I proceeded very cautiously. "That means you have five more months, give or take, until the baby comes." I hesitated, but it had to be said. "Some women try to end their pregnancies. But a lot of the time they die in the process. The later in term you are, the more dangerous an abortion is."

"I won't do that," Lucy said, and I could tell this had already been discussed. "I carry life, and I have to honor God's decision I should do this."

I figured God hadn't had a lot to do with this. Somehow, these two, neither of whom wanted the other sexually, had nevertheless done the deed.

Eli had been following another train of thought. "Lucy," he said, his voice dark and cold. "You consented? This was not done without your consent?"

I would not have wanted to be Felix in that moment. I didn't even want to be in the room.

"I may be many things, Eli, but I am not a rapist," Felix said, just as coldly.

Lucy nodded, a jerk of her head. "I consented." Her cheeks were dark red. She clearly wanted the floor to open and swallow her.

"If you're right about your times of the month, the baby will be due in May or early June," I said, trying to sound brisk and matter-of-fact. "Have you felt movement yet?"

If Lucy had been a horse, she'd have reared and whinnied. I could see the whites of her eyes. "No!" she said, very alarmed. "Movement?"

I never understood how these families thought leaving girls ignorant was a good idea. It didn't keep girls innocent. It kept them stupid.

"You need to go talk to your mother," I said. "Not only has she had four children already, she's expecting again."

I probably shouldn't have added that. If Lucy could be even more discombobulated, she got that way. She looked at me as though I'd grown another head.

"My *mother* is going to have a baby? But my mother is old!"

"Well, she and Ford have sex, and babies happen when you do that," I said, trying hard not to sound impatient. Still trying to get this back on a steady course.

"Then how come you haven't had one?" Lucy said, like she was accusing me of something.

It was stupid to feel like I'd been smacked in the face. "I lost our baby," I said.

All of a sudden, Lucy's anger drained away. "I'm so sorry," she said.

I nodded.

Then there was a strange silence. Everyone was regrouping.

Eli gazed into the distance, his eyes not meeting anyone's, especially mine. Eli was trying to make a policy about how he should react to this. He decided. He rose and went over to his childhood friend, who had only ever loved Eli. "Felix, I congratulate you on your fatherhood," my husband said, shaking Felix's hand. "I hope you and my sister have a healthy baby, who will be a blessing to you."

Felix decided to run with that. "Thank you, Eli. I will do my best to bring your niece or nephew up right. Lucy and I will learn about this. If thousands of people go through this every year, we can, too."

To my huge relief, Lucy decided to get on board that train. It wasn't a happy train, but at least it was calm and steady and moving forward. "Felix, you're right," she said. "I can talk to my mother. At least I will not have this baby on a boat in the middle of the ocean, like my mother had us."

"Good point," Felix said, almost smiling at his wife. "Some women go to a hospital to have their babies now. Or we will find the best midwife in San Diego."

Lucy nodded: short, sharp, decisive. "It will be all right," she said, mostly to herself. "We will have a healthy, intelligent child. And it may be a grigori, like its father." She actually smiled.

Felix brightened quite a bit at this thought. "That would be a great thing," he said.

The odd couple looked at each other directly and smiled at the same moment. The resolution had passed.

We all took a deep breath.

Felix said, "You must have had a reason for your visit. Is there something we need to talk about?"

"Yes," I said, before Eli could. "Here is a secret you have to keep. Felicia has decided to marry Hans Goldschmidt, the Jewish grigori—or magician, if that's what they call 'em in Germany. And you know what will happen there, since you were at the meeting with the seer. This can't become public until Hans has gotten to Switzerland. His family's wealth is there, jewelry smuggled out of the store where his father was killed."

"By whom?" Felix said. "That is, who killed his father?"

"By this Hitler's followers. And Hans's mother died, too, after getting the jewelry out of the country to give her kids something to live on."

I thought I'd summarized it pretty well, but maybe not. Felix and Lucy had a lot of questions. Felix understood why we needed to keep Felicia in circulation, as if she were still deciding which of her suitors interested her.

Lucy was very pleased to be included in the conversation, which made me wonder how much Felix had shared about what was going on behind the scenes of this week's activities. She had a lot of questions, good ones. Eli answered them as clearly as he could.

Gradually the tension in the little living room ebbed. Lucy and Eli got up to make some tea.

I was alone with Felix. I told him what was on my mind. "Lucy has a good head on her shoulders and she's trying to be a good wife to you. Please talk to her more. Tell her where you're going, and why you do the things you do."

"I was thinking the same thing," he said.

And that was the end of our little talk.

Eli had taken a moment to talk to Lucy, too. She was looking happier when she returned with a tray and teacups.

I can take tea or leave it. Though I'd had an awful lot of it lately, I wanted to keep Lucy smiling. I took a cup and emptied it.

Everything had changed in a few days.

Veronika was having a baby who wouldn't be a Savarov, but a McMurtry. Lucy was having a baby that would be a Drozhdov. Felicia had decided to marry a young man with a sad background and a dubious future, a man she didn't really know.

The safe marriage I had been determined to help her find did not suit her. It was never going to happen.

Something in me had known that all along.

I hadn't listened to myself.

CHAPTER FIFTEEN

A s Eli drove us back to his mother's house, we didn't talk. That was all right, for once. We had a lot to think about.

I gave up worrying about Felicia. She was going to do what her heart told her to, despite the danger, despite giving up a future that could have been secure and comfortable.

The future was not for me to know.

I was glad of that.

Why didn't seers kill themselves? Did they ever see anything good?

I'd made that big decision, to leave Felicia's life in her own hands. So I went back to something more familiar: I struggled to remember what her schedule was for tonight, since we were obliged to go ahead with the pretense she was still in the market for a suitor.

"The talent show," I said out loud. Eli shuddered.

"I don't know who thought it was a good idea to put all these grigoris on a little stage to show off their *other* talents," he said.

"Did you have a talent? Six years ago?" I was fascinated with the Eli of a previous Wizards' Ball Week, the Eli who had looked at all the talented grigori women and not picked one.

Eli laughed. "Hell, no," he said. "But Isabella danced."

"Danced?" I tried to imagine Isabella dancing in front of a crowd. "Like . . . square dancing, or what?"

He laughed again. "No, flamenco. It's a kind of Spanish dance, with these things you click attached to your fingers. It's very dramatic and fiery."

"Was she good?"

"She looked good in her costume, and she had the drama down pat."

"I wonder why she never found anyone. She's really pretty, and a Dominguez."

"Everyone, including me, was scared of Francisco. It was clear that if you married one of the Dominguez children, he'd still be the leader of the family. You'd never get away."

"That's why they were all single, I reckon."

"All except Valentina. She married your father, got cut from the family tree, and maybe died because of that. After that story went the rounds, courting Maria Rosa, Diego, Fernanda, or Isabella became even less attractive." Eli shook his head. "I have to admit, it was brave of Isabella to help Felicia. I don't know how she got money to the Karkarovs, or how much of that Felicia even got the benefit of, but at least Isabella tried."

My husband had a little too much admiration for his former flame.

"She did," I said, giving the devil her due. I was glad when he dropped the Isabella topic in favor of the party this evening.

"I got a list of the performers. Clayton is going to play the guitar. Mateo and one of his cousins will juggle. One of the German girls is going to play the piano. An Irish boy is playing some kind of harp and singing. Two of the Chinese kids have an acrobatic act."

"I don't know what that is." I was learning so much this week. Most of it, I didn't really care to know.

"Contortions, mainly, for the very limber and young. You'll enjoy it."

"Do you think anyone will try to kill Felicia tonight?"

"The good side of keeping her engagement a secret is that everyone will think she's still on the market, and they'll be trying to get close. They might feel they still have a chance to get her over to the German side. No matter what she's said through me."

"Even if we got to talk about her being promised to Hans, the Germans and Japanese would realize she's engaged to a Jew. They wouldn't have any hesitation in mowing her down."

"Unless they kill Hans first," Eli said. "Then she'll be free to marry again."

"I can't see a way out of this," I admitted, after thinking for a moment. "The only idea that might work would be to take Felicia away from here and hide her until she and Hans can marry. She'd miss the last months of school. I don't know where we could hide her that a good magician couldn't find her. They sure found her when she was in Segundo Mexia."

Eli had nothing to say about that. My thoughts drifted off. Not for the first time, I assessed how my life had changed the minute my sister entered it.

Death follows Felicia, I thought. Maybe that was not too surprising, since death was her specialty. If she had been an earth grigori, for example, her life would have been very different. Or if she'd been an air grigori, like Eli and Peter. It was hard to imagine Felicia without the burden and glory of her frightening power.

I didn't blame Felicia for having such power and not being shy about using it. I would have, too. Or for not loving Peter. You couldn't help that. But having her for a sister had changed my life, and I couldn't deny it.

My sister was the center of a struggle between two powers. My sister was in love. My sister could kill many people in a matter of minutes, even seconds.

My sister was awesome and terrible and a teenager.

I loved her.

Death followed me, too.

CHAPTER SIXTEEN

Another night, another hotel, another occasion for dressing up. At least this wasn't formal.

This time I was wearing one of the dresses Lucy had left at home when she married. It was a little young for me, flowered and with touches of pink, but it had fit better than the others.

I'd tried it on late that morning, asking Veronika to judge. Leah, who had helped me with the buttons, told me I looked lovely. Veronika had turned greenish and dashed for the bathroom, though I didn't think me in the dress had anything to do with that.

Eli had heard the noise. He came in and stood waiting until his mother staggered out. Eli said, "Mother, is there something you want to tell us?"

Veronika had turned red, almost as embarrassed as Lucy had been. "Ford and I are expecting a child," she confessed. "I wanted to be sure before sharing the news."

"I'll bet Ford is excited." I liked the man.

"He's pretty much beside himself," Veronika said, smiling. "We both assumed that at my age, I wouldn't get pregnant." She looked at Eli hopefully.

He didn't disappoint her, as he hadn't disappointed Felix and Lucy. "I'll be glad to have another brother or sister," he said, and kissed his mother.

Veronika beamed at him, all misty-eyed. Eli left the room without looking at me.

At least we got that piece of family news taken care of. We would leave it to Lucy to tell her mother that she was pregnant, too, when and how she chose.

When we gathered in the foyer to set out for yet another event, Felicia looked beautiful, as always. The Polish families were sponsoring this evening's talent show. Felicia had gotten friendly with one of the Polish girls, so she was anxious to go.

"I'll be glad not to dance or eat a huge late meal for one night," Felicia said in a world-weary way. I didn't know whether to laugh or cry. I thought she was putting me on, but I wasn't sure.

There wouldn't be as much moving and mixing, since the entertainment would be on a stage and all the attendees would be sitting and watching. That was fine with me, too. Easier to watch my sister. Easier to watch her enemies.

When we got to the hotel, we found it was hopping. Several groups (both ordinary human and magical) had rented special occasion rooms for this evening, and there was a lot of coming and going. We found an employee who could direct us to the room the Poles had rented, only to discover it was in a state of polite turmoil.

Everyone who had been invited had actually arrived. (Felicia was not the only person glad to have an evening to simply sit and watch.)

The seats had been set up in two sections, with narrow aisles on either side and a broader one down the middle. In both sections, there were ten rows of six chairs apiece. Despite the flurry of chairs carried in from other rooms by hotel employees, some of us would have to stand.

I told Eli I would be glad to stand first, and after a while we would switch. I didn't mind. Though my days were far longer than usual, I wasn't getting enough exercise.

"We'll rotate when the halfway point is reached," he said. "It's on the program."

A woman without a chair was a shocking thing to the men standing. They kept trying to get a chair for me, despite everything I could say, until Harriet came to keep me company. She had parked Soo-Yung with Felicia and Agnieszka, the Polish girl Felicia had befriended. The three were chattering away in no time. Eli, who sat on Felicia's left, was keeping a sharp eye on them. I would watch the people around them.

"How's Bo-Ra?" I asked Harriet, picking out people I'd met (or could identify) in the crowd.

"She's a tough old bird. Couldn't walk for two days after the explosion, but then she got up and started moving again. Her arm is broken. It's healing faster than mine would, for sure, but due to her age it'll be a while. How are you?"

"I got some stitches in my back. They're due to come out next week. I'm better."

"You got some healing."

I nodded, still looking through the people milling around the room. "I did. The stitches pull, but I'm not nearly as sore."

A bell rang to alert the audience the entertainment was about to start. Everyone who could sit did. The lights went down.

Turned out to be a tradition that the oldest Listed person from Poland (this year, a woman in her late twenties) made the opening remarks. She spoke good English. Even if she'd spoken in Polish, I would have known she was telling us we were welcome, apologizing for any discomfort a few of us might feel at standing, and promising us an evening of good entertainment.

She wasn't lying. No terrible singers, people reciting poems, or dancers with two left feet.

The first performer was a teenage French boy. You'd think a magic act would be run-of-the-mill in a room full of grigoris and other wizardy people, but it wasn't. Instead of cleverly making a card vanish up his sleeve, Henri actually made it vanish. And when a rabbit appeared, Henri needed no puff of smoke to make the rabbit vanish again. Then Henri stabbed swords through a rotating box with the Polish hostess inside. Blood ran out of the bottom of the box, and everyone gasped. She was quite well by the time he reopened the box, though there were stab marks all through her dress. Henri received quite a round of applause, and so did she.

Two Chinese girls were next on the low stage, the acrobats. I had never seen human beings as flexible and agile. "Like human pretzels," I told Harriet, who tried not to laugh. They raised and lowered each other with magic, hanging in contorted positions above the stage.

The two performers were completely covered, but the very fitted one-piece outfits left nothing to the imagination. I had never seen anything like that, and from the expressions on the men's faces, neither had they. "I would have a more adventurous life if I was that limber," Harriet whispered, as the girls arched backward on their hands. I had to smile.

A young woman from Italy sang. She had a wonderful voice and a very talented piano player, another Italian.

"She's been professionally trained," Harriet said. "That was an aria from *Gianni Schicci* by Puccini."

"If you say so. No matter what she was singing about, that was beautiful."

After two more acts, my program told me were halfway through the scheduled performances. There was a ten-minute break, the Polish woman announced.

Time to switch places with Eli. I'd been keeping a keen eye on my husband in case he was going to give me a signal. He looked back and raised his hand.

I'd already realized the Poles had not invited any Germans to the party. But Harriet pointed out a Japanese family.

A mother, father, and two Listed daughters were seated in the row behind Eli and the girls. There were two Listed boys sitting with them, from some other country. Harriet was keeping an eye on them, because Soo-Yung would not speak to the Japanese and they would not acknowledge her, which was not only pointed but awkward.

The Japanese mother who'd been sitting behind Agnieszka stood up and began to move down the row. Maybe she just needed to go to the bathroom. Or maybe she wanted to get behind Felicia or Soo-Yung and do something small and awful. I began to move down the narrow aisle until I was at the correct row. I faced her. My movement caught the woman's eye as she was sidestepping along the row. We looked at each other. I shook my head. I put my hand on the pocket of my dress, to let her know I was armed. This close, if I threw the knife I'd catch her right in her chest.

The Japanese lady scuttled back the way she'd come and dropped into her chair, her eyes strictly forward.

I was almost certain she'd just needed to go to the ladies' room.

Almost certain was not good enough.

Eli rose to swap places with me. Felicia leaned over to pat my arm, and Soo-Yung bowed in her seat. Agnieszka beamed at me.

Good to be wanted.

And that was all that happened the rest of the evening. We watched more talented people do talented things. Clayton Dashwood turned out to be an excellent guitar player, and his sister sang. She had a very pretty voice. It was kind of homey, after the opera singer.

I saw Clayton as we were leaving. I waited until a very pretty girl from Hungary had fluttered her eyelashes at him and left with a backward glance. "I sure enjoyed your music," I said, making sure my own eyelashes stayed absolutely still.

"That's real gratifying," he said, and he sounded sincere. "I think you're a hard woman to impress."

I narrowed my eyes at him. "Depends on why you're trying to impress me, I guess," I said, and caught up with Eli and Felicia. They were doing goodbyes with the hosts.

The Japanese woman who'd gotten up was talking very rapidly to her husband, with many side glances at me. He scowled in my direction. Well, I wasn't here to make friends.

He could scowl all he wanted. I was not afraid of him. I let him see that.

Which was stupid, because he might could kill me six ways from Sunday before I could raise a hand.

But he didn't.

So I counted the evening a win. I was glad Felix hadn't come. He would have been bored and spoiling for a fight.

We were back at Veronika's house and halfway up the stairs when Ford and Veronika came out of the sitting room and called to us. Back down we went. Ford was smiling so hard I thought his face would seize. Now that we officially knew the big secret, he was waiting for our good wishes with all the delight of a seventeen-year-old.

"We told Alice tonight," Veronika said. "She was so excited!"

I wanted my mother-in-law to be happy. Apparently Alice did, too, and had kept her real reaction to herself. Veronika would be an older mother, facing her fifth childbirth, and I figured she needed all the good will she could gather up.

Finally we were able to escape to our room. We weren't talking much. We were both tired, and I was feeling relieved because for once my feet didn't hurt. I was still glad to take off my shoes, and I wiggled my toes with a contented sigh. Looked like Eli was going to spend the night here, and I was too tired to have any more words with him.

"Has Felicia said Ahren and Hans have gone?" I asked. She hadn't said anything to me, but I hadn't asked.

"They left last night. So she was being brave tonight. That was what all the smiling and laughing were about." Eli had peeled off his evening coat and his good grigori vest. His shirt seemed to have twenty little buttons. A lot of work.

"So Ahren won't get to finish Ball Week. I don't know if he found anyone he admired." I had only thought of Hans.

"The boy has enough to worry about," Eli said as he finally got rid of his shirt and dropped it into the clothes hamper. "Getting married is probably the last thing he should be doing right now. Ahren will have other Wizards' Balls. Two or three more, perhaps. Plenty of time."

I was rolling my stockings down as another thought made me pause halfway. "If this Wizards' Ball is this tense, if the Koreans already hate the Japanese because they're occupying Korea . . . and Japan is allying with Germany against the rest of the world . . . and England and all its colonies, present and past, are against Germany and Japan . . . and Germany may invade Belgium and France . . ."

Eli had pulled on his pajamas, since the night was chilly. He sat abruptly in the easy chair. His face was bleak. "This may be the last Wizards' Ball for some years," he said.

"Maybe ever. Think of all the ill will that will build up. All the magicians who will die at the hands of other magicians. That's going to happen, in the war that's coming." I took a deep breath and asked the question that had been haunting me. "Do you have a side in this fight? Will you go?"

Startled, he swung his head toward me, his hair trailing over his shoulders. "I suppose that depends on what the tsar decides to do. And what he decides to do may depend on what side the godless Russians choose. What do you think about your country?"

"Texoma won't do anything. It's small and poor, and I can't see us picking a dog in this fight. If you mean what used to be the United States of America . . . Britannia will go with England, for sure. Dixie? Whoever will pay the most for cotton, I bet. New America . . . New America is organizing a militia to take over Texoma and any other land it can grab back from Canada and Mexico. That'll be a war fought in this country. If I were New America, I'd pick this time to do it, since everyone will be in a tizzy over the bigger war."

"There will be war all around us," Eli said.

We looked at each other. Grim moment.

"If all the worst things happen, yes," I said. "I got no ideas about the rest of Europe—Spain or Portugal, Romania, Czechoslovakia. I know there are lots of little countries I haven't even heard of. Ahren's folks have settled in England. Hans's money is in Switzerland with his uncle. What do you think the Swiss will do? Any idea?"

"There's one Swiss alchemist here. I talked to him. He thinks his country will remain neutral. It's too small to do otherwise."

"I think we'll have to do something," I admitted. "We probably can't sit out the war in Texoma. Maybe someone will shoot this Hitler and it will all be over before it's started." I got up to brush my teeth. "If I had to pick right now, I'd say I was against the Germans and Japanese and whoever joins up with them. It's awful to pick Jews to kill. It's like picking people with black hair, or people with grigori vests. It might be us, next. Also, if Felicia marries this Hans, I want to be on the same team as her."

"What if the tsar decides to align with one or the other?" he said. "What if he wants me to go overseas?"

"I bet people all over San Diego are having this same conversation in different languages," I said. "The tsar has been yanking you backward and forward for a couple of years, Eli. Your dad was bad. You are good. He can't seem to make up his mind whether to trust you or not. Or whether . . . well, what it looks like to other people at the court if he does let you back in."

Eli would have liked to have denied that, but it was true, so he couldn't. My husband's unhappiness made me want to kill his father all over again, and spit on his grave. But then, I was depressed by all the choices in front of Eli and me. Choices we would have to make.

I hoped he and I would make the same one. But I wasn't counting on it.

CHAPTER SEVENTEEN

F elicia got a telegram the next morning while Eli and I were
eating breakfast with her. We were alone in the dining
room. Ford had gone to work, Veronika was throwing up
in her bathroom, Alice had gone to the grocery with Leah in attendance. She was all starry-eyed. Evidently, the second visit with the
Volkovs had gone well. Veronika and her husband (and Alice, of
course) were invited to the Volkovs' place for dinner in a week.

Eli excused himself to make one of his mysterious phone calls in
the library, which had been his father's office. Since the main telephone was in the foyer, the library was the only room where you
could talk in private.

We heard the back doorbell ring. "Leah's gone," I said, and
pushed my chair back.

"Mrs. O'Clanahan will get it," Eli said, and left to make his
phone call.

Sure enough, after a moment the cook came into the dining
room with a yellow envelope on a little tray. I was about to tell her
where Eli was, but she went to Felicia's chair.

"Telegram for you, Miss Karkarova." Mrs. O'Clanahan looked a
little excited. We didn't get a lot of telegrams.

Felicia's whole face lit up as she took the envelope. "Thank you,"
she said, with a decent pretend calm. As soon as Mrs. O'Clanahan

left the room, she tore it open. Her eyes ate up the words. "Hans is in New York," she said, just about vibrating with excitement. "He and Ahren are about to board the *Normandie*."

"Where will they dock?" I put down my fork.

"They'll dock in Southampton in England." She said this very carefully, as if she'd memorized it. "Ahren disembarks there to get a train to where his folks have settled. Hans will go on to Le Havre, in France. Then he'll get a train across France to get into Switzerland, to Geneva. He might be in Geneva in as little as six days. More likely seven or eight. I found maps in the library."

I would need to study some myself, if everything the seer had predicted began to happen. "Listen to you," I said admiringly.

"I don't know if I pronounced all of those right," Felicia admitted.

"I'll never be able to say you didn't." My sister would have (more or less) a week of suspense until Hans had reached his uncle in Geneva. And then he would have to get all the business about the jewelry settled. I had never had business that big to manage, so I couldn't guess how long that might take. "He won't try to go to Germany, right? To see his sister?"

"He has to stay out of Germany. We hope his sister's husband can protect her, but he wouldn't be able to do anything for Hans."

"So then what?" I asked.

"Once Hans has gotten his financial situation squared away, he'll come back. He'll find work to do for a year. And then we'll be married." Felicia was willing herself to believe all this would happen, could happen. That war would not break out and destroy her one little plan.

"Doesn't seem like much to ask," I said.

"It doesn't, does it? Everything could go all right."

"It could," I said, not letting any doubt into my voice. "Who was he working for, before?"

"What do you mean?"

"When he showed up in Texoma. To have a look at you."

Felicia's face went blank. She'd never thought about that part of Hans's story. Love, it blinds you.

"He does belong to some group of Jewish wizards. And they had heard about me. And they sent him. But he didn't explain more about them." Now she sounded uncertain.

"Maybe it's better we don't know," I said.

"Why?"

"We can't tell if we don't know."

"You really think someone will try to get it out of us?"

I hadn't really believed someone would try to kill my sister during this festive week. I hadn't believed a mother would sit silent while a bomb was ticking away at her daughter's feet. "I don't know," I said heavily. "I do know you have to keep on pretending you're open. To Mateo and Clayton, and the others circling around."

Felicia looked at me with an arch expression. "Not just me that's getting circled around."

"Who? Katerina? Fenolla? Anna?"

"I've hardly seen Anna." Felicia looked troubled, just for a second. "And since Katerina's mother and brother . . . left town, Katerina's kind of at a loss. Her dad came down from Los Angeles to escort her. You think maybe we could take her with us, to something?"

"I don't mind. I'll talk to Eli." That was a good thing. If I came face-to-face with Irina again, I'd have to kill her. But that wasn't Felicia's problem. "What were you saying before we got sidetracked with Katerina?"

"Ohhhh. Clayton has paid me a lot of attention, but the last two times I danced with him, he just wanted to ask questions about you."

"What?" I could make no sense of that.

"Lizbeth this and Lizbeth that. How old are you, what family do you have in Texoma, how long have you been married to Eli, was it a legal marriage . . . on and on and on."

"Why would he do that?"

"Lizbeth! He's got feelings for you, dodo!"

"But I'm married. He knows it." That settled it, as far as I was concerned.

"Maybe Clayton thinks he can edge Eli out of the picture." Felicia was openly grinning now. She thought this was hilarious.

I was married. That was the last word: again, as far as I was concerned. Our marriage was tottering, but it was still a promise I'd made.

Clayton Dashwood was good-looking. He had financial security. He lived in an agricultural state with lots of water. He could play the guitar very well. I liked him.

But Clayton had told Felicia and me, when he'd appeared in Texoma, that he needed to marry a woman with magical ability since it was running low in his bloodline. I pushed this new and unwelcome confusion out of my head and slammed the door on it.

Eli returned to get a cup of coffee. He seemed to be thinking hard about something, which he usually was nowadays, but Felicia wasn't interested in his mood. She was a teenager in love. She told him all her news about Hans and his journey. I didn't mind listening twice, because I wanted to be sure I got it straight. None of these places seemed real to me. I hadn't even seen them on a map. I hadn't heard of them before.

I had a small world.

Ford had left the newspaper on the table when he left, and I decided I better start reading it every day like he did.

The news about Germany was pretty scary. German troops were beginning to move toward the Polish border. Looked like they were preparing to invade. I shook my head, thinking about Agnieszka, who surely must have some family there.

The next thing my eyes fell on, like the story had a magnet attached, was a little two-paragraph item. A woman's body had washed ashore and been discovered. Probably it was Maria's, from the description. I wasn't surprised. Felix and I had just dumped her in the surf. From time to time, I'd seen bodies that had been in the water for more than a day. Not salt water, but I couldn't imagine that would be any less destructive. There wouldn't be a way to find out how she'd died, and I'd made sure there was nothing on the body to say who she was. Maybe the sister in Encinitas would see the story and view the body. She'd at least know why she hadn't heard from Maria.

I was just being silly, sentimental. (That was one of my mother's least favorite traits in other people, being "sentimental." "Silly" was a close second.) Maria's sister had barely been able to write in Spanish, and the chances of her reading a newspaper in English were about zero.

Just as Felicia was coming to an end of the Hans saga a second time, and Eli's patience was also coming to an end (I was an expert in spotting that), I noticed another article.

Two bodies, that of a middle-aged woman and a young man, had been found close to Lake Murray Reservoir. They'd been identified as Irina and Mikhail (also known as Paul) Swindoll of Los Angeles.

It seemed someone had believed me when I'd said that Irina knew about the bomb ahead of time. And the only people I'd told had been Eli and Felicia.

I looked up to give my husband a narrow-eyed look. He raised his hands, palms up, to ask, *What did I do?* Maybe he hadn't read the paper.

"Felicia," I said, to stop the river of Hans-talk.

She shut up, surprised.

"I don't know if Katerina will be going to any more events this week," I said. "Her mom and brother are dead."

"Really?" My sister didn't try to look surprised. Neither did Eli.

"I don't know if I've pointed this out before," I said. "But I really, really hate not knowing things. *Important* things. Things I'm part of."

Eli and Felicia both looked pretty damn guilty. Of course, Felicia decided to get angry, because she knew she was in the wrong. I saw her tuning up. "No, ma'am," I said. "You don't get to bawl me out. You two need to tell me what you did."

CHAPTER EIGHTEEN

"You're right," Eli said, to my surprise. "Let's go to the backyard and talk."

Felicia lost the attitude. With a slightly sullen face, she rose when I did. We trooped through the kitchen out the back door. Felicia remembered to thank Mrs. O'Clanahan for breakfast as we went through.

In the large backyard, there was a fully grown tree with a table and chairs underneath its branches. I didn't know what kind of tree it was, but it had a beautiful spread. The branches were bare and the air was cool, but we'd grabbed jackets and sweaters from the rack by the back door. We were comfortable.

I so needed to be outside. The walls of the house, the streets and cars and tall buildings . . . they constricted me like a rope.

I waited, enjoying breathing in and out and calming myself. It didn't take long for Eli to crack.

"After you told me about Irina, I began asking around about her," he said. "I was very angry. If the old Korean witch hadn't been with you, you and Felicia would have died."

Since it had happened to me, I hadn't thought how it must have made Eli feel. I remembered his face when he'd found me in the hospital.

"One of the waitresses ran across the street to call for ambulances," Felicia said. "While I was waiting for one to show up, and trying to stop your bleeding, Irina came dashing out from behind the building—as much as a woman her size can dash. Irina was making a big show of blubbering and wailing for her dead daughter. Swearing vengeance on the Japanese, who had obviously taken the chance to kill Soo-Yung, daughter of a Korean who was organizing a rebellion against them."

"What happened when Irina saw Katerina and the rest of you?"

"She screamed," Felicia said scornfully.

"Not with happiness, I take it."

"Even Katerina could tell her mother was horrified to see her alive, not glad. Katerina'd been about to run to Irina, but she stopped dead and her face—I just felt so bad for her."

Eli had been looking at his feet. It was like he'd never seen them before.

"Tell me if I'm wrong, but I suppose after you brought me home you two went hunting. That's why Leah checked on me so often? Why Callista sat with me?"

"It wasn't hard to grab Irina," Felicia said in a reassuring kind of tone, as if that had been my big concern. "She and Paul were at the train station when we caught up with them. Before they even realized we were there, Eli laid a spell on them to keep them quiet. They came with us because they didn't have a choice. We picked up Felix along the way."

Of course they had picked up Felix. Why kill anyone without Felix along? "How did the bodies end up close to this . . . reservoir?" Another word I'd never said before.

"A friend of mine owns a cabin in that area," Eli said. "She agreed I could borrow it if I cleaned up afterward. I was planning to tell you, but things just kept happening." Eli shrugged.

He was right about that. Things just kept happening.

"Eli and I could have handled it," Felicia said with a bit of anger. "But he simply had to bring Felix."

My eyes met Eli's. He hadn't wanted Felicia to come with him. But she had insisted, so he had wanted Felix there in case something in her went out of control. Eli knew my sister now in a way he hadn't known her before.

"I'm sorry you were there," I told Felicia. Eli knew I was telling him this, too. He looked at his feet again.

"I didn't mind," my sister said calmly. "That woman and her bomb-making son needed to learn their lesson."

All of a sudden, very unpleasantly, I understood I hadn't yet gotten Felicia's measure. The expression on her face was chilling. She wasn't the half child, half woman I'd been dealing with for the past several days. She was something else, too. Something grim. I'd always known that, but I hadn't looked at it square on before.

I was no walk in the park myself.

I took a deep breath. "Why did Irina agree to kill her daughter, anyway?"

"Paul did it," Felicia said. "Irina really was stupid. She loved him more than anything. Katerina was just a . . . mistake to Irina. Nothing Katerina did was good enough, though Katerina's grades are excellent and she is a competent fire grigori and and a loyal friend. But Paul! What an asshole. He flunked out of Rasputin after talking back to all the teachers, and he was just coasting in his college classes. He did have a knack for chemistry and mechanics, so instead of learning how to make a living with that knack, he learned how to make a bomb." Felicia made a face. Bombs were her specialty, and here Paul had made one. "Stupid Paul got approached by a Japanese wizard, who offered Paul a lot of money if he'd take out Soo-Yung. It's true her father is a dissident, and it's true the Japanese would love it if the loss of his daughter shut him up. He has other children to lose."

"Irina went along with this?"

Eli said, "For the money. Irina had been spending more on Paul than her family could afford. She didn't want her husband to find out. She actually said, 'He's always had it in for Paul.'" Eli shook his head.

"Paul was willing to kill his sister," I said. I could believe it more easily of Irina than I could Paul, because I'd heard Irina talk about Paul.

"He told us all about it," Felicia said with a shrug. "He went to the tearoom early. He attached the bomb to the table reserved for the group. One of the waitresses told him which one, after Paul said he was planning a birthday surprise for his sister and her friends. I think the waitress believed there would be some kind of movie projected over the table. Of course, Paul thought the waitress would die in the explosion."

"And Paul and Irina got paid for this." I wanted to be sure they'd done it for money.

Eli nodded. "Quite a lot. From Irina's point of view, this was a great thing. Her son would have more money to make his way in a world that didn't appreciate him, and she wouldn't have to devote any more time to Katerina, who detracted so much from Paul."

"That's vile," I said. It was not a word I'd used before, but it was the only right one. "What about Katerina's father? Did he know?"

"He didn't," Felicia said. "We asked several times, and that was the answer we got."

"Does he know anything about what you have done?"

They both shook their heads. "It's a mystery to him. He's just grateful he's got Katerina, even though he had to turn down a job on a movie to get her through this week."

"You found them at the train station the night of the day the bomb went off," I said.

They nodded again.

I thought it had been three days, but the way things had been going, it could have been less. "When were you going to tell me this?"

"Soon," Eli said. "But between the Hans situation, the social schedule, and your recovery, it just never seemed like the right time. Don't pout about it," he said, trying to lighten up the atmosphere.

"Okay," I said. "No pouting." I got up and walked into the house, up to our room.

I didn't have anything else to say.

CHAPTER NINETEEN

I spent two hours brooding. After letting myself have that time, I admitted I was being stupid. My husband and my sister hadn't done anything I wouldn't have done, if I'd been able. Their only (very big) mistake was not telling me about it right away. I actually *was* pouting, as Eli had said.

Time to be a better person.

When we were alone in the car on our way to the afternoon party we'd been invited to—well, Felicia had been invited, and "with escort" had been added at the bottom—I told them I was sorry for overreacting. The words were bitter in my mouth.

"It's okay," Felicia said, before I'd even finished. "I understand."

Eli nodded. "Me too. We should have told you right away."

"The whole thing made me sick," Felicia confessed. "Irina begged and begged. Not for herself, but for Paul."

Ugh. "Was Paul sorry, even a little bit?" I know, it was dumb to ask.

"He was only sorry we took the money from them. That was his future, he kept saying. Until he knew he didn't have one."

"What did you do with it?"

"The money? We gave it to the fund for indigent grigoris," Eli told me.

"There are indigent grigoris?"

"Not many, but some. We have a building for them, small apartments but nice. Their food is served to them in a dining room in the building, and one of the nursing grigoris checks on them every day."

That sounded pretty good to me. Gunnies had no such organization. Of course, most gunnies didn't live to get old. I thought maybe that was one of the reasons I hadn't kept up with what was happening in the world. I had never expected to live long enough for it to matter to me.

I fell to imagining old grigoris who didn't even remember what the herbs in their vests were for, what damage they could cause. Working in the home for indigent grigoris would be hazardous. The nursing grigoris truly earned their wages. It was something to think about, besides my own ignorance, and why my husband and sister had chosen to keep the deaths of Irina and Paul from me . . . as if I would mind that they were dead.

Felicia's party that afternoon was a games party, grigori style. It had been well organized by the Swedish group. A small city park had been reserved for two hours (don't ask me how they swung that). Of Felicia's friends, only Anna had been invited, and Anna was only a sort-of friend. There were forty Listed there, twenty girls and twenty boys, most of them on the cusp between youth and adult. Hormones and power pulsed through the air like dandelion fluff in the wind.

"I'm glad to be a bystander on this one," I muttered to Eli.

He nodded. "Keep an eye on that Greek boy; he means mischief." Eli was relieved I was talking to him like everything was okay between us.

"Got it." Linus, the Greek boy, whom I'd seen at other gatherings, looked a little like a bull. Linus's face was broad and his eyes small; his brown hair was curly and thick, and he was muscular. He also had a very broad sense of humor and could make fart noises with his hands. The younger girls made big eyes at him, and that made him behave even more outrageously. Anna in particular was openly admiring. Linus must have money, or maybe Anna had a hankering to live in Greece.

When the Listeds were paired up in teams, Anna and Linus were together. She did a decent job of not smiling too happily.

Jason Featherstone and his mother, Penny, had been invited. Jason was glad to see Felicia, who had been so nice to him and introduced him to Fenolla Gregory.

Felicia had told me Jason and Fenolla really liked each other. Since Fenolla had not been invited to this party, Felicia was a safe partner. Felicia and Jason smiled when they were paired.

The oldest Swedish man, in his forties, stood in front of the teams to explain the rules. They were simple. No sabotage by magic or by human means, and if he blew his whistle, everyone stopped where they were.

"Do you all agree?" he called. He looked from Listed to Listed.

"We agree," they said, every one of them.

There were German and Japanese Listeds mixed in with the others. Eli was keeping a close eye on them. Today they might be simply carefree young people like the other guests, but they might not. The haughty young woman who'd approached Felicia in the Japanese Friendship Garden was there. Her partner was an Italian about the same age.

The "games" were not hard. There was a sack race, with each of the two Listeds having one leg in the sack, so they had to hop together to the finish line. There was lots of squealing and yelling and general enjoyment. A Norwegian team won. They each got silly crowns to wear. Much laughter followed.

Some folding chairs had been provided for the "escorts." Neither Eli nor I sat down. There was too much going on. So far, this party looked like youthful silliness, but after the past few days we weren't taking chances.

The contests went well, for a while. I was almost ready to relax. The Listeds were blowing off steam, out in the open, dressed in everyday clothing. Felicia's hair came down and she didn't seem to mind. Everyone had followed the rules so far. It was all smooth until the obstacle course.

There was a net of ropes knee high to get through, then a wall about chest high to climb over—the idea being the boys would help the girls and then scramble over themselves, since of course girls would not know how to do that—and then another wall probably three feet tall and five inches wide at the top. Each Listed had to walk the wall. It zigzagged and was actually about twenty feet in length. After that, the Listed jumped down to run the last few yards, going over four low hurdles, only a foot off the ground. One of the Swedish escorts was timing this for each Listed pair.

Felicia did well, but I'd known she would. Jason was less awkward than I'd expected. When he was not in a social situation, he was much more relaxed. (I could appreciate that. Same for me.) He and Felicia were in the lead until Linus tripped Jason when he jumped down from the balancing wall. Jason hit the ground and yelled in pain. Felicia was beside him in a second, ready to defend Jason while he was down. She wanted to raise her hands so much that she was shaking.

Immediately, the whistle blew.

Eli and I hung back, since the Swedish man was on top of the situation. Linus, who obviously didn't realize he was in trouble, laughed. I could see Felicia's temper popping.

So could Linus's partner, Anna, who stepped back from Linus, palms out, as if to say, *I had nothing to do with this. It's all him.*

The Swedish referee decided Linus needed to quit laughing, so he punched Linus in the face.

I almost clapped, but decided since I was an adult, I shouldn't. Some of the Listeds did, though.

Linus hadn't come with any escorts, so he was on his own. He was too shocked to bluster much. But he did protest, loudly. Since he was speaking in Greek, no one understood.

Then Linus made his second mistake. He pointed at Jason on the ground with scorn and made a "boo-hoo-hoo" face to mock the boy, who was in real pain.

Penny Featherstone was hurrying to her son when she saw Linus being an ass. Here's another thing Linus didn't expect: Penny stepped up to Linus and slapped him full in the face with all the force she could muster. I'd been pretty sure the Swedish referee's punch had broken Linus's nose. His shriek after Penny's slap told me I was right.

Felicia turned her back on Linus pointedly. She crouched by Jason and began asking him questions and touching him here and there to find if he'd broken any bones. He shook his head and held out his hand so she would help him up. Felicia gave a yank, and Jason shot up like a cork, though he leaned heavily on Felicia's shoulder since he didn't want to put his left foot on the ground. He even managed a smile. He got a round of applause from the other Listeds.

Penny, seeing Jason was up, walked back to the sidelines to stand beside us.

"Well played," Eli said quietly. I clapped silently. Penny gave a jerky nod as she began trying to come down from her surge of anger.

Linus was marched out of the park by the older Swedes. I kept my eye on him, just in case. He stood on the sidewalk, wobbling back and forth. Maybe he was trying to figure out how to get back to his hotel. Finally, he started walking, his bloody shirt causing passersby to shrink away.

It was very satisfying.

After that, the party ended with punch and cake. Even the Germans and the Japanese Listeds had a great time.

"That's the most fun I've had this week," Felicia told us on the way home.

They'd gotten to act like kids for a while, I thought. Playing silly games out in the open.

"There's more to Jason than I thought," I said. I was driving, this time.

"I hope he gets along with Fenolla," Felicia said. "And his mom is a firecracker. She's on her own. Mr. Featherstone died two years ago."

"What kind of magician is Jason?" Eli was interested.

"He's a pattern seer."

"Explain?" I'd never heard of that.

"He can see patterns in events, and deduce the probable outcome of those patterns, so he can predict money things? And political stuff?" Felicia sounded none too sure. "He explained it to Fenolla. She was really impressed."

"He'd be very valuable to the English armed forces, if the English weren't so willfully blind about magic. But then, they are excellent about closing their eyes when they don't want to see," Eli said, sounding especially grim.

"You're referring to something in particular," I said. "What?"

"Tsar Nicholas II and his family escaped from the godless Russians and took to sea with many of their court, but he never thought he would still be wandering years later. Our tsar, his wife, his children, and Rasputin expected to go to England. They were sure they'd be welcome there. He and King George V were first cousins.

They could have been twins, they looked so much alike. Instead, George refused to give refuge to our tsar. That is the true reason for the Long Sail."

That was what the Russians called the wandering of all the boats, some almost derelict, that held what was left of the Russian court and their servants. Some had died, some had married on the sea (like Eli's parents), and some had been born, like Eli, Peter, Alice, and Lucy.

"Now that you think England's going to be overrun, isn't it a good thing the tsar landed here, and was made so welcome?" Felicia said, sounding a bit dry and testy.

"I see your point, but my mother said it seemed like the worst thing in the world when they weren't given asylum," Eli said, his eyes ahead on the traffic. "They all wondered if they would die on the water."

"Are you saying the grigoris . . ." I didn't know how to end the sentence.

"Are you saying you won't help the English when the Germans invade?" Felicia asked. She was indignant already. "There are refugees already in England from Germany, and Belgium, and even France. If the Germans do have a big group of magic users, what will happen if the others of our persuasion don't rise up to fight them?"

This was all stuff I hadn't even thought of. I felt small and dull. Again.

I forgot about myself when the full meaning of Felicia's little speech dropped on me. I wanted to turn and slap her, the way Penny had slapped Linus. I took a deep breath, my fists clenched. "Felicia, are you actually saying you think my husband should go to England to fight the Germans? When none of the countries in North America are at war with Germany?"

Felicia was in the back seat with her lower lip stuck out like a child's. Eli was looking straight forward. That was what he did when he didn't want to meet my eyes. Or if he knew I wasn't going to like what he told me.

"That's what you all have been talking about," I said. "That's why you've been going to all these meetings."

Eli nodded, one sharp jerk of his head. "The debate is very hot," he said.

"You made it clear you weren't a fan of the English royals. But you don't want this Hitler and his pet magicians to win. What side are you on?" I asked.

"If all the magic adepts in Britannia, Canada, and the Holy Russian Empire—and the ones now living in secret in New America and Dixie—agree to help England and France in the fight, it could make the difference between those countries being occupied or free. Otherwise, the Germans and their allies, which seem likely to be Japan and Italy, will win. They'll occupy all the countries they can. France and England, Belgium and Poland . . . they'll go under. All the people Hitler blames for Germany's problems . . . they'll be killed in those countries as well. Millions upon millions." Eli's eyes shut as he saw this happening. His eyes crinkled up. He looked so fragile, just for an instant.

Felicia scooted up so her head was between ours. Her eyes were blazing. She was ready to go right now, no doubt about it. "We have to stop it," she snarled.

My heart sank. We'd driven into the garage behind the house. I turned off the car. No one moved. Finally, I had to ask. "Eli, are you leaving me to go to Europe to fight in this war?"

He took a deep breath. "I am thinking of what is best to do."

And that was it.

"If you go, I will go with you!" Felicia was on fire. "I will fight side by side with Hans and you and Felix!"

"Felix must not go," I said.

"Why not?" Felicia was outraged.

"Because he's going to be a father."

Felicia's face was a picture. I wish I could have photographed it, even at such a grim moment. "You're kidding me?" she said.

"Not at all."

She knew I was serious, and she finally believed it. A wide grin made her look like a different girl. "Those rascals!" she said. "The two of them!"

I had to smile a little, but Eli didn't. "Lots of grigoris who have children, or are married, think they should go," he said.

Just like that, my smile was gone. "Felicia, would you mind going into the house?"

Without a word, my sister climbed out of the car and went to the back door.

We were alone.

"Let me just say this, so you're clear how I feel." I would not sit by and let him make this decision on his own. It was our lives, not just his. "I do not want you to go out of this country to fight this war that isn't ours. If we are invaded here, of course we have to fight. We have to kill them all. But otherwise? I say no."

He looked straight ahead, and he thought about what to say in reply. Just when I thought I would scream, Eli said, "I understand your feelings. If I were you, I would feel the same way. But there are a lot of factors in this decision. You are the most important, but there are others."

That simply meant I was not the most important.

I let that lie there for a minute. "All right. What factors?" I was proud of how calm I sounded.

"Maybe you should have married that Dan Brick," Eli said. For the first time, he sounded . . . defeated? Exhausted?

"Don't you ever say that, you ass," I said.

That startled a half-smile from him. "You are honest," he said. "I have tried to be, but I haven't always succeeded."

Oh, that wasn't worrisome. Not at all.

"If I ever want to go back into the tsar's service, I have to do what the tsar wants his grigoris to do. If he decides we should go, I have to go. If he decides we won't take up that battle . . . here I stay."

"You want to go back into the tsar's service." I wasn't really asking a question.

"That was what I was raised and trained to do," he said, sounding only tired. "I have been happy with you in Texoma, helping the people there with little jobs. But it's not what I . . . expected in my life."

"And not better than what you were doing here." *Before you got thrown out.*

Eli shook his head. "Not better. Good, but not . . . what I was born to do."

So he'd finally spoken the truth.

I'd lost, already. It was like he'd stuck a knife in me, but I didn't bleed on the outside. I opened the car door and went into the house, thinking any second I would sink to the ground. But I didn't. Eli did not come after me. He stayed in the car for a long time.

I had nowhere to go except our room. There wasn't time to go anywhere else, if I could have thought of a place I'd rather be. Maybe I should have gone to talk to Felicia, but she had her own dreaming going on. Alice was too young. Eli's mother was, well, Eli's mother, so she was out of the question.

The telephone rang as I passed it on my way to the stairs. For lack of anything better to do, I answered it. "Savarov residence," I said, hoping that was the right thing to say. Leah answered the telephone that way.

"Lizbeth, is that you?"

"Yes. Who is this?"

"Harriet. Listen, I need help. Bring your guns."

It was like the Almighty had heard my prayer, if I was a praying person. "Where are you?"

"I'm at Ainslie Boardinghouse, 831 Nutmeg Street. There are at least three men outside, maybe four, and I'm pretty sure they're waiting on me and Soo-Yung. They may rush the house if we don't come out. I'd be grateful for your help." It wasn't easy for Harriet to say this. "Park on Sage, the next street over. The back door is the best way to get in. They probably won't know you by sight."

"On my way." I dashed upstairs, put on my city pants rather than my Segundo Mexia blue jeans, and packed my guns in a leather over-the-shoulder bag that Eli used sometimes for spell ingredients. My hair was still fixed, so I figured I looked respectable. Not out of the ordinary, anyway. Eli was on his way in as I was going out. His shoulders were slumped in an unhappy way. Too damn bad.

"I need the car," I said, and took the keys off the hook I'd just hung them on. I was gone before he could ask any questions. I'd grabbed the map I kept in the room, and I drove a block or two before I pulled to the curb to pick my route. I'd been afraid Eli would try to stop me if I gave him time to think.

I am quick with maps. I found Nutmeg Street and figured out how to get there. It took me twenty minutes. First, I drove past Ainslie Boardinghouse so I could fix its location and appearance in my head. That would make it easier to approach from the back. It was a narrow, two-story white building, as old as the teahouse but not as well kept.

I spotted the men, though I took care not to look at them directly. They hardly spared me a glance. There were four of them. They were all Asian, all wiry, and all armed. These weren't young thugs, but serious men.

I found a parking spot against the curb on Sage. Lucky for me the backyard of the boardinghouse wasn't fenced. I walked on the property line between two houses. I paused to push myself against a tree so I could survey the backyard of the Nutmeg Street house. Harriet was right. None of the men were behind the house or in the yard. I thought that was strange. Maybe if they were actually in someone else's yard, the property owner would call the police.

With a lot of confidence, I walked across the yard to the back door and found it unlocked. I stepped in, to meet Harriet's gun. She lowered it when she recognized me. She looked very relieved.

"Thank you," she said. "Soo-Yung is upstairs locked in the bathroom. She's in the bathtub. I figured that would be a good position. Might be stray bullets."

"Sounds like the best you can do," I said. It felt so good to talk about something I knew how to do with someone else who was a professional. "How long have they been here?"

"Less than an hour. I spotted them before I called a cab for me and Soo-Yung to go shopping. The closing reception is tonight, and she says she's run out of hose and needs another pair of shoes."

"Where's Bo-Ra?"

"In bed in her room upstairs. She was getting better, but she whacked the broken arm against the door yesterday. Knocked her back a few steps."

"Since she's a hundred years old? I'm not surprised, but I'm sorry."

"Me too. She's effective."

"Who do you think sent these guys?"

"I think they're local thugs sent by someone in the Japanese group attending. Soo-Yung's father is a famous guy in Korea. He thought she'd be safe over here, but obviously they know who she is. Killing her would be a great way to make him lose heart."

"Or make him decide to kill even more of them."

Harriet shrugged. "Either way, we're in a pickle."

I agreed. "How do you want to play this?"

"I've been thinking about that. We could call the police, but the men would be gone the minute the police roll up. They'll come back right after the police leave. They may have eyes in this neighborhood, though there aren't a lot of Asians around here."

I nodded. If they'd been paid to do a job, these men would come back and finish.

"The landlady and her daughter have gone to visit friends a few streets over. They're Korean, too, a family connection of the Kims. I told them to stay away a long time. The daughter is way younger than Soo-Yung. These guys will know it wasn't her leaving. They know we're in here. Do you think you can leave as quietly as you came in and circle around them?"

"What then?"

"I guess we have to kill 'em. If you don't want to get dragged into this, because of the no-guns policy in San Diego, just say so. I shouldn't have called you. But there's no one else from Iron Hand in the area right now."

"I'll help," I said, and wondered if I was signing my own death warrant. Or jail term. "Here's what we need to do. We need to not get caught."

Harriet laughed, but it sounded rough. "Sure, let's do that," she said.

"So I sneak up behind 'em and I take out who I can?"

"And I come out the front and take out the rest."

"That's not much of a plan." I looked at her sideways.

"You've got a better one?"

"We sure know a lot of young grigoris who might be willing to give us a hand."

Harriet was doubtful. "I don't think we can drag the Listeds into this. We'd draw down all kinds of shit on our heads if one of them got hurt or arrested."

I had to agree. I didn't know what I had been thinking.

Not like a gunnie, that's for sure.

"Okay, what's our signal?" I said, moving toward the back door.

"Gunfire," Harriet said, smiling for the first time. "You leaving the bag here?"

"No, I better keep it. Someone might call the police if they see me with guns in my hands."

We gave each other a nod.

"Easy death," Harriet said politely.

"Easy death," I agreed. Right now I didn't care too much.

With the bag looped over my shoulder, I left the boardinghouse as quietly as I'd come. Maybe because having four thugs in the neighborhood had scared everyone inside, I didn't see anyone as I walked south on Sage. Turned right for a short stretch on Pepper, then north on Nutmeg.

This was the most basic plan ever.

I spied two little girls playing in the front yard at the corner house on Nutmeg. They were really involved in building something out of sticks and odd bricks. They hardly looked at me. I thought they were going to be far enough away from the action, but bullets went all directions in a gunfight. I paused and turned back. "Girls," I said. They looked up, not afraid. "You need to go play in your backyard. Now." The older one's face sharpened, and she grabbed her sister's hand and they trotted out of the front yard and around the house. I resumed my stroll down the broken sidewalk.

Just another woman in pants and sensible shoes, strolling north on Nutmeg Street, ignoring the thugs scattered along the way (they thought) inconspicuously. I counted again. Only four. The flap of the bag was undone. I was ready to start this. Closer was always better. I felt the familiar hum in my nerves rising. I took a few more steps, not hurrying, casual, planning my action.

Then one man glanced my way and did a double take. Shit, he knew who I was. He opened his mouth to yell a warning, and then my guns were out and I began. *One two three four.*

They spun and fell like tops.

Their guns were still coming up when they died.

A quick look to verify none of them were moving, and my guns were back in my bag. Then I turned around to retrace my steps. Didn't want to be connected with the boardinghouse. Harriet had stepped out on the porch with her gun drawn. She took in the situation and popped back inside. People were beginning to emerge from their houses, mostly women and children. A couple getting out of a car down the street got right back in and drove away.

Didn't see the little girls again. I was glad.

I almost made it. In a very few minutes I'd be able to get in the car and drive away. There was an old truck pulled to the curb, the back full of paint cans and ladders. The driver's door popped open and a man stepped out in front of me. He was big and burly.

"Did you just shoot those men?" he said. Though he had for sure just watched me do that, he couldn't believe it.

"Do you want to find out?" I said, my hand in my bag.

Suddenly, he understood his situation.

"No, no," he said. "I do not."

"You didn't see me."

"I didn't see you, sister."

I turned the corner and reached the car. I glanced back to make sure the painter hadn't followed me to see what car I was driving. He had not.

Then I was gone.

Harriet would not expect me to return to the boardinghouse. She'd call me, or maybe she wouldn't.

Bo-Ra had saved my life and Felicia's. Now I'd saved hers.

I had finally gotten to do something I understood, something I did better than almost anyone.

It felt good.

CHAPTER TWENTY

E li was in our room when I got back, sitting in the armchair. He'd been checking the pockets on his grigori vest.

"Where have you been?" he said. "I looked for you everywhere."

"Why? What more could you have to say to me?"

He actually looked surprised. "Lizbeth, you're my wife. I'll always have something to say to you."

"Do you want to tell me again that serving the tsar is more important than our marriage? Do you want to remind me how unfulfilled you felt living with me in Segundo Mexia? Do you want to let me know what your plans are for going to Europe to fight Hitler?" I was so angry I was shaking. To cover that I sat on the side of the bed.

It was hard for me to tell if this was a delayed reaction to the excitement of the shooting, or simply more rage escaping. I'd never seen a volcano, but I had seen newspaper photos of the cloud of steam that rose before an explosion.

"Lizbeth," he said. And then he stopped. He couldn't think of what he could say to make this better. He didn't want me to be angry. He didn't want me to be upset. He wanted me to somehow be all right with his plans and decisions.

Too late for that.

Tonight was the closing ceremony, the last Wizards' Ball. Tonight everyone would return to the tsar's grand reception room where the week had officially begun. Tonight many of the Listeds would make public their engagements, or their opening negotiations toward such a contract. It would not include the invitees who'd come to the opening, the more-or-less regular people the tsar and tsarina had wanted to please. All the attendees would be magically gifted or protecting the magically gifted.

"I'll go tonight, so Felicia will be covered," I said. "After that, I'm going home."

Eli said, "You don't want to stay to find out how Hans fares in Switzerland, or when he will return?"

"Felicia can write me a letter. When she goes back to school, she'll be safe. You and Felix can take her there. If she'll agree to go."

Eli looked uncertain, not something I'd ever seen on him. He also looked lost. I was glad that he was struggling with this.

That was something.

"You did love me," I said. "Right?"

"I still do."

But he was willing to give me up. So, the unspoken end of that sentence was "but not enough." I deserved more than that.

"Moving my stuff to Lucy's old room," I said, and got my suitcase out of the wardrobe.

"Don't bother, for one night." Eli sounded ten years older, and tired. "I'll get my overnight things and put them downstairs." He got his evening clothes and his pajama pants, then added his shaving kit. I watched him silently.

We'd always had tense moments, but I'd thought that as time passed and Eli got used to living in Segundo Mexia that would pass. He would get used to our ways. He would enjoy the slower days.

Maybe he had thought that if I spent more time in the Holy Russian Empire, I'd enjoy the faster pace?

We'd both been disappointed. Maybe we should have talked about it, but would that have made a difference? There still would have been too many people I was supposed to please here.

Less than an hour after he'd left the room, Felicia came bounding up the stairs. "Okay, what's happening?" she said. She was scowling.

"We've come to a parting of the ways."

"No," she said firmly. "You love each other."

"Maybe. He doesn't love me enough. He wants to stay here and work his way back into favor at the court, even if it means he has to go to war. I have no interest in that. I can't live here."

My little sister looked at me with big sad eyes. "But you had a happy ending. You met your prince—he was actually a prince! You fell in love."

I felt bad for her. I felt pretty bad for me, too. "Sometimes even when you meet your prince, it doesn't work out," I said. "I'll be going home tomorrow. But listen, just because it didn't work out for me, doesn't mean it won't work out for you." If it didn't, Hans would have to answer to me.

"Where did you go this afternoon?" she said. "I saw you out the window. You looked like you, for the first time in forever."

I told her.

And Felicia said, "Oh, golly, I wish I'd gone with you!" That seemed to surprise even her, and after a pause, she said quietly, "We're just scary people, I guess."

"I guess we are."

"Everyone whispers about me killing my family," Felicia said, sounding a little sad and bewildered. "But they were only my family in a technical way. They were never my kin. All they wanted to do was use me when I got old enough to be used. They wouldn't have cared if I'd starved to death when I was little."

"True."

"And you killed our father."

"He raped my mother and left her without a backward glance. I don't think he ever knew her name or cared. That's all I knew about him. I felt like I owed it to my mother."

"I can understand you feeling that way," Felicia said. "I loved him most days, but if I had to call up any single fond memory of Father, I couldn't do it."

It was the first time she'd really talked about that. "You're not holding a deep grudge that will cause you to suddenly turn on me?"

"No," she said simply. "You're real family."

"What about Isabella?"

"I love her too, most days. But I don't trust her."

"I think that's wise."

Felicia smiled. "Sometimes I am. Listen, after tonight . . . you're really going to go home?"

I nodded. "I have to, sister. I can't stand this anymore. Too much aggravation. I like Lucy and Alice. Felix has always rubbed me the wrong way. Veronika has never thought I was good enough for Eli."

Felicia was still smiling. "You're tired of wearing the clothes and following the rules. Listen, I'm proud of you for sticking it out."

"You knew all along. I did try. And I was glad to do it for you."

She nodded. "You're a great sister. One more thing before I leave you to get ready . . . for the last time. The last party! I think you better take your guns tonight."

"I will, then," I said. Felicia knew carrying guns on Imperial Island was strictly forbidden. She would not have told me to do it without good reason. "Got to clean the one I used this afternoon." The other one had not been needed.

Leah came to the door to tell Felicia the hairdresser was waiting for her. Felicia rolled her eyes but got up. "See you in an hour," she said.

I nodded. After Felicia left, I opened the wardrobe to find there was a new dress in it. It was beautiful, the light golden brown of seasoned wood, with a figure-hugging drape to it. Not fussy. Oh, Eli. My heart kind of cracked. I actually put my hand to my chest as if I could feel that happening.

Then I shook myself. I cleaned my gun rapidly, I bathed rapidly, and I pulled on the dress. I looked . . . very pretty. While I waited for my turn with the hairdresser, I packed up all my things in a large duffel bag. Then I worked on how to take my guns to the Wizards' Ball. Evening purses were small and the dress was slinky. I could fit one gun in a somewhat larger day purse. It didn't go great with my dress, but to hell with that. If I took one gun, I'd have seven shots, plus I strapped on two knives. That would have to do.

Since the tsar and tsarina weren't going to put in an appearance (Ford had told me that), the gun might not be a killing offense. Better yet would be not getting caught. I tucked my extra gun away in the duffel and put it by the door.

Eli watched me coming down the stairs. His expression was complicated.

"You look beautiful," he said quietly.

"Thank you for the dress. It's my favorite of all the things I've worn this week."

"I didn't get it. But when I saw it in the wardrobe, I knew it would look good on you." He was wearing his evening outfit again.

We waited for Felicia.

I was about to ask Eli who had bought the dress, though it must have been Veronika, when I heard Felicia coming down the stairs in a hurry.

She looked gorgeous, grown but young, powerful but pretty, all in a bluish-green dress. It was new, too.

Alice waved goodbye to us, and Ford hoped we would have a good evening. Veronika was up in their room being sick. I'd have to write her a note.

As we had done before, Eli drove the car to the ferry landing. The ferry was not as crowded as it had been a week before. We three stood in a cluster, silent, all the way across the water to the landing on Imperial Island. There were armed guards waiting there as there had been before, and there was the line of determined ladies. No one searched me, or even thought about it, as far as I could tell. We walked up to the reception hall without a word.

Felicia was keeping her face blank and her eyes to herself. She was thinking real hard about something. What Hans was doing at the moment, over in Europe? Me separating from Eli? Who knew?

I was too unhappy to ask questions.

I hadn't worn a wrap tonight, simply because I didn't want to go through the procedure of checking it in at a booth and standing in line to retrieve it when we left. I was shivering by the time we got into the building. At least if you had to be surrounded by people you didn't know, they helped to keep you warm.

The first person I saw was Isabella. She was standing with a nice-looking man with dark hair, a little older than her, and after a moment I recognized Mateo's uncle. What had been his name? Agustin. Clearly, he'd followed up on his interest in Isabella. In fact, he was holding her hand, which made him a very brave man. Maybe it would be Isabella who would live in one of the beautiful houses on the beach in Baja California.

Eli saw someone he knew and muttered an excuse before he took off.

Just then Isabella glanced my way, and I nodded and smiled.

Despite the times she'd tried to kill me, she was in Felicia's corner. Isabella nodded back, with a small upturn of her lips. She looked at my dress particularly and raised her eyebrows as if to say, *Do you like it?* I understood, with no small shock, that she was the one who had picked out our dresses. Was it Isabella who'd told Felicia to ask me to bring my guns?

The crowd was still milling, people were still entering. Felicia had found her friend Fenolla, and Fenolla had told her something that had Felicia wide-eyed and beyond excited. Felicia threw her arms around her friend. Katerina joined them. I was surprised the girl had found the heart to come tonight since the bodies of her mother and brother had been found the day before. The man with her must be her father who worked in Hollywood. He was short and a little paunchy, with heavy dark eyebrows and a pleasant face. He looked friendly and open and smart. I wandered over to meet him out of curiosity. I didn't know where Eli was or what he was doing. I didn't see Felix, either.

"Hello. I'm Felicia's sister, Lizbeth Rose," I said. I'd decided to stop being a princess, no matter what it got me.

"I'm Evan Swindoll." He shook my hand heartily. "I have a lot to thank you for, I understand."

Well, my husband killed your wife and son, I thought, but that would not make him especially thankful. Or it might? Irina had been stupid and brutish. "Nothing to thank me for," I said.

"You got them all out in time," Evan said. "You saved my daughter."

"Katerina is a sweet girl," I said, since that was always the right thing to say. "She's a good friend to my sister."

"I understand you were hurt pretty badly," he said, his whole face radiating concern. "You seem like you're feeling pretty well now, and it certainly didn't tarnish your good looks."

It seemed like a month ago that I'd had a giant wooden splinter in my back. "I do feel well," I said. "I had some healing done, and I rested for a couple of days." I was dodging the remark about my looks. I never knew what to say to compliments from people I didn't know. Or people I did know, for that matter.

"Well, if you'd ever like a guided tour of Hollywood, I'm your man."

"If I ever do, you'll be the first person I think of," I told him. Evan clapped me on the shoulder and shook my hand again.

"Me and my daughter are going back to Los Angeles tomorrow morning, and I don't know if she'll go back to school. This whole thing with her mother and brother dying, the circumstances . . . it's shaken her up pretty bad."

"Of course," I said. "I hope you get to spend some time with her." I bit off the "now" that should have gone on the end of that sentence.

"I will for sure," Evan answered, and he sounded sincere.

I saw a few more people I knew after Evan and I said goodbye. After Evan and I parted ways, I spotted Felicia talking to Fenolla. I asked Fenolla where her parents were, and she pointed over to a potted palm. The Gregorys were standing with Penny Featherstone. Suddenly I understood what the excitement was all about. Jason and Fenolla must have gotten engaged.

I didn't know whether or not to say anything to Fenolla until the official announcement. Probably better to wait. The girls were acting a bit odd. Whispering, and making little gestures to some of the other Listeds.

I put my hand on Felicia's shoulder. I gripped it hard. "What are you up to?" I said, keeping my voice low but pretty damn fierce. Something was up, and it couldn't be something good.

"Just be calm and collected," Felicia hissed at me. "We've got a plan. We're sticking to it. Stay by the wall." She yanked her shoulder out of my grip. She and Fenolla got lost in the crowd.

I said something terrible, but under my breath. I caught a glimpse of Eli and began making my way toward him. He was talking to a Frenchman; I believed the man was a wizard. They were looking very serious. I grabbed Eli's wrist, startling him. "What is it, Lizbeth?" he asked, trying to be calm about being interrupted so rudely.

"The kids are up to something. They have a secret plan," I said, as close to his ear as I could get. Suddenly he didn't mind being interrupted.

"No," he said, but he wasn't really denying that was possible. "No."

"Yes," I said.

"What is it?" He'd forgotten all about the Frenchman, who was looking from me to Eli with narrowed eyes. I figured he spoke English.

"Felicia wouldn't tell me. She ditched me. She and Fenolla are in on it."

Eli was thinking furiously.

A voice, magically amplified, boomed through the room. "Good people of the magic way! Tonight is the last event of our special week! I hope all of you have had a week full of fellowship, making ties, and perhaps even finding love."

There was a gust of laughter.

"Please form the great circle," the voice directed, and people began to shuffle around with a purpose. Eli took my hand and drew me to the edge of the room, where we turned to face inward. His face was grim and hard.

"She said we should stay by the wall," I told him.

We took steps back. Now we were literally against the wall, the outermost circle in a greater circle of magic practitioners. Only the middle was empty. It was obvious most of the others had done this before.

"Let's celebrate our countries! First, from Argentina . . ." the voice droned on, listing all the Listeds in the Argentinian group, who came out of the circle to stand in the middle, smiling, their chaperones and bodyguards around them. They all waved and smiled and received the applause of the other attendees.

The recognition went on and on, each nation stepping into the middle, getting praised, melting back into the circle. Britannia came and went, and I looked hard at the small group, finding Camilla and Clayton in the center. Clayton waved at me, and I managed to smile back. Camilla looked very pleased indeed, and I thought I saw a ring on her hand as she waved. The Canadian horse guy, I guessed.

Yep, he was in "Canada," and he was beaming, too.

There were countries I hadn't even realized were here. Some of them had two representatives, some of them forty. I'd only seen a little corner of the week's celebrations. Maybe the rest hadn't had any assassination attempts or explosions.

There were about ten people in the Finland group. Then a large crowd from France. "G" would be coming up. At that moment, all my alarm systems began tingling.

I'd lost sight of Felicia and Fenolla. "They're gone," I said to Eli, and he jerked around, looking at me with real alarm. "They've got a damn plan."

We had thought this was the end of our watchdog duties, and we'd let our guard down.

As the very large group from Germany gathered in the middle of the floor, looking proud and cold as befit the future conquerors of the world, I caught sight of my sister. She was at the front of the circled audience, all the way across the ballroom. She looked to her left, and I spied Fenolla, forty-five degrees around. To Felicia's left was Jason Featherstone. He didn't look like a tall goofy wallflower anymore. He looked grim and determined. And opposite Felicia, several people closer than me to the edge of the circle, was the Polish girl, Agnieszka. There were more Listeds I didn't recognize, who'd all worked their way forward to be next to the empty space where the countries were recognized.

I could not stop this. Eli actually took a step or two forward, his mouth open, his hand upraised, but all he could do was distract them now. If they were going to do this, they had to do it completely. I jumped forward and wrapped my arms around my husband for the last time. I pulled him away from the circle around the Listeds from Germany and their companions.

I was still restraining him with all my strength when Jason, Fenolla, Agnieszka, and Felicia killed all the Germans.

It took maybe three minutes.

Most of them really didn't know what had hit them.

CHAPTER TWENTY-ONE

I had a lot of thoughts in the immediate aftermath. Not while people were screaming and running, because even the magically gifted are afraid when a whole bunch of people drop dead in front of them. But soon after that. When the Japanese contingent decided to retaliate.

After that the room became the site of a terrible free-for-all.

The Polish girl died immediately. She was closest to a cluster of the Japanese who'd been assembling for their turn in the spotlight. Then a paralyzing spell intended for my sister hit the man behind her, and he toppled over without any means of stopping his fall. Felicia, quick and light on her feet, dodged through the crowd headed for the cluster. The Japanese began shouting in rage and alarm. They spread out so they wouldn't make as easy a target and they began shooting invisible bolts at her, like little lightning strikes, I guess.

Eli fell during those few seconds. I still had my arms around him, and when he collapsed, I went down with him. That saved my life. But it changed his forever.

I screamed his name, but his face was blank. I could feel his heart beating, but it was slow and sluggish. I never felt so torn in two. I needed to stay with him. He should not be alone if he died. I also needed to find my sister and either kill her or help her get away.

Clayton Dashwood knelt by me. "Did you know about this?" he said, and somehow I heard him clearly.

"Good God, of course not," I said. "This is so wrong."

"I believe you, but a lot of people won't. I advise you very strongly to get the hell out of here."

I couldn't seem to think at all. "But Eli is dying," I said. "I can't leave him." I looked down at Eli's blank face, and he blinked.

"It's the Japanese paralyzing thing, their favorite spell," Clayton said. "I believe he'll come around. More or less."

"Eli, what should I do?" I tried to pat his face, but my hands were shaking too badly. "I don't usually have any problem knowing," I said to Clayton. "Dammit!"

Eli blinked furiously.

"He's telling you to get out of here," Clayton said.

Eli blinked again.

"Okay, that's a yes." I knew Eli so well, I even knew what his blinks meant. Clayton was right.

"You got some money?" Clayton asked.

"No."

"Here." He dug out his wallet and handed me everything in it. "Go get on a train. Go somewhere. Anywhere. Get out of San Diego."

"That's like saying I knew what she was going to do before she did it. I did not."

"I believe you, but no one else will."

Good point. In the wake of this massacre, everyone would want to hold me responsible. And Eli. But if he was out of it, they would leave him alone.

"You just keep being paralyzed," I told him. "They won't blame you if you got hurt."

He blinked.

"Divorce me, if you live," I said. "You've got to. We were headed that way anyhow."

He did *not* blink. But he would see the wisdom of it. This might have queered his chances of ever going back to his former life, but he'd be alive to make a new one.

"Thank you, Clayton," I said, and took the money. "Can you get more to go home on?"

"I can go by a bank tomorrow," he said. "And Camilla is going home with her Canadian to meet his family."

"Thank you," I said again. "I'll see you, maybe." That was just one of those things you say.

"Yes," Clayton said. "You will."

"And I'll pay you back," I said, because that had sounded very personal, and in front of Eli.

"Of course you will," Clayton said easily. "What's Eli's family's address?"

I gave it to him and rose, looking around. People were still dying, and my sister was still not to be seen. I couldn't run in this dress. I had to go back to the Savarov house.

"Come on," Felicia said, appearing out of nowhere. She was wearing pants and a jacket.

I didn't know what to say to her.

"That can all wait," my sister said. "We got to get out of here. Now!"

"Go," Clayton said.

I looked down. Eli blinked.

"Okay," I said, and we ran for the exit. We joined the throng of people making for the ferry. For the first time, I realized Felicia was in disguise. The change of clothes included a coat and hat that covered her upswept hair, and she was wearing glasses. Veronika's reading glasses.

We pushed our way onto the ferry. It was chaos. This was the very thing all those guards were supposed to prevent, and they hadn't prevented it. I guess they were rushing to the ballroom to make some order there.

We were packed in with frightened people, and I was terrified someone would recognize my sister and throw her overboard. I stood right in front of her, blocking any view of her. When the ferry docked at the parking lot, I began walking as fast as I could.

"Hold up," Felicia said, the first time she'd spoken since the ballroom. "We have to stop by the car."

"I don't have the key," I said. I felt numb.

"I do." She held it up. "I picked Eli's pocket earlier. There's another key back at the house. They can come get the car later. We've got to open the trunk."

"Why?"

I found out why pretty quickly. She'd packed our bags and put them in there. "When did you do this?" I said, almost unable to get the words out.

"When did I put the bags in the trunk? While you and Eli were waiting for me to come down. Since you'd already packed, it was a cinch."

"No! When did you plan this massacre?"

"We've been working on it since Hans left. Fenolla and Jason were gung-ho, and Agnieszka, too. There were a few more who joined in when they saw what we were doing. Hitler's going to hit Poland probably tomorrow, and then England will be next."

There were a few cabs waiting for guests who didn't have their own car, and after a short wait we were able to get one.

"The train station," Felicia told the driver.

It wasn't a long ride. I couldn't even begin to think of what to say to my sister. I don't think I was really myself.

I did realize there was no one else at the station in evening clothes, after I caught a few startled glances.

"Go change," Felicia said, handing me my bag.

I went into the ladies' room and shut myself in a stall. My breathing was very uneven, and I couldn't decide whether to cry or not. I felt very odd. It wasn't easy getting out of the beautiful dress in a little space, and even more, trying to put on my jeans, my shirt, and a jacket. And my boots. What a pleasure to put my feet into something they were used to. I stuffed the evening clothes in the bag. Better not to leave them here.

Then I sat staring at the stall door.

I'd lost my husband and seen my sister start a war all in the same day.

The bathroom door opened. "Lizbeth! Are you going to spend all night in there? The train is leaving in thirty minutes!" Felicia sounded aggravated. Like everything was as usual. Like an impatient sixteen-year-old.

I'd only understood the first few layers of my sister. Today I'd seen the core.

She'd paid for the tickets herself. Where had she gotten the money? I didn't even want to ask, at least not now. I was pretty sure I knew. Fucking Isabella.

"Where is this train going?" I asked her, but only after we'd climbed on board and sunk into our seats. There wasn't anyone sitting right around us.

"To Tulsa," she said. "There you can catch a train for Dallas, and then to Sweetwater." That was the closest train station to Segundo Mexia.

"You don't think they'll be able to follow us?"

"Who's going to do that?"

"The HRE police," I said.

"Why? It was a grigori crime."

"Okay, then the grigoris."

"I don't think so, not after the prophecy they heard."

I thought Felicia was being pretty naive. They would have to be seen to be doing something, if they wanted to keep on speaking terms with the Germans until war broke out. There had also been considerable side damage to other people who'd just been attending the ball because they'd gotten engaged. And the Japanese! What a retaliation, so quick! Those people were organized. The Japanese had already tried to kill Felicia at least once. The target on her back had just grown enormous.

"I won't change trains at Tulsa," Felicia said, after we'd been quiet for a while.

For the first time I looked at her directly. "Where will you go?"

"To New York. To wait for Hans to return."

"How will you live in New York?"

"Isabella gave me money."

Fucking Isabella. "I should have known."

"Don't blame her. She didn't know about this. Until right before, when I warned her, so she and her new man could get out of there."

"You told her but not me. And now Eli is paralyzed."

"Hey, I . . ."

"Don't speak." I closed my eyes and pretended she wasn't there. That Eli was up and walking. That my sister had plotted all this behind my back because she knew I would try to stop her. You bet your ass I would have tried.

"Not because I wanted to save the Germans," I said out loud. "But because you ruined your life." I kept my eyes closed, struggling with myself, struggling to not lay into her with my fists. A wonderful life had stretched before Felicia, and all she'd had to do was reach out and take it. Not now. After everything many people had done to offer her this chance . . . Veronika, Ford, Eli, me, Madame Semyonova, Felix . . . I had never been so angry in my life. She hadn't wanted what we'd worked to offer her, but why hadn't she told us that? Why? I finally calmed down, at least just enough to fall asleep.

When I opened my eyes an hour later, Felicia was gone.

I could have searched for her on the train, but I didn't. She'd probably left at an earlier stop and then caught the next train, because I didn't catch a glimpse of her when I went to the restaurant car or the bathroom, or just walked.

After the multiple shocks wore off, I had an unexpected feeling.

I felt good. No one knew me. No one was judging my clothes . . . or if they did, it wouldn't reflect on anyone but me, and I didn't care.

I didn't have to eat when other people were eating or wear anyone else's clothes. I didn't have to follow anyone else's schedule, and best of all—I didn't have to make small talk with anyone.

At Tulsa, I changed trains with only a two-hour wait. I had found the ticket in my bag. I had only spent a little of Clayton's money on food.

What did I think about during this long trip?

I tried not to think about anything, but that wasn't possible.

I wondered if Eli was still alive. I was pretty sure he was. I had a reasonable amount of hope he would recover, since he'd been showing signs of life so soon after the spell had hit him.

Pretty sure Veronika would never speak to me again. I could bear up under that. Maybe after a while I could write Lucy, and after longer, Alice.

I wondered if Felix had stayed away because he knew what was going to happen. Or maybe he'd just skipped the last event because he was going to be a father. Maybe both.

I bought a paper in Dallas.

Everyone in the German contingent was dead. Hitler had had a drastic response to the loss of such a big chunk of his magical community. He had invaded a piece of Poland and hunted down every magician in it. He had killed every single one he could find, including Agnieszka's family.

The list of the injured included Eli. The attached article said he was recuperating at his family home, and that his wife had been reported missing, presumed dead.

Wait. What?

"She rushed to the ferry to get help from the mainland," Veronika McMurtry, wife of the tsarina's aide, Captain Ford McMurtry, told our representative. "That ferry was swamped by a wave, and her friend Harriet Ritter saw my daughter-in-law go overboard. She has been missing since then. I fear she perished."

Well, that was . . . convenient. I had figured Harriet would want to kill me for having exposed Soo-Yung (and herself) to such peril. Then I realized I hadn't seen Harriet that night. Had she been there at all? Or had Veronika somehow tracked Harriet and suggested she could help me out?

"I fear she perished" my right foot.

I got home the next day. I walked from Sweetwater, and it was quite a distance. I could not think how to call someone to come get me without explaining a lot of things I didn't yet understand. It felt good to get the exercise, after San Diego. I knocked on my mother's front door that night. I had hoped to make it up to my cabin, but I had to stop.

My mother's face when she saw me was like that of someone who'd gotten a ticket to heaven. She hugged me, and she cried, and she called to Jackson, and baby Sam started crying, and it was perfect to be there.

When I'd explained enough to let myself off for a while, and my mother had given me a huge sandwich, and my stepfather had patted me on the back in a big burst of emotion (for him), and I'd held Sam until he fell asleep again, I went to bed on a cot in Sam's room. That was the nicest thing that could have happened to me. No kidding, I slept like a baby. For most of the night and the next day. Then I got up, ate as much of my mother's cooking as I could stuff into my stomach, enjoyed every bite, and went to sleep again.

My mother gave me the telegrams the next morning. "They were for you, but the telegraph boy knew you weren't in town, so he brought them here," she said. "I didn't know whether I ought to read them or not. I didn't, but if you hadn't shown up in a couple more days, I would have ripped them open."

I nodded. "Would have been fine." I took a deep breath and opened them myself.

The first one said, *He's going to mend. I didn't know.* It was signed "Felix."

The first sentence made me very glad. Eli and I had both tried, I saw that now, and it just hadn't worked. Maybe if I hadn't lost the baby, maybe if he hadn't always had that bit of hope he could return to his place at court . . . but maybes don't amount to a hill of beans. We had loved each other. I had had that.

The second one said, *Made it here, F and J and his mom here, too.* It was signed, "S." I knew many people whose names began with F, but I had only one sister. I couldn't figure out how she'd gotten to New York before I made it back to Segundo Mexia, or met up with Fenolla, Jason Featherstone, and his mom. But I would worry about that later.

Possibly she hadn't gone to New York at all.

The third one was from Harriet. *We're even* was the whole message. I'd killed those men for her, she'd "witnessed" me getting washed overboard to keep the heat off me. And maybe so that Eli could declare me legally dead sooner. That was four lives for one, but I wasn't going to quibble.

"Thanks, Mother," I said. "I can't tell you the whole story right now, until I know if someone's going to come looking for me." I'd told her what Felicia had done, and that Eli and I had come to a parting of the ways. That was enough.

My mother, still beautiful, still with only a tiny thread or two of gray in her hair, was changing Sam's diaper. She'd had to work all through my infancy and for years after. When I'd been a baby, her parents had kept me every day while she taught school. Mother had made the big decision to retire when she'd found she was pregnant this time, and Jackson was all for it. The new schoolteacher, Miss Widmark, was only twenty-two and the object of a lot of attention among the local men. Mother laughed and said she'd done Segundo Mexia a favor by retiring, so a single woman could take her place. "Honey, you tell me what you can, when you can." She pinned the diaper expertly. "I am only glad you are home. I know this is a painful time for you, and I'm sorry. But you're only twenty-one, and you have many years ahead of you." She gave me a beautiful smile.

"I'm half-mad at Felicia, and I'm half-frightened for her. I don't know where she is, or what she'll do, but I know she'll be in this war."

"That's her say-so. It seems pretty clear she's declared herself an adult, and it's pretty clear she's going to make her own decisions. It also stands to reason some of those decisions are going to be bad ones, dangerous ones, or both. That's her nature, Lizbeth. She was never going to think things through like you do. I like the girl, but she is who she is."

There was so much truth in this. I knew in time I would not worry so much about Felicia. My mother was right: my sister would do what she would do, and nothing I could say or do, even if I were right on the spot, would change that. I knew that now. She had not even given Eli and me adequate warning before she and her friends let loose hell. We might have looked like we'd be okay, at the back of the circled crowd. But that was only a "looked like." Felicia simply hadn't wanted to risk us stopping her. And I figured she hadn't wanted any of the Germans to escape, so she had attacked as quickly and thoroughly as she could. To accomplish that, no one except her teen accomplices could know.

I picked up the duffel bag I'd carried along for so many miles. "Heading up the hill," I said. "Going home."

Mother smiled at me over Sam's shoulder. "Pretty soon he'll be able to say 'bye-bye' when his sister leaves."

"I can hardly wait," I said. And I meant it.

Four weeks later, I was on my way home from hunting. I had gotten three rabbits, which would make a good stew. I knew I had an onion in my larder, but I was wondering about carrots. I'd come up the back of the hill, and when I got to the top and walked around my cabin, I found someone sitting at my picnic table.

"Clayton Ashley Dashwood," I said. "I bet you never thought you'd come to Segundo Mexia twice in your life." I fetched a piece of wood and threw it on the table. Kept the blood off the surface. I threw the rabbits on it and got out my skinning knife.

"Oh, I knew I'd come back to Segundo Mexia," he said, perfectly at ease. "I had to wait awhile, because I wanted you to have time to recover."

"From my drowning death?"

"That, and other things. You look good for a dead woman."

"Thank you," I said. "I'm going to set to on these rabbits. Would you see if I have any carrots on the shelf in the kitchen? I couldn't remember as I was coming home. I should have an onion or two."

"The door's unlocked?"

I appreciated him not trying the knob.

"It is. My neighbors always know if someone's at my house. They keep an eye." Especially since I'd started giving Chrissie's boys a nickel a week to be my warning system.

"The two boys? I thought they were going to tie me down and start asking questions," Clayton called from inside the cabin.

"That's what I pay 'em for."

Clayton was smiling when he came out, three carrots and the onion in his hands. Doesn't take long to cut up rabbits, and in thirty minutes I had the meat, carrots, and onion in the pot with some salt and pepper and a little spring water, which I'd add to from time to time if the liquid got low. I threw in some cilantro my mother had grown, and some dill I'd gotten from her, too. Time to put it on the stove. The glowing coals fanned up into a small flame pretty quickly. It was cool enough at night to cook in the house, made it pleasant.

I was at a loss after I'd finished that task and cleaned my hands. But Clayton wasn't.

"You got any cornbread to go with that?" he asked.

"You bring some?"

He laughed. "No, but I can make some if you've got the cornmeal."

"I do." I watched, wondering, as Clayton Dashwood made cornbread in my kitchen and put it in the oven.

"How's your sister?" I asked him, when he'd washed his hands.

"Got married last week," he said. "She's grown-up and he's grown-up and they didn't see any reason to wait."

"She's gone up to Canada?"

Clayton nodded. "Feels kind of lonely at our house. My mother even commented on that."

There was a little pause before he added, "How is *your* sister?"

"I don't know," I said. "That makes me sad, but considering—well, not what she did, but how she did it—maybe it's for the best. Maybe she and her Hans will survive the war. Maybe not."

"You not going to fight?"

"It's not my war. New America is raising a militia just in case we get overrun, they say, but I don't think that's their real plan."

"What do you think they aim to do?"

"I think they want Texoma, and maybe some of the land Canada took at their border."

"Will that be your war?" He leaned forward, and the fire glinted on his blond hair.

"This may sound stupid. But I feel like I've had my war."

He thought about that, then nodded. "I understand."

"Thanks. Oh, I just remembered! Here's your money." I got it out of the coffee can I'd kept it in. I'd made up what I spent in supplying game to the two local restaurants that used anything besides cows and chicken.

"Thanks," I said again, and handed it to him.

He accepted it without comment and put it in his pocket. I had a strong feeling he'd forgotten all about it. "You know I didn't come here thinking you owed me money," he said after a moment.

I nodded. We sat there until the stew was done and the cornbread out of the oven, and then we ate. It was good, and it was peaceful. We did the dishes, and then it seemed like the most natural thing in the world to take him to my bedroom. When we'd gotten to the point, for a little while I felt awkward and odd, after being with Eli for so long. It was like learning a different language. But soon, it seemed to come so easy to my tongue.

"You have to go back today?" I asked the next morning.

"Nope. My mom's good running the farm, at least for a week. After that, she gets pretty restless."

So he stayed.

"Felicia said you had feelings for me, but I didn't believe her," I said after a couple of days.

"That's one thing she was right about."

"What about you needing strong magical power to add to your bloodline? Not that I expect anything," I said hastily, "but you were heading for higher ground, so to speak."

"You feel like magic to me," Clayton said.

No one had ever said that to me. Anything like that. All of a sudden, I realized this might be a serious thing, and I was speechless.

"I'm still married," I felt compelled to say.

"You'll be declared dead in the Holy Russian Empire next week."

"What?"

"Usually, when someone vanishes, it takes five years for them to be declared dead," Clayton told me. "But since there was a witness to you getting washed overboard, and the tsar was interested in speeding it up, it'll be done."

"If I'm dead, I can't be married to Eli, I guess."

"I guess not."

"I'm glad you told me." But I looked at him doubtfully.

"I was hoping Eli would have," he said. "The only reason I waited."

"What does this mean to you?" I had to know where this was going.

"It means that someday I'd like you to visit Virginia, if I don't get drawn into this war that's brewing. I'm doing my best not to. All my magic is for the farm, for growing things, not killing. If I can keep the farm producing, I can send food to our troops."

"No one in their right mind wants to go to war," I said. I imagined my sister had found that out by now.

"Do you think you'd like to see Virginia?" Clayton looked pretty anxious, for the first time.

"I might," I said. I smiled. "After I'm legally dead, you can meet my parents."

"And your little brother?"

"If you're real lucky."

"I'm already lucky," he said, and smiled back.

After Clayton left, it felt funny the first day, and then I was back to normal.

When I went down to see Mother and Jackson and Sam, my mother led with, "I hear you got a man up there. You not going to bring him down here?"

I told them about Clayton. I told them about being dead in the HRE.

"Good," my stepfather said, right away. "You can never go back there again, and that's fine with us."

My mother nodded, and she made Sam wave his little hand.

"I don't know what's going to happen," I said. I'd been sure before and look where that had gotten me.

"Who does?" my mother said, and for a moment she looked sad. She was remembering finding out she was pregnant at fifteen, and that the man who'd caused it was long gone.

"If Clayton gets pulled into this war, I'm not going up to visit him," I said. "No point."

My mother nodded. "But if you have a chance to be happy, you take it," she said, her voice hard. "You grab it with both hands."

Jackson handed me a newspaper that he'd folded and left on the table.

I flattened it out. The headline was big and black. "HOLY ROMAN EMPIRE DECLARES WAR," the print screamed.

I closed my eyes for a minute, knowing at least a few people I knew in the HRE would not be coming back.

Jackson and Mother were tensed, waiting for what I'd say.

Some thoughts and feelings that had been rolling around in my head came together to make certainty.

Since I'd gotten back to Segundo Mexia, I hadn't looked for a gun crew to join. I thought I'd just needed to get over all the events that had happened at the last Wizards' Ball. But I realized I'd changed.

Now that I wasn't on a gun crew, I didn't feel certain I'd die any time I went out on a job. That made a big difference.

I had a new horizon.

ABOUT THE AUTHOR

Charlaine Harris is a *New York Times* and *USA Today* bestselling author who has been in print for more than forty years. She was named a Grand Master by the Mystery Writers of America in 2021. Harris has written five series, including the Gunnie Rose series, and two stand-alone novels, in addition to numerous short stories, novellas, and graphic novels (co-written with Christopher Golden). Her Sookie Stackhouse novels have appeared in over thirty different languages and on worldwide bestseller lists. They're also the basis of the acclaimed HBO series *True Blood*. Harris has co-edited five anthologies with Leigh Perry (Toni L.P. Kelner). Harris now lives on a cliff overlooking the Brazos River. When she's not writing, she's an omnivorous reader, and she's also surrounded by rescue dogs.